PUBLIC LIBRARY

Justice Warrior

THE ADVENTURES OF FOX RUNNING
AND JOHN DOOLEY, BOOK 2

JUSTICE WARRIOR

RUSTY DAVIS

THORNDIKE PRESS
A part of Gale, a Cengage Company

Copyright © 2022 by Rusty Davis.
Thorndike Press, a part of Gale, a Cengage Company.

ALL RIGHTS RESERVED
This novel is a work of fiction. Names, characters, places, and incidents are either the product of the author's imagination, or, if real, used fictitiously.
The publisher bears no responsibility for the quality of information provided through author or third-party Web sites and does not have any control over, nor assume any responsibility for, information contained in these sites. Providing these sites should not be construed as an endorsement or approval by the publisher of these organizations or of the positions they may take on various issues.
Thorndike Press® Large Print Hardcover Western.
The text of this Large Print edition is unabridged.
Other aspects of the book may vary from the original edition.
Set in 16 pt. Plantin.
Library of Congress CIP DATA on file.

**LIBRARY OF CONGRESS CIP DATA ON FILE.
CATALOGUING IN PUBLICATION FOR THIS BOOK
IS AVAILABLE FROM THE LIBRARY OF CONGRESS.**

ISBN-13: 978-1-4328-9275-3 (hardcover alk. paper)

Published in 2023 by arrangement with Rusty Davis

Printed in Mexico
Print Number: 1   Print Year: 2023

JUSTICE WARRIOR

Chapter One

April 1883, Tongue River Valley, Montana

Pete Bigelow sneered at his victim, filled with the power of his men behind him, arrogance mingling with the sweat that trickled through three days' worth of gray and white whiskers. The smells of whiskey, coffee, and rotting teeth came with each breath. He rocked on the heels of his hand-crafted boots, bloodshot eyes blinking against the unusually hot April sun as he considered how he could most enjoy killing the scrawny Indian boy in front of him.

The boy had stolen a steer. The kid seemed to think tying a rope around its neck and pulling as hard as a kid more bones than meat could pull would get him off Bigelow's sprawling Tongue River Valley ranch before he was caught. He made it farther than Bigelow thought he could, but not far enough.

"Want to hang you, son," Bigelow told the

boy, who looked about twelve. "Want your family to see your body rot. Want your kind to know the Circle B is not to be trifled with. Would you like that? Want to hang?"

Bigelow pantomimed hanging and made a face like a man dying. The boy spewed a stream of heathen gibberish at him and fought against the restraining hands that held him until a rifle butt in the side sent him back down to the dirt.

"Want to hang you. But we ain't got enough rope to waste, and there ain't no tree nearby that would serve," Bigelow said, gesturing at the rolling grasslands and rocky ridges that covered most of the landscape except for a few stunted oaks that were not tall enough for what he had in mind.

"So I'm gonna have to shoot you. Usually, that's quick. Too quick." Bigelow shook his head, bemoaning the deprivation of the joy of killing the boy slowly.

"Tell you what I'm gonna do. 'Cuz you are such a brave Injun boy, I'm gonna shoot you in the guts and let you bleed out while we watch the fun. And when they find you, after you finally die and we get to scalp you, that will send a message that this here Tongue River Valley belongs to me, not you, not your kind. Not now. Not ever. And son, so's you know, I ain't one of these men that goes mincing around with secret plans and secret handshakes that's out to play politics in Washington, or some high-toned come-lately who thinks his money matters more than my hard work. I'm a man with a gun, and I am going to kill anyone dead who steps on my land without my say-so. Especially you Cheyenne, but, you know what, brave who ain't so brave? I'd kill anyone who covets it. Like the Commandment says. Vengeance is mine because the land is mine, and I'm going to hold it until an hour after I am dead, boy. Stick that in your peace pipe, Injun scum."

The boy's blank look told Bigelow his speech was mostly in vain. Bigelow felt like killing him even more.

He'd thought Montana was rid of the Cheyenne when the army marched them off back in '77, but they refused to rot in exile and had returned to Fort Keogh a few years later. Last year, the numbers had risen so much that, while the army and Washington argued over giving the Cheyenne a reservation, the soldiers at the fort sent them south into the valley to start homesteading. To Bigelow, it was the equivalent of letting loose a plague of locusts. He missed no chance to graphically express his anger and had established a system of bonuses for hands who killed Indian trespassers.

The boy's face showed pure hatred. He rose to his feet and glared up at Bigelow in silence. He knew he was going to die, but he would die as a Northern Cheyenne should.

"Usually I have my men do the chores, but I think this is one I'll do because I just plain want to." Bigelow turned to mount his horse. "Now, boys, I want to show you a game. It's a good game," he said as he lifted his bulk onto the animal. "You let that boy run, and I get to chase him on Roper here. Should be a good laugh for everybody. Well, maybe not the kid, but he don't count."

Bigelow settled into the saddle, which was made in distant Mexico and cost more than a year's wages for any three members of his crew, and pulled out a pistol. He would not need the rifle. Not at all.

"Let go of him, boys, and let the fun begin!"

A small grove of cedar trees stood some 150 yards to Bigelow's left. To the right, if the boy could make it about fifty yards, a formation of rocks looked like it led to a ridge where the boy could escape, except for a twenty-foot break in the tumbled boulders that no one could leap. The rock formation might provide shelter but could only delay the inevitable.

"Now, boys, stand back, here," drawled Bigelow, surveying the sober faces around him. He knew just the thing to make them smile. "Tell you what. If he heads for them scrub oaks there, just so you boys can have some fun along with me, if we get him corralled in there, and he climbs one of them trees, you fellas can help me shoot him down! How's that sound?"

Bigelow's men hooted. The one holding the boy shoved him to the dirt and danced away out of range.

"Well, go on, worthless savage," said Bigelow, pointing toward the Plains beyond, where white clouds dotted a wide blue sky. "Let me enjoy killing you."

The boy seemed not to understand his role in the drama. He once again stood but did nothing more than look at the men and then out at the land. Bigelow clucked at the horse, which walked a step closer. "Sonny, you don't start running, I'm a-gonna start shooting you in places that will take you forever to die. You ruin my fun, you'll pay."

The boy leaped up, colliding hard with Bigelow's horse. He tried to pull Bigelow off in a frantic effort to gain control of the animal and managed to yank one of the man's legs out of the stirrups, but the rancher was bigger and stronger. He kicked the boy loose as he struggled to control his mount. Bigelow's riders all closed in on the boy, who managed to elude the hooves and make a run for the rocks. A round of wild shots followed him.

"Stop!" bellowed Bigelow. "Nobody cheat me out of what's mine. Now I'm mad. I'm gonna do this personal!"

He spurred his horse savagely and reached the rocks as the boy started climbing. Bigelow's prey moved out of sight, clambering around to the far side of the rocks in search of handholds. Bigelow followed. A few riders noted a stray wolf watching from the ridgeline, probably waiting to eat the loser.

From behind the rock formation, they could just about make out Bigelow's thunderous voice. Two shots followed. Bigelow's men grunted at each other and nodded knowingly. Their boss had a powerful hatred of Indians. When he found out some Indian kid had stolen one steer, he insisted on being there for the kill. LeRoy Harris, who would do anything Bigelow told him, was ready to do the scalping. He was waiting for Bigelow to drag the kid's body out, or say he was done doing whatever he might have done to the corpse. Whatever it was, his men were going to swallow hard and tell him over and over what a great man he was. Bigelow was a hard boss.

"Let's get him scalped, boss, and get back to the range," called Harry Washburn, the oldest of the nine riders with Bigelow. He was new to the ranch but had worked very hard to ingratiate himself with Bigelow, something the rest never bothered to attempt. "Maybe we can have extra steaks to celebrate!"

There was no immediate reply. Washburn was about to send Harris over when they heard, "Don't shoot," in a voice that sounded like Bigelow's but at the same time was nothing at all like his usual harsh, commanding tones.

The man who reappeared a second later, coming around the edge of the rocks, was a shadow of the domineering, driving force behind the Circle B. He looked pitifully like a bizarre ghost, his white, ankle-length drawers visible and sagging everywhere except where they were tight on a bulging stomach normally hidden by the coat Bigelow usually wore. The humiliated rancher wore a white linen shirt as well. His face was red from the outdoors, a sharp contrast to the pallor of his bald, hatless head. He limped and staggered as he walked in stocking feet across the baked rocks and sticker weeds. His hands, sun-reddened like his face, were way up in the air, and he was almost cringing.

Behind the boss walked a young Cheyenne man, a lithe, fearsome shadow. A piece of red cloth was tied around his head, and his black hair fell almost to his shoulders and danced behind him like a battle flag in the breeze. His copper skin was stretched tight across a scarred, gaunt face that looked much older than the rest of him. His clothes were the usual collection of castoffs Indians wore. A thin shirt and pants covered his slight frame, and moccasins covered his feet. He looked like a bag of discarded rags. But the gun he pointed at Bigelow was all business. Another gun sat in the holster on the Indian's left hip. His eyes flashed as he looked at the cowboys; his teeth showed in a fierce battle smile.

"Move," Fox Running told Bigelow, when the big man halted at the sight of his ranch hands watching with wide eyes. "Keep going."

"I will kill you," seethed Bigelow.

"Perhaps you will, but not today," Fox Running replied evenly. One of the few joys he owed to his time at the Indian School of Boston was the ability to mock ranchers in their own language. "I think you are a coward, Pete. A cowardly old man." He raised his voice to carry to the assembled hands. "I keep hearing that the Circle B wants to wipe out all the Cheyenne in the Tongue River Valley. If you want to start, you can start right now with me."

No one answered. "I can make it a fair fight, if you are afraid." Fox Running holstered the pistol. He lifted his hands and beckoned the riders to advance.

Harris and Evan Kalendish, another member of the crew who would do anything Bigelow ordered when it came to killing Indians, looked at each other. The next second, they spurred their horses forward.

"No!" Washburn snarled at two other riders who started to follow. "Fools!" he muttered under his breath.

The two Circle B riders swiftly covered the distance. Kalendish wasted three shots riding; Harris sent two as wide as bullets usually went when men on horseback tried to hit a small target.

Twenty yards.

Fox Running waited. His hands were poised above his guns. His black eyes snapped with calculation as the predator watched the prey.

The Circle B hands didn't slow. They meant to ride down the Indian.

Fifteen yards.

"If they keep going, they might hurt you, old man," Fox Running called to Bigelow, humor and sarcasm coloring his tone. "Good for you I am here to save you!"

Ten yards.

The old man's eyes widened as he saw his hands were all but coming straight at him!

They opened fire again. One bullet kicked up dirt near Fox Running. Bigelow started to yell, but his men never heard what he said.

Fox Running drew his right-hand gun and emptied it with a speed born of experience firing a pistol at white men for almost half of his short life. He grabbed Bigelow by the undershirt and pulled the man behind the rocks as the two horses galloped past. Harris flapped in the saddle like a scarecrow in a tornado. Kalendish slumped on his mount like a torn-open flour sack.

"Stay there," Fox Running cautioned Bigelow, who was paralyzed with fear and stared wide eyed out at the world.

Fox Running holstered the revolver, drew his left-hand gun, shifted it to his right hand, and faced the Circle B men. He wasn't a good left-handed shot, but life often called for more than one gun's worth of bullets. "Anyone else?"

There was not.

"Let the boss go," Washburn called out, walking his horse forward a few steps, hands held out from his sides.

"Planning to," Fox Running called. "He's too tough to eat." He grabbed Bigelow by the ear and pulled him closer. "Probably can't train him to watch anything, either. Useless. You want him, you can have him!"

"Kill you," hissed Bigelow. Fox Running grinned. Taunting men he knew possessed the power to kill him was a game — deadly, but a game he had come to play with a defiance born of unquenchable anger and a confidence that nothing could stop him.

He whistled loudly, a series of notes that a trained ear would recognize as part of an Irish rebel song from long ago and far away. A roan horse emerged from around the rocks where Fox Running had been hiding. The wolf on the ridge loped away.

"This is what is going to happen," Fox Running called out to Bigelow's crew. "The boy and I are leaving. You are staying. If you chase us, I will kill every single one of you. I do not want to do that, but I will if I must."

"We won't follow," Washburn said.

"Red Calf," Fox Running called out. "Get over here."

The boy, clearly in awe of Fox Running,

came meekly.

"You have dishonored the Cheyenne people by stealing, even from a man like this. What is it you must do?"

The boy frowned. "Do you mean I have to . . ."

"Apologize? No," replied Fox Running. "You can choose to do so and ride with me. Or you can refuse to apologize, and I will leave alone."

The boy looked at Fox Running, an unhappy realization crossing his face. "You are the Justice Warrior. The one they say does the work of the spirits."

"I have heard this talk." Fox Running dismissed it with a wave of his left hand. "What I have not heard is an apology. Adding to the mountain of wrongs does not bring honor to The People."

The boy swallowed. "I . . ."

"Look at the man you wronged," ordered Fox Running.

The boy looked at Bigelow. He was smaller than the rancher and had to tilt his head back to look Bigelow in the eye.

"I am sorry I stole your cow," he said lamely. "We were hungry."

Bigelow glared, hate and fear choking off any response he wanted to make.

"If this man were honorable, Red Calf, he

would accept your apology," said Fox Running. "He is not. He is a foul man who preys on anyone weaker than he is, white or Indian. But even men like him must be treated in the fashion required to be a proper Cheyenne warrior. If you wish to steal from the Shoshone in a raid, and ride up to them and declare yourself a man so strong they cannot stop you, that is one thing. To steal from a man only because you want it, to do so when no one is looking; that is wrong."

"Are you done?" grumbled Bigelow, who was regaining confidence now that he knew he would emerge alive. "Then let me add one thing: you ever set foot on Circle B land again, I will kill you. Both of you."

Fox Running looked at the rancher.

"The day you try to kill me will be your last to feel the sun and the wind." He stepped closer. Although inches shorter than the older man, he radiated a larger presence by his anger. "I hope you try soon," Fox Running breathed, his teeth showing. Bigelow feared no man, but he gulped and felt a quiver in his spine as Fox Running's face, split by a scar between his eyebrows and peppered with smaller ones across his cheeks, twisted in a small, deadly, humorless smile. "Very soon."

Fox Running ordered Red Calf to mount. He gathered Bigelow's clothes and gun.

"Those are mine!" Bigelow snarled. "I had that coat made for me, and those boots, too!"

Fox Running spread the clothes on the ground, setting each item out and fussing so that all were laid flat. He stood up the boots. Then he met the gaze of his roan horse. Coyote Horse looked back with a glint in the eye. Coyote Horse had been a gift of the spirits, sure-footed, loyal, and as full of tricks as his namesake.

With one last look to be sure Washburn and the other Circle B men were keeping their distance, Fox Running mounted. "Let us go, Coyote Horse," he called out.

Bigelow screamed in outrage as the roan rode hard over his clothes, sending one boot flying as a hoof came down on it.

"No, you contrary beast, the other way!" Fox Running said, laughing as the horse, knowing the rider's true intentions, kept on with his work.

Bigelow jumped back as the horse galloped over the pants, coat, and remaining boot, ruining what was left to ruin as the animal, Fox Running, and Red Calf rode past a line of Circle B riders doing their best to take in every inch of the boss's humiliation while not being seen to do so.

"And now we must leave," Fox Running sang out as the wind blew full in his face and the sun lay warm ahead of him.

It mattered not that he and the world were at war; he had survived the worst of what it could bring and was still here to defy it. A Cheyenne who had been more welcome with the Lakota than with his own people, until the spirits had led him to the Tongue River Valley, a place where he would never be a stranger again. He had a home now, and before long he would have a family.

"Morning Shadow comes soon from the land of the Lakota, and I want to be there to welcome the woman who will be my wife!" Fox Running urged Coyote Horse to a gallop as he turned his back on the fading sounds of Bigelow's curses.

CHAPTER TWO

June 1883, along Rosebud Creek, Montana
"No!"

Rides a Crow sat up with a start, sweat standing out on her forehead. The young woman gasped deeply, swallowing huge gulps of air.

"Mama?" Wrapped in a Blanket, who always slept near her adopted mother, touched Rides a Crow and then drew back her hand, looking at it oddly. "You are wet."

She was. Rides a Crow was saturated in sweat, not the kind that came from a day pretending she was an ox hauling a plow, but that kind that boiled over in a body consumed by white-hot nightmares.

She touched the little girl. Something real. Alive. Someone to wipe away the looming threat of death that was once again coming for her Northern Cheyenne. Her nightmare made that clear.

She was known as a Spirit Walker, a Wise

Woman, from the days she helped The People find their way home from exile in the south. Even during those months of 1878 and 1879, with all the death, hate, and violence that surrounded them for weeks as they walked hundreds of miles, she did not feel the cold, steel-edge blackness of the threat now descending on the lands of the Northern Cheyenne. The People were a sitting target, strung out as they were over dozens of miles south from Fort Keogh, now that they were trying to become farmers and not hunters.

Her dreams had become increasingly violent. The wind dream was the one that recurred most often. In it, a relentless wind blew through the Tongue River Valley. Cheyenne and white men and women — and children — were tossed like sticks in its path. But this was not a violent tornado, like The People had experienced in Indian Territory several years ago. This storm had no funnel and no dark clouds, but carried the sound of thunder or a thousand guns firing at once. Some of those tossed by the storm rose in a kind of ecstasy; others lay still and dead. Those who rose marched in the direction of the wind, trampling everything in their path as the past gave birth to the future. Then they vanished in a cloud.

This dream was dark, with no redeeming hope. Death was coming. Death was coming. Death was coming. The dream said it with the rhythm of the white man's railroad. Rides a Crow drew in a sharp breath. That was it! Whoever or whatever was coming, it was coming on the railroads, the ribbons of evil that chopped hunting grounds into smaller and smaller parcels. She closed her eyes and tried to dive past the revulsion and fear she felt to learn what the spirits were saying so that she could warn others.

There was a gun. A Colt or some other pistol. The gun loomed huge in her sight. Fire spewed from its barrel in the dimness of her nightmare, and the acrid smoke of gunpowder filled her senses. Around her, just out of sight, lay the bodies of those who had died. Her lips tasted a mixture of gunpowder and splashed drops of blood from the victims.

The hand that cocked the gun was lining it up with its next target. Her own distant scream came to her ears. The gun exploded in fury just as its target turned, and Rides a Crow saw the round, gentle face of Two Moon, the leader of The People. Then, as though she were the gun, she could see the bullet as it left the barrel and headed toward the head of the man the whites had declared the chief of the Northern Cheyenne. The man who had tried his best to keep the fragment of The People who had survived from being wiped away.

In the dream she screamed at Two Moon, who smiled and changed shape into Little Wolf, the disgraced former leader of the Northern Cheyenne who had led them from exile in Indian Territory — the only leader from those days who remained alive since the death of Dull Knife. Little Wolf was smiling the gentle smile he had worn the day they surrendered to the soldiers; the one that said there was hope and peace and a future for The People.

Thunder from the gun enveloped her; flame obscured everything.

Then it all went black.

"Mama?" The child was feeling her terror.

She opened her eyes and looked at Wrapped in a Blanket, and tried to smile. "The trickster sent Mama a bad dream," she said. "It is just a bad dream."

"It will be better if I braid your hair."

The little girl liked to braid her mother's long, black hair. Rides a Crow slept with it free.

"Of course, little one."

"And then I will sleep in your bed and keep away the trickster," said Wrapped in a

Blanket. Found as an infant after her parents were killed seeking freedom, she used any pretext to be as near to Rides a Crow as possible. "No more bad dream."

Rides a Crow knew there would be no dream because there would be no sleep. She had received other warnings from the spirit world, as if any were needed that the simmering cauldron of the Tongue River Valley was ready to explode. That was why, weeks ago, she fought with the spirit wolf that protected her and demanded he watch for attempts on the lives of others, not just hers. The spirit horses had remained nearby to scout for trouble but had so far found only the usual frictions between the Indians and settlers.

What bothered Rides a Crow the most was not that she was warned, or that there was hate against The People, for there had been that always. No other warning had been so graphic, or brought with it the sense that the future had already happened, and for once there was nothing she could do to change it.

June 1883, Sickles, Montana

From the looks the passengers were giving him, Sam Rickett knew he'd done it again. If it weren't for the fact that the lurching train was now making them all worry more about falling off their benches than whatever he'd been screaming, he'd be sitting again in a peck of strangers with his head down, trying to be invisible, wondering what sent his mind back to the Wilderness.

He'd been a sixteen-year-old kid afraid he'd missed the war when he caught up with the Texas Brigade that morning back in 1864, so excited he ran half the way to catch up. A few hours and five hundred casualties later, that kid was lost and gone forever, with images of men blown apart and a forest burning with fire and death seared into his mind.

Funny thing. The Wilderness seemed like it was yesterday. Other than the first and the most recent, he could barely recall anything about the thirty-four men he had put in the ground with his gun. Maybe because that was just business. Just like this, except these were ones no one would be counting except him, because they had been very clear that no one was supposed to know.

He would have said he could not have fallen asleep on the swaying, rickety rail line that connected the tiny town of Sickles with Laramie down in Wyoming, but after more than a day on some form of train or other

— or waiting for one — a man just wore out.

The train had stopped. Other passengers moved quickly to get off. His eyes lingered for a moment on the little bald man in the Eastern suit who seemed preoccupied with keeping dust off of his clothes. *Wrong world to be in, pilgrim,* he thought. Maybe they didn't have it east of the Mississippi, but west of it, dust and death were the two most constant companions life had to offer.

The young, red-haired woman riding with the handsome young, black-haired army officer let him lift her down. They had loudly proclaimed they were brother and sister, as if anyone believed it or cared. Rickett had observed them with what he was certain was more circumspection than they did him. The soldier radiated aggression. Rickett knew the type. Some soldiers were men doing a thankless job. Some were bullies preying on others. This one was the latter. Their Boston accents were strong. Their inability to lower the volume of their conversation — even when they talked about him — made Rickett wonder what kind of crosscurrents and conflicts were really flowing in this valley. The Indians were everyone's target. Once they were disposed of in whatever way folks wanted, Rickett was betting that the ones who fought the Cheyenne would turn on each other.

Not his problem. He wasn't paid to care, just shoot.

Didn't take long before he was the only one left in the train car. The east side of the Tongue River was a long way from anywhere. Long way from Texas. No one would know him. No one would be prepared. He stretched, a tall man with his hair just starting to gray out. The large, raggedy mustache was leading the parade. He hated the way it looked, but he hadn't shaved his upper lip in twenty years and wasn't planning to start now.

He lifted the long-barreled .44 from its holster, checked to be sure it was loaded. Never knew what kind of welcome there might be, who might know he was coming. He had gripped the knapsack stuffed with his spare shirts and socks, extra ammunition, and a copy of the sketches of the men he needed to find on this trip. Each sketch had a number. They told him that when they knew which of the ten it would be, he would be informed by telegram, so no one could identify who had hired him. It was an odd job, and they were very odd men, who were almost as clever as they thought they were, but it was what it was.

He flung the sack over one shoulder and walked toward the cold air streaming into the railroad car. He didn't like cold. Never cold in Texas in June. Cold made his hand stiff, and in his line of work, that kind of thing could be the reason one man went in the ground and another walked upon it.

He'd had a bad feeling about the job when he took it back in Texas. Something more was taking place than he was being told. Never had a job like it or worked for people like them. Secrecy. Zeal. Men who had the smell of army about them. Bad men. Then there was that smooth talker who first told him about the job. Man had enough riders and money that he could have raised an army of his own to chase Sam Rickett to death across a lot of states and most of the territories if Rickett had refused. All but threatened to, talking about important friends back East as well as all his connections. Rickett did not like being threatened.

But the money? It could set him up for life, and a man who had put as many men in the ground as he had knew there was always a faster hand and a better aim out there somewhere. If he could get out now while he was breathing, he would be ahead of most of the ones he knew.

Well, he could whine about it or get the

job done. He walked out of the rail car onto the platform and looked across the river, off to where the Northern Cheyenne lived in dissonance with their white neighbors. Then he looked around the town. Maybe there was a decent place to buy a horse. Then it would be time to start the job. He looked around some more, his instincts telling him there was something wrong, something that would make him wish he had stayed in Texas. This was going to be work.

June 1883, Lame Deer, Montana
"Come back to me, lad."

John Dooley knew Fox Running did not hear a word. As had become Fox Running's habit in recent days, when he was physically present at all, he just stared out the window of the cabin that served as their home and the office of the agency they had just begun that spring.

The idea was grand. Fox Running's Boston benefactor, Katherine McGillicuddy, dreamed up an agency to investigate complaints between the Northern Cheyenne and their white neighbors, find the truth of disputed events, and stave off another Indian war. She also saw it as a way to channel the restless, unending energy of Fox Running, whom she knew from his days at the Indian School of Boston, from which he'd escaped after being both its brightest student and its biggest behavioral nightmare.

That energy had all but vanished now, replaced by lethargy at a time when Fox Running's vitality was sorely needed. For all that the Tongue River Valley was filled with beauty, in this year of 1883 it was also filled with hate. After the army encouraged the Northern Cheyenne to settle lands in the Tongue River Valley beginning in 1882, conflicts between whites and Indians escalated as white and Cheyenne homesteaders lived together in a crazy-quilt pattern of land ownership. The army had supported the Cheyenne in carving out lands for themselves, pending creation of a formal reservation, pitting soldiers against politicians. The little town of Lame Deer had emerged as the central point for the settlements, and so Dooley built a cabin there. He was not sleeping in an Indian lodge!

Dooley felt sorry for the young man as he watched him gaze aimlessly at the landscape. Dooley had been a guard at the Indian School of Boston when Fox Running was the school's most rebellious student and all but lived in the detention cells, where he and Dooley became friends. The

Irishman, a former police officer too wounded by the Civil War to remain a policeman, had helped Fox Running escape back home. Dooley came West when McGillicuddy, a wealthy Boston woman who had tried to befriend Fox Running with mixed results, wanted to use her money to help the Northern Cheyenne recover from near extinction and give Fox Running a direction for his rootless life.

The war-weakened Northern Cheyenne had surrendered in the spring of 1877 and were sent to Indian Territory in the south despite being promised a home in the lands they had roamed for generations. In the fall of 1878, they escaped the reservation. Although many died and some were captured, a remnant of about 150 Northern Cheyenne reached Montana in early 1879, where they initially settled at Fort Keogh, at the northern end of the valley. Soon, so many scattered Northern Cheyenne flocked there that they needed to spread out to the south.

The death of Dull Knife in the spring of 1883 and the self-imposed exile of Little Wolf after killing a man in 1880 meant the Northern Cheyenne were led by Two Moon, who believed the first order of business was to rebuild the size of the Northern Cheyenne and use the tools of the white man — the plow, the ox, and the soil — to reestablish social, cultural, and religious foundations that had been all but wrecked during the tribe's years of turmoil.

Protected by spirit helpers, such as the spirit wolf that warned Rides a Crow to send Fox Running to find the boy Red Calf before his steer-stealing escapade turned fatal, Dooley and Fox Running had tried to stop small incidents from becoming large. It was too soon to tell, but one thing was clear to both men: there would never be a shortage of work.

In fact, Dooley was drowning because Fox Running had only recently returned after vanishing for weeks. The previous fall, the young Cheyenne had pledged himself to Morning Shadow, a Lakota girl who lived on the Pine Ridge reservation in Dakota Territory. He had planned to bring her and her orphaned siblings to Lame Deer with him. But a few weeks ago, instead of his bride, he had been visited by a delegation of Lakota elders who said they would not allow the marriage because it took the daughter of a major Oglala leader and her brothers and sisters away from Pine Ridge. For the good of the Lakota, it could not be permitted.

Fox Running understood the Lakota perspective, even though he sensed more opposition from the elders than he could have imagined. Morning Shadow would have been told before the elders came to him. If she had wanted to defy them, she would have been in Montana by now. That she had not come meant she had complied with the elders. He could hardly ride to Pine Ridge and kidnap her. Nor could he leave. He had made a commitment to the Tongue River Valley after the Spirit Walker told him that here — and here alone — he would find his path. He had no choice but to abandon his dreams.

Dooley had felt uneasy when the Lakota men visited. He sensed there was a deeper story beneath their words. He knew well how men could mask one truth with another when the false excuse had a gloss of respectability, but he knew nothing of Lakota or Cheyenne culture. Dooley kept his concerns to himself, not that Fox Running paid attention to anything he said these days.

Losing Morning Shadow did to the Cheyenne whirlwind what years of battles could not — left him feeling defeated and utterly lacking in purpose. After living without a real home since the 1876 raid that destroyed his village, he had been planning to sink deep roots in Montana. The unexpected blow broke him. He vanished the day the elders left and had only recently returned, without explaining to anyone where he had been or what had happened.

Listless or not, Fox Running's condition alarmed Dooley. Not that long ago, the young Cheyenne had been a powder keg of emotions. He was good with the guns he wore on his hips like a white gunfighter and was not hesitant to use them. It was a combination that could touch off an explosion in the volatile Tongue River Valley, where Dooley felt like he was often throwing smaller and smaller bits of water on a fire that burned hotter and hotter.

Yet since his return, Fox Running had said nothing more than one-word answers . . . as though he still existed, but on a separate plane from the rest of the world. Nothing interested him. Nothing even irritated a young man Dooley knew had the thinnest of skins. When the explosion building inside finally came — and Dooley knew his young friend well enough to know he couldn't help but resent anyone interfering in his life — Dooley feared it would be terrible to behold.

With Fox Running fighting whatever internal battle consumed his soul, Dooley had risen to the challenge of trying to sort out the rising number of grievances between the Northern Cheyenne and their neighbors. His gift for getting along with all people in almost all arguments, and his belief that all people had good in them somewhere, had served him well. The fact that the army had shown itself expressly unwilling to punish Indians purely on the say-so of a white farmer limited the number of trumped-up charges with which he dealt. Mostly, his lot was education. Teaching a Cheyenne that a steer that showed up in his field one day was not free to be taken for meat; teaching a white farmer that sacred dances were not a return to the warpath; teaching both sides to leave rifles at home while working the fields, even if it meant passing up the chance to shoot at game (while sending a bullet far too close to a former enemy).

Dooley was a big Irishman who viewed life as a daily chance to find a way to outwit the misery endemic in existence. His sandy, reddish hair, with bits of gray creeping in that gave him an air of authority, had grown shaggy now that he was removed from the world of barbers, and his sideburns were full and puffy. He was usually clean-shaven, but his whiskers grew in when work took away time for primping, which was often.

Dooley's kind blue eyes, ready smile, and creased face reflected the warmth and sincerity that glowed within. A bulky man who had been turning to fat in Boston, he found the active life of Lame Deer a perfect tonic. He who had never done more than build a table and chairs had built a cabin, albeit with help from those who had done it before, and a wee bit of luck. He was busier than he had ever been, and in some ways happier, for he was helping people. The clouds on his horizon were the zealots who — whether they believed the Cheyenne must have land or must not — stood in the way of people simply seeing each other as people and making the best of each day. Without him, Fox Running might have been one of them and thrown away all the second chances the younger man had been given. Dooley would not let that happen.

His even temper was often tested. The army had discovered that an investigative agency with a white man and a Cheyenne was a perfect vehicle to resolve disputes and had become their best customer, if for no other reason than because there was no one else.

Little feet slapped outside. "Big Bear, come quick! They want to shoot Golden Turtle!"

A small Cheyenne girl with hair cut by an inexpert knife poked her head in the doorway, clearly sent by someone who knew it was quicker to call for Dooley than send for the army, even though a small post was maintained at Lame Deer.

He knew who she meant. Golden Turtle was a Cheyenne who not long ago had been a mediocre warrior and a poor hunter, but a man of great respect who had walked from Indian Territory to Montana when the Northern Cheyenne escaped captivity. Since settling in the Tongue River Valley, he discovered that he not only liked to farm, he was excellent at growing everything he tried. As a result, he enjoyed telling everyone else how much better a farmer he was than they were. Most Cheyenne were happy to let him brag, since his advice helped them, but his boasting often grated on white ears.

Dooley sighed as he rose. The legs start wearing out after thirty, he often said. Fox Running remained staring out the window. Dooley, blending irritation and concern, decided not to bother asking this time. "Where are we going, Grasshopper?"

"You know my name is Spotted Dawn," the fragile-featured girl said.

"You sound like a grasshopper when it sings the Hay Song," Dooley replied, mussing her hair. He had come to find Cheyenne songs and customs delightful. "Where are we going?"

"You will get lost again. Come on," she said in the chaffing tone many of the Cheyenne children used for their favorite white adult. She grabbed his hand and pulled it hard to make sure they reached Golden Turtle in time.

The single gunshot Dooley heard while still far away was not echoed by a response, which made him run faster. A crowd had gathered around Harry Miller's General Store, which was good. When bullets were flying too close for comfort, crowds melted. He pushed through. Spotted Dawn held his hand, unwilling to miss a minute of this excitement.

"Apologize or I finish it," said Portage Lawrence, a man who ate too much, drank too much, worked too little, and annoyed everyone around him as a matter of course.

Golden Turtle was on his knees, angry after having ducked in premature fear to miss the shot fired well over his head. Now the town was gathering to watch his shame. Lawrence waved the gun in his face.

"And is the problem here that his turnip is bigger than yours?" asked Dooley in the lazy way he started when dealing with the inebriated.

"What's it to you?" Lawrence waved the gun in Dooley's direction without taking his eyes completely off Golden Turtle. "Whoever you are."

"John Dooley. Tongue River Agency detective," he replied, using the agreed-upon way to distort things to make it seem like they were part of the army. "Golden Turtle likes to brag. What did the wee man say?"

"Told me my crops would grow better if I didn't hit my wife! What kind of thing is that to say?"

Golden Turtle rose and was nodding.

"Her tears drive away the good spirits from his land," he said. "A house with misery and hate cannot grow things that are good. If he does not want his wife, others might. Unhappy people cannot grow good crops. Every Cheyenne knows this is true. I do not eat of his crops for this reason. Everything he grows tastes foul, because there is a foul spirit breathed upon them by this man. I fear that, because he lives so close to me, this hate will poison my crops as well."

"You been eatin' my food? Without payin'? Why, you thievin' . . ." The gun in Lawrence's hand started rising toward Golden Turtle.

Dooley stepped forward. "Now, now, shooting the man isna' the answer."

"Out of my way, Irish! Not being told off by some so-called farmer who was out scalpin' white men until a few years ago."

"Perhaps it would be wiser to walk away instead of getting yourself killed," Dooley replied. "It may even be wisest of all to stop hurting your wife, for the children do not need to see that sort of thing. Put the gun on the ground, Mr. Lawrence, and walk ye away. Golden Turtle meant no offense."

"Make me, if you think protecting that red filthy —"

"Ah, laddie," Dooley began, moving closer until he was in range to deliver a sharp kick to the inside of Lawrence's right ankle. The man tumbled, and the gun that had been in his hand went flying to land in the dust of Lame Deer's busiest street, which was little more than a strip of flattened earth barely worthy of the name.

"If anyone here is a friend of Mr. Lawrence's, please help him recover from drinking too much, and would ye please hold his pistol for him until he has safely returned to his home," Dooley called out, addressing the crowd. "I believe, gents and all ye ladies, that this ends this portion of today's entertainment."

Walt Carruthers, a small rancher, came to grab the pistol. He helped Lawrence to his feet, scolding the man about being a fool.

"Golden Turtle," called Dooley as the Cheyenne farmer tried to melt away. Dooley beckoned the Indian closer with one finger. The man looked guilty as he abandoned his escape and obeyed the summons. Spotted Dawn stood next to Dooley, glorying in the way her white hero had faced down a bad man!

"Glad I am you enjoy the farming, but I wouldna offer Mr. Lawrence advice again about his marriage and his farm. He is an unpleasant man and if —" The sound of shouting interrupted him. Dooley had never fully taken his eye off Lawrence, even as he turned to face Golden Turtle to show appropriate respect. The abashed white farmer had not taken well to being humbled. Indians and their white neighbors alike lost all control when they drank. Lawrence was raising the pistol he must have wrestled away from Carruthers. He pointed it toward them.

Dooley, unarmed, shoved Golden Turtle away with one hand. With the other, he pulled Spotted Dawn behind him.

Two shots rang out together. Lawrence staggered a step from the impact of a bullet, turned to look over his left shoulder, then pitched forward and fell to the dust. A *thunk* behind Dooley said Lawrence's shot did nothing but plow into the side of Miller's store.

But standing in the street behind Lawrence's prone form was a young Cheyenne with a red cloth band around his head and a smoking pistol in his right hand.

Fox Running's bullet had caught Lawrence in the midsection. The young man moved toward Dooley. Lawrence struggled to his knees and tried to raise his own gun again, even with blood dripping from a wound on the right side of his ribs. He slowly cocked it and was pointing the wobbly weapon toward Dooley, the child, and Golden Turtle when Fox Running's second bullet struck him dead center, spinning him around until he collapsed.

Carruthers, who had been standing next to Lawrence, looked ashen as Fox Running, gun still drawn, slowly approached. "Were you injured, Mr. Carruthers?" Fox Running asked, as kindly as if offering refreshment at tea time.

Speechless, Carruthers shook his head.

"I regret he could not let it alone," said

Fox Running. He looked down at the large ungainly lump Lawrence made within a circle of darkened dirt. The man was quite thoroughly dead. "I wonder what his wife will say and whether that will make his crops grow better."

"It didna have to end that way," Dooley maintained as he and Fox Running returned to their cabin. "If I shot all the drunks, this would be a deserted town. Too hot ye are to kill the fools."

"It was cleaner," said Fox Running tersely.

Dooley's brow furrowed. He thought in straight lines, where Fox Running leaped to conclusions without the bother of logic and then grew testy when having to explain himself. Dooley waited him out. He knew the lad.

"Lawrence has never let go a grudge in his life, and he was a devious man," Fox Running said. "Captain Evans told me that for years he took pot shots at a soldier who rode through his corn once — just once — until that soldier was no longer posted out here. Golden Turtle would have had some terrible accident sooner or later that would have ruined his crops, with nothing traced back to Lawrence. We would have known Lawrence did it but have had no proof.

Golden Turtle would have taken some clumsy revenge to uphold his dignity, and the army would have had to arrest him. All this would have wasted time and failed at achieving justice."

There were times when, looking at a young man whose preference in clothing was for the worst rags the frontier could offer, Dooley could forget Fox Running was one of the smartest students at the Indian School of Boston, as well as one of the most rebellious. Then there were times when he remembered the doors that started opening to a smart young man and slammed shut suddenly because the young man was an Indian. He said nothing further. Fox Running's logic was cold but correct. Lawrence was a fellow who sought trouble too often, and finally found more than he could handle.

"Back is it, you are?" Dooley said. Fox Running nodded. "Well, kind it was of ye to step into the festivities. I know this was not about Golden Turtle as much as it was that little Grasshopper and I were probably going to be shot."

Fox Running let that pass. He did not want to hear compliments. "You had a crowd. Who was the tall man with the big mustache? Big man. Just going gray."

"Didn't see him."

"If you see him again, talk to him. He has to be a gunfighter, from the look of him. Everyone else was looking at Lawrence, but he was studying me."

"Maybe that's because you were gone for so long, and he didn't know you."

"There was another man. Little man. He had a notebook and was writing. He didn't look like the swaggering types who write for the newspapers, but he was scribbling furiously in his little book. Short, like me. He mopped his head twice. Bald. A little gray hair left on the edges. Eastern suit. He looked scared, as though all he wanted to do was run, but he had to stay and watch."

"Because you just killed a man in front of him?"

Fox Running looked downward.

"I did not mean to desert you. I . . . I had to ask Rides a Crow again. She told me once I was not cursed, but I did not believe her. I needed time on the Buffalo Spine again. There is comfort for me on those rocks. I am alone there. Well, not. It is bleak and windy and harsh, but the spirits speak in the wind. The Lakota . . . I was once as much a Lakota as anyone. I was Crazy Horse's ward. I felt as though my own people had betrayed me when the elders rejected my marriage. I understand. I was a Cheyenne in a Lakota world as a boy. I do not want to do that to anyone. And I knew. I knew that what I wanted and what the spirits wanted were not the same, but I did not listen. I fought them as I have fought everyone else. I wanted . . ." Dooley could see the struggle within played out on Fox Running's face. "I wanted something that was not what the spirits have planned for me. I have fought against this in my soul, but I can only accept it. Now I am at peace, or such peace as there is while being alive. Rides a Crow had been seeking me as well. She had a disturbing dream."

Dooley's suspicions about the Lakota returned, but he let it pass. Fox Running had suffered enough. It was time to heal.

"You can tell me as we eat, lad. There is a Basque gentleman who came to town this past month who believes his people were the ancestors of all the Indians some number of thousand years ago. He cooks wonderful stew and plays a fiddle so sad and sweet that he can believe we are made of bear grease for all anyone cares! He says he cannot cook just for one, and so, when he does, he feeds everyone he can find to invite. He will be cooking this night, and we shall celebrate your return, laddie!"

■ ■ ■

Howard Porter was miserable. He wanted to be in his cramped garret in Boston, and not in a drafty, dirty boardinghouse in Lame Deer, Montana. However, he did not have a choice. His employer, Michael McGillicuddy, had ordered him to come to the West. McGillicuddy hated Indians, and Porter had learned very early that pandering to McGillicuddy's ways was the only way to keep his clerk's position. He knew that Mr. McGillicuddy and some female relative were locked in a war of wills that involved the Indians — with each out to break the other and frustrate each other's purpose.

He did not care about his boss's motives. He cared about survival. Nearing fifty, having failed at other positions, he could not lose this job. He had made a point of sharing his condemnation of every Indian action he could find in the newspapers, particularly the adventures of this Cheyenne Kid that were chronicled and repeated in the various sheets.

He had said many times that he wished he could do something to help his boss fight the Indian menace and had claimed he shared his employer's reverence for Custer, who had seemed more like an arrogant lout than any sort of hero. Now he was trapped by his own words, for the truth was, he cared little for anything besides a job that would allow him to scratch out a meager living.

Porter had been startled when McGillicuddy called him into his office and told him he was going to get a large increase in salary, but first he needed to do one thing, and the one thing was something that McGillicuddy was certain Porter would very much want to do. That one thing had not seemed as difficult in Boston as it had during the endless dusty train rides and bone-rattling coach trips that took him oh so perilously far from civilization. There was also a very large hint that, if he did not do this one thing, McGillicuddy would find someone else, and Porter would lose his job.

His assignment had been clear: he was to document every possible reason why the Cheyenne should not be allowed to have a reservation. McGillicuddy said he had powerful friends in Washington who warned him that the inspector sent to examine Lame Deer as a possible center for a reservation would be controlled by the army, which seemed to be partial to the Indians.

Porter's report would oppose that, McGillicuddy said, and he would be helped along the way by friends of McGillicuddy's in Montana. These friends were supposed to contact Porter once he was in the territory, although they had not done so yet. Porter had papers that identified him as an official investigator, which seemed to mean much less out here than it would have in Boston.

He certainly had enough to start with! That Indian shooting a white man because the white man confronted another Indian was one reason not to give them control. What if gunfights like that happened every day? He shivered and wished he had a cup of his Boston landlady's tea as he wrote up his first notes so as not to miss any details.

"Do ye think it is Bigelow who wants Two Moon dead?"

The rancher was the loudest, boldest, and most virulent Indian hater in the Tongue River Valley.

Fox Running shook his head. Bigelow was a bully who liked to see others cringe. If he wanted Two Moon dead, he would have picked any day to ride up to the chief's lodge near Fort Keogh with all of his men and kill him, for Two Moon lived without ceremony in the middle of his people.

There were other stockmen who were equally evil, but more devious. There was the railroad, which wanted to expand and was endlessly frustrated by trying to build around areas where the Indians purchased land, because the army was doing its best to avert war, which meant protecting the Indians from being arbitrarily thrown off their farms. At the northern tip of the valley, Miles City was trying to grow into another boom town like Cheyenne. Some towns would stop at nothing in the fever to be important. Violence among frontier towns was always possible.

There were still men with old scores to pay. Custer was not quite seven years dead, and many frontier cavalry officers felt cheated in their quest for revenge.

Two Moon had Cheyenne enemies as well. Some parts of the Northern Cheyenne Nation believed he was too quick to shed some old ways to protect others. Many young warriors Fox Running's age looked down on the old man and wanted to hunt, kill, and ride as their ancestors did. Dull Knife's death earlier in the year also caused ripples in the Indian world, for his age and long suffering on behalf of The People made them respect his wishes that they live in all possible harmony with their white neighbors. Two Moon had been at Fort Keogh when Dull Knife, Little Wolf, and the rest were fleeing from Indian Territory and risking their lives. He had long encouraged young warriors to scout for the army as a way to keep their restless energy from getting them in trouble. Some other Indians, particularly the Lakota, looked askance at this. In short, there was someone irked with someone else every day, and the peacemakers found themselves beset by all sides at all times.

"If what you say is so, enough people want the man dead to kill him ten times over. Should we try to drum up what you said they had at Pine Ridge, much like an Indian police force?" Dooley asked.

Fox Running again shook his head. With no formal reservation, there was no land Indian police could patrol. Two Moon would never accept an army escort. The army would never officially embrace creating Indian police on non-Indian land, even though everyone knew the Cheyenne had guns and went around armed.

"Rides a Crow needs our help because, whatever this is, it is not something easy for her to detect, even with her spirit horses and spirit wolf to protect her and to protect The People," Fox Running said. "I think we need to find out who really wants to kill Two Moon, not just who hates my people, and we have to do it out there." He gestured at the valley in general. "If we wait to guard him, whoever it is will find a way. I think that, from the terror Rides a Crow felt, her dream has more to it than one man killing another."

Dooley mulled over the task. As if there was a choice. He had lost little by leaving Boston behind and coming to Montana, for life there had passed him by and relegated him to the status of someone no longer needed. Here, he had a purpose.

He was also starting to realize that, with this new lease on life, and a partner who seemed destined to blow the valley wide open as a path to healing it, there was also a very good chance he would never need to worry about growing old.

CHAPTER THREE

June 1883, Fort Keogh, Montana

Captain Jack Evans listened to the soldier's tale. These were the moments he missed the clarity of a fight. Then, he knew who the enemy was, and who was on his side. Now, with swirling alliances and devious plans taking shape all around him, he was in a fight with no front and no rear.

Peace was also elusive. It had been more than four years since he received Little Wolf's pitiful band of tattered Northern Cheyenne survivors in a clearing near Fort Keogh. At the time, he naively thought there would be an end to conflict between whites and Indians. But instead of war across an open field, there was smoky talk, politics, and a realization that war did not end when the fighting stopped. Within the army, factions demanding loyalty could be as great a foe as any external enemy. It was in some ways a battle that would never end, and one that was wearing him down day after day. He could obey orders. He could be true to himself. It was getting increasingly difficult to do both.

The short, thin captain had long experience with Indians. When others in the prewar army were finding glory in the War Between the States, he had been posted to Minnesota, where the Dakota War of 1862 gave him a harsh lesson in how quickly death could erupt when Indians decided to avenge broken promises. The subsequent mass hanging of the Dakota and the harsh terms inflicted upon them had ensured the war would never be repeated and that, in the eyes of the Dakota, the white men would be their forever enemy until the children who watched their families starve were dead.

After the war, he had fought Indians across Kansas, Nebraska, Dakota, Wyoming, and Montana. He would kill anyone who fought him and share bread with anyone who did not. He had been one who pushed for a hard war because he knew the Lakota and the rest needed to be defeated to make room for settlers. Followed by a just peace, people who were no worse than the former Confederates so quickly welcomed back into the Union could learn that there was a better way than their age-old traditions, even if it lacked the glorious freedom of riding across the plains looking for buffalo.

At thirty-five, the West was his home and the army his family. Fate had put him in the right place to welcome the Northern Cheyenne home after their exodus from Indian country, and he had worked to ensure the transition to peace, if not smooth or perfect, was fair. He viewed every obstacle to peace as an enemy, whether Cheyenne or white.

As the messenger spouted irrelevancies, he stroked his bristling black mustache. Finally, his snapping brown eyes bored into the messenger.

"They're dead?" he asked. "Is that what all of this hemming and hawing is all about?"

"Not just dead. Butchered, sir."

Ben Rawlins had been one of the few white ranchers who hired the Cheyenne as helpers. His was a small spread on indifferent land near the town of Sickles, located just east of the Tongue River some forty miles southeast of Lame Deer.

Rawlins had about a half-dozen Cheyenne working for him as well as another half-dozen whites. They had been working together a year. Now, Rawlins had been killed along with two white men and four Cheyenne. The rest of the hands had been away from the ranch house along with the stock. Some cattle and horses were stolen.

The bodies were not simply scalped; they were desecrated in a fashion not seen since the year when Custer was slaughtered and the Cheyenne village at Rosebud Creek was destroyed. Evans knew that white ranchers disliked Rawlins for hiring Indians. Some Cheyenne disapproved of their young men working for white ranchers instead of helping their own people. He would ride down to Sickles, because, regardless of whoever committed this crime, it must be solved and solved quickly before it became a pretext for more conflict.

First, he would stop in Lame Deer at the agency whose past and purpose were both murky. Apparently, some woman from Boston offered the army a lot of money if it allowed her to fund this agency, which was not an official part of anything but seemed to be involved in everything. He had been told this would make his life easier as he oversaw the transition of the Northern Cheyenne from hunters to farmers, but he had been told that before. He wondered why this woman did not simply dole out the money directly if she wanted to perform an act of charity, but the ways of the rich were known only to themselves.

He had heard mixed stories about the Irishman and the young Cheyenne. The Irishman was a marvel. The Indian was wilder and less reliable. The incident earlier in the spring with Pete Bigelow had been retold a thousand times, and probably magnified in the telling. Bigelow may well have deserved what he got, but it did little to settle restive nerves among ranchers who looked for the least evidence the army was coddling Indians.

There had been, he was told, other cases. Fox Running came with a violent past. Evans had heard rumblings of concern over letting the young Indian run wild, but an equal number of what a blessing Dooley was. He sighed deeply. Since someone with connections well above his rank had put them in business, and connected them to the army, they were as much a flawed weapon as the new cannon that arrived and were too heavy to be drawn by cavalry horses.

He had not wanted to look closer at this Tongue River Agency until it had a few weeks to operate. Now, he had no choice.

Half of the brass and politicians were trying to create a reservation for the Cheyenne. The other half were fighting against one. Each side would want this incident to prove a point, which was why it needed to be handled with care and caution until he received the direction he knew would be coming as to how the army wanted the truth to be told.

June 1883, Rawlins Ranch near Sickles, Montana

Dooley watched Evans watch Fox Running as the young man walked around the ranch yard, while wispy dust wiped away even more traces of whatever had transpired.

It had been a week now since Rawlins and his hands were killed. The remaining hands who came upon the massacre described the stolen animals, but the horses and cattle had not been seen in the vicinity of Sickles. Dooley listened closely as the hands explained where all the men were found and in what state the bodies were — limbs severed with what appeared to be an axe, and violent blows inflicted on the heads of men who had already been shot. All the bodies, since buried, were left in a row.

Evans was trying to share everything he could and was being very gracious. Sadly, the same could not be said for Fox Running, who did not seem to understand that Evans was one of the truest friends the Cheyenne had, but also one who could not show prejudice for either side.

Fox Running had half listened. He seemed to spend more time looking at the roan horse he rode, a horse Dooley could see at a glance was full of mischief. If he did not know better, Dooley would've sworn Fox Running was talking to the horse. Now if he would only be as polite to the captain!

"Lad? Could ye join the parade?" Dooley called. Fox Running was wandering off toward one of the outbuildings. Dooley turned to Evans. "His company manners, sir, have their moments."

"I have heard he often has moments," replied Evans. "I am aware that the benefactor who is paying the bills has apparently unlimited faith in him, but I am concerned that we have a Cheyenne with a hair-trigger temper and two guns he wears with defiance trying to keep a warehouse of dynamite from exploding. If I may speak bluntly."

"Being the proverbial wet blanket is my stock in trade, sir."

Evans was forced to smile. Both the prickly Cheyenne and the genial Irishman were exactly as advertised. Perhaps the results of their investigation could be so as well. "What do you make of this, Mr. Dooley?"

Dooley sighed. "Glad I am they killed

both red and white, sir. Not that I wish anyone dead, but that makes it less obvious that one side or the other did the deed. I would think this was the work of Indians, from all I read in the East, but my partner said it is not."

"It is unusual," Evans admitted. "Most of the time if there's rustling, the object is to steal, and the farmer or rancher becomes a victim by defending his property. This seems to be a case where the men were killed deliberately, regardless of the stolen stock, but I know of no reason why. Nothing stands out about them. Perhaps your partner has discovered something."

Fox Running was approaching Dooley and Evans now, his brow knitted in thought. The scar between his eyes, suffered in the November 1876 battle at Rosebud Creek, seemed to glow hot pink.

"Was Rawlins the only white rancher to hire Cheyenne?" he asked Evans.

"He was among the first to do so, and he hired the most," Evans said. "I think he knew he was taking a chance." He met Fox Running's glare; the young man had clearly taken his words to mean the Cheyenne were inept. "I mean that, with hard feelings running high, he knew adding them would likely cause fights among his crew."

"Did it?"

"It might have, but if so, it was nothing he couldn't handle. I never heard he had trouble with his crew. Small ranches and farms have so much work that in the end, the hands get along because they can't take the time to hate each other. Hands come and go, but I rarely hear of bad feelings that would cause the level of violence we saw here."

"Could you and your men give Mr. Dooley a list of the farms and ranches that have hired young Cheyenne men or women? I know it will not be complete because they do not need to ask permission from you, but I think there will be few enough that it will be a short list. How many animals were taken, and what was Rawlins's brand?"

"The hands said there were four or five horses taken and a few head of cattle. Maybe five or six. Some of the cattle were penned because they were just ornery; a couple of others were set aside for the Indians to butcher when their work was done. That's how they wanted payment. Bar-R was his brand. The letter *R* with a line below it."

Fox Running looked at Dooley. "Mr. Dooley, would you mind visiting any of the ranches nearby that hire Cheyenne? I will be back in a day or two once I find a reason."

"A reason?" Evans asked.

"Yes, a reason why a gang of white men would slaughter these men."

"How do you know the killers were white men, lad? You are not exactly unbiased, Fox Running," Dooley called out, aware that the soldier was giving his partner a hard and skeptical look.

"I am not, that's true," he replied as he walked to Coyote Horse. "What kind of Indian would I be then?" He grinned at his friend, but the smile faded quickly. "The spirits know what they know, and the foulness left behind from killings that were coldly planned is not that of Indians. I do not pretend Indians never kill, or even that they would never kill for the sport of it. But not once in all the descriptions of the bodies has anyone said they were stabbed or cut with a knife. An axe is a white man's tool. And you know how 'them Injuns' are with their knives!"

"Lad?"

"If I am right, Mr. Dooley, at least one other rancher has had a visit recently — either just before this murder took place, or just after. We need to know what was said at those visits. They will talk to you and the captain where they will not talk with me, for obvious reasons. I will be back and meet you here."

Evans and Dooley watched Fox Running leap onto the back of the horse, which seemed almost playful as they galloped off far faster than any reason would allow.

"Should I be concerned?" Evans asked.

"Only if he is right, sir," replied Dooley, who had grasped Fox Running's implication. "Only if he is right."

The Tongue River Breaks were one of the delights of the broken lands east of the river. With the streams, trees, rocks, and rough terrain, a man could hide forever and subsist forever on the game that roamed freely there. The topography gave the impression of a child who built mountains in the sand, had a tantrum and tried to crush them, then rebuilt them and crushed them over and over.

Hanging Woman Creek flowed through the rugged terrain. Fox Running picked up the creek about a mile from the Rawlins ranch, about three miles east of Sickles, and followed the water.

Coyote Horse was one of the smaller spirit horses, a collection of animals with special gifts that helped protect the Northern

Cheyenne people from extinction. He picked his way through the creek as Fox Running let him walk any way he chose. After about five miles, he lifted his head and snorted.

"Good horse," said Fox Running, who had been warned by Rides a Crow that Coyote Horse, named after the trickster of legends, was liable to be impish. She was the link between The People and the spirit horses and had asked that one be given him to help protect him.

They had settled who was the boss early on. After Fox Running refused to be thrown off as planned, despite several attempts, and informed the horse in no uncertain terms that he thought all the tricks were great fun and could they have more, the horse seemed to decide it had met its match and had since been a faithful friend. In return, Fox Running cared for the animal as he never had for any living thing.

He looked ahead and saw horses. Three of them, all with saddles and bridles as though they had been in the process of being readied for a ride. The dappled light hid the brand at a distance.

"Just a little closer," Fox Running told his mount, picking up the reins he had let fall slack. "Let me see the brand."

The animals ahead were well aware of Coyote Horse and preparing to dart away. Fox Running felt the tensing of muscles in Coyote Horse's back, that meant only one thing.

"No, you will not . . ."

He could not tell which came first, whether the three riderless horses began the chase or Coyote Horse did, but two miles later, when it ended, Coyote Horse had proven how fast he could run, and Fox Running was thoroughly soaked from water splashed up by Coyote Horse's hooves. His legs were caked with mud.

However, Coyote Horse had headed off the three horses that were their quarry. After they all stopped, Fox Running dismounted and glared into Coyote Horse's eyes. He pursed his lips and examined the mess he had become, then patted the roan and laughed. "Well done, my mischievous friend," he said. "You have done your work and played a prank at the same time!" He stroked the horse's muzzle. "And now I know why Talks to Horses was anxious to be rid of you!" he added, mentioning the leader of the spirit horses, a black mare with whom Rides a Crow could communicate.

Coyote Horse's expression was one of total innocence as Fox Running, still laughing, moved to gather the reins of the three horses they had pursued. Upon close inspection of their brands, he saw they came from the Bar R.

Evening came early amid the trees and crags. Fox Running built a fire to dry out and tethered the three Bar R horses to a nearby tree. He offered to do the same for Coyote Horse just to see the animal's reaction, then laughed and hugged the roan's neck.

As he warmed himself by the fire and dried his clothes, he debated going further into the rugged country, considered a wild place that was a refuge for white men and Indians hiding from someone as well as those men who had come West because they wished never to be found. By now, any missing Rawlins cattle were in the process of becoming steaks.

No, he would return to the ranch in the morning with proof that whoever attacked Rawlins had so little interest in the animals that they turned them loose in the Breaks. There was no question in his mind — the raid had been aimed at the men.

Dooley and Evans were waiting when Fox Running led the three horses into the Rawlins ranch yard. They both looked somber, and Evans somewhat chastened.

"Let me guess," Fox Running said to them as he dismounted. "Mr. Dooley found there have been visitors to the farms around here that hire Cheyenne. They wore some kind of crude mask with eyeholes ripped out of the cloth. And, later, a warning came in the night. Something tangible left behind. Something small, but terrifying. Something like . . ."

"Teeth," finished Dooley. "The teeth Ben Rawlins would no longer need, they were told."

"How do you know this?" exclaimed Evans. "You were not with us!"

Fox Running held out a hand. Four teeth reposed in it. All had been painted black.

"I found these on our first day here, tossed on the floor of the pantry. I wondered if they were a warning. When I was at the Indian School in Boston, there was a woman who helped me learn about the world. I had books and magazines — all anyone could ask to read," he told Evans. "I read about the activities of the Ku Klux Klan in the southern states after the War Between the States was over. When I heard about the violence here, it sounded like something done to intimidate. Do you know from the other Rawlins hands if Ben Rawlins talked about a warning?"

"I believe he collected a rather vast number of them, lad," Dooley replied. "The hands also said the Cheyenne told them that some of their own people did not like them working here because Cheyenne should not work for white men. They all believed it was just talk."

"Some of the talkers do more than that. It seems to me we have a gang of local men trying to make other men so afraid to work with the Cheyenne that any attempt to create a new home for The People will fail. Did the ranch hands you talked to notice anything familiar about the riders or their voices?"

"Why do you think they're local?" asked Evans.

"The horses they turned loose could have been sold. Look at them. They are fine animals. The killers did not want to be seen with them, which is only a risk if the killers live near here. If they lived far off, they would not care."

As he spoke, he also considered another alternative — that those who took the horses lived deeper in the wild country and would be looking for the animals when next they emerged. But outlaws would not care about farms that hired Cheyenne men as workers, unless they were hired by someone like Bigelow. He shared that possibility with Evans and Dooley.

Evans had been told that Fox Running was clever. "An Indian who thinks like a white man" was the way one had described him. That could make him a useful man, and a dangerous one in a delicate situation. There was no question the young Cheyenne believed the Tongue River Valley should belong to the Cheyenne and the Cheyenne alone. Evans, like Dooley, believed Fox Running would be happy to kill anyone who stood in the way of that happening, something he could personally understand but could not officially support.

Evans needed to be sure that what came next was the truth and not something that favored one side over the other. He knew many of his superiors believed the Cheyenne should get a reservation, but for the army to even appear partial right now could set back that effort and wreck the career of anyone who contributed to a disaster. "Could you meet with the ranchers again?" he asked Dooley. "See if any of them recall anything that might help identify who these 'visitors' really were?"

Dooley agreed. He understood that Evans wanted him to do the work, to avoid getting

Fox Running too involved. He accepted Evans's offer of some troopers to assist, since Evans himself could not remain away from Fort Keogh indefinitely.

Fox Running wanted to prowl the Tongue River Breaks. "You want to go look for trouble, lad," said Dooley, who knew his friend was always far too willing to take risks.

"I think it already found us, Mr. Dooley."

Chapter Four

Fox Running packed food and spare ammunition as he rode slowly into the glorious jagged madness of the Tongue River Breaks. Its wildness had called to him on his first encounter with the land, and whether or not he was right that he would find out more about the thieves who followed the murderers, he could at least have a few moments to explore.

In one spot, a pine tree grew on a sandstone outcrop that had eroded almost level with the ground. There should not have been enough dirt for a tree to grow, but there it was. This was a place to come often. He rode slowly, losing the thoughts with which he'd entered the Breaks amid sights and sounds that enveloped him. Soon, he was not only hearing and seeing, but feeling the rhythm of life that pulsed beyond the narrow, beaten path that wound through the trees. The route through the trees was hardly visible as such, little more than dirt tramped down harder than anywhere else, with fewer dead leaves and needles strewn across it, except for places where it appeared human hands had tried to hide the trail.

The sun filtering through the trees illuminated bits of soundless movement here and there at the far edges of his vision. Fox Running knew he had been seen. He had expected it. The watcher remained. As he crossed one of the tiny rivulets that fed the creek, his patience — nearly nonexistent to begin with — began to wear. The birds had gone silent. He dismounted at last.

"This game is silly," he called out in his usual blend of Cheyenne and Lakota, for he had grown up among both. "You can come out and we can talk, instead of you leaping from tree to tree like a squirrel. I am called Fox Running. I am of The People. The Lakota knew me as Blazing Hands, if you are Lakota. Come and show yourself so I may properly honor you and your father."

"What do you know of my father?" The voice was a young woman's.

Fox Running did not show his surprise. His watcher would not know she had already gotten one up on him. He could roughly guess which tree the voice came from and looked directly at it as he replied.

"Enough to know that the horses he stole from some white men a few days ago are from a place where men were murdered, as are the cattle he has butchered. He may be in deeper water than he knows, because the army is looking for the man who did the killing, and they will find him in the end."

"My father does not kill," she replied.

"All men kill," he argued back, flatly.

He could see a rifle barrel move slightly. A tiny flash, but it was there.

"The army will not believe whatever story you wish to tell when they follow the trail from the ranch where the men were murdered to the place where you hide by the rocks, where the trees cover the entrance to the cave," Fox Running called.

"Who are you?"

"I am who I said: a Cheyenne who hears what the spirits speak and knows what the spirits know."

"If you are Cheyenne, why do you wear guns like a white man, like those who shoot guns for their pay?"

"I have lived many years among the white men. It is how I survive."

"Lift your hands." He did so. "Try no white man's tricks. I have a rifle. I can shoot you dead if I must."

"I shall try no tricks, but please do not

dawdle further," he said. "I have many things to do this day other than speak to talking trees with guns."

"The only thing that matters to you is that you not trick me," said the young woman as she stepped out from behind the tree. A piece of leather looped across her forehead and around her hair, which hung in two long braids on each side down her back. She wore a dark buckskin shirt that hung to her knees, buckskin leggings, and unadorned moccasins. He could see a string of white at her throat — some type of bone necklace that stood out against the dimness of the trees.

As she moved closer, he realized she was about his age. She was about his height as well, if not taller, for he was short even for a Cheyenne, and built along the same wiry lines as he was. Her face had a large white blotch on it — a scar she had clearly gotten long ago. From the time she was taking in moving closer, he assumed she was inspecting him much as he was inspecting her.

"You took the horses," she said at last. "When I came for them, I was too late, and I saw you!"

"I did. Or perhaps, to be fair, I should say my horse captured them, for they tried to run, but none can match Coyote Horse."

Fox Running glanced at the spirit horse with pride.

The young woman looked from him to the roan with an expression that said she did not find the animal impressive. Then she looked back at Fox Running, who was on the receiving end of a baleful glance from the spirit animal.

"Could you please stop pointing that at me?" asked Fox Running, nodding at her rifle. "Because I was raised by the Lakota and spent many years among whites, I do not always keep Cheyenne customs, but since I did not shoot at you when your foot dislodged pebbles at the gray rock shaped like an arrowhead, or when you scared the deer by the very bent cedar tree, I believe that proves I have no plan to kill you. Which means you should not have one to kill me."

"I do not trust you."

"That is wise," he replied. "But, by now, if I was leading others, they would have arrived. What is your name?"

"I am Cut Sky." She glared at him, radiating pride and defiance. For an odd moment, he felt as though he were looking in a mirror.

"Lead me to your father so we may all talk. What is taking place involves more than horses and cattle. He and those who help him need to know."

"How do you know I am not here all alone?"

"The spirits told me." She gave him a scoffing look, and he went on. "I also saw the small mark on the ground from the stick your father leans upon when he walks. It made no sense to me at first, but the spirits took the scales from my eyes, and now it does."

"How so?"

"A man who cannot walk easily is also one who cannot ride well. If he walked this far, it must have been important. He would have seen his choices and decided to take that which matters most. The cattle were food. Food is rare here. The horses were less so. This is poor ground for horses, and those with whom you live have little space to hold them, so, if they walked away or could be held and sold at a later date, it was all the same when placed next to taking meat that could fill hungry bellies. Am I not correct?"

A grumble was all he got for an answer.

"Walk this path," she said, pointing to a track that wound uphill to his right. "I will follow with my gun on you."

"I do not like guns pointed at me."

"Did you hear anyone ask what you like?" she said. "I do not care. Go."

He did as he was told, leading Coyote Horse. "It is a shame we are walking," he said. "You should see my horse run."

"Keep going," she replied.

"He can run!" Fox Running added with increased animation, looking Coyote Horse in the eye. "Run!"

"I don't . . ." she said, then broke off as the horse appeared to bolt. Fox Running ran a few steps to catch him, crossing in front of Coyote Horse and putting the animal between himself and Cut Sky. When he popped back into sight, he had a pistol in his right hand. She was still holding her rifle across her chest.

"I said I do not like guns pointed at me," he said, in the tone of a parent reminding a child of a basic rule. "Set your rifle on the ground, please, until we can come to an understanding."

She eased her finger off the trigger, showed him her right hand as she took it off the gun, and then set the rifle down with her left hand.

"That is good. Keeping your hands away from the knives in your belt would be a good idea also. Now, please lead the way."

He holstered his pistol. Eyes met eyes in a challenge as she thought about kicking him when he picked up her rifle. He waited calmly for her to decide. She looked at the ground. He picked up the fallen rifle.

She walked ahead of him, refusing to take the bait every time he made an attempt at conversation. After about two miles of silent walking through old, dense forests, he could smell smoke. Having made his point, he would not march her into her own camp as though she was a prisoner.

"Cut Sky." She turned. He tossed her the rifle. She grabbed it in anger. "That is a fine weapon," he said. The 1860 Henry rifle — one of the fastest guns to work and fire — was rare.

"It was used by a warrior at the Greasy Grass," she told him. "It knows well how to kill an enemy."

"I am no enemy."

Her glare said otherwise. He laughed.

"Shall we greet your father together? Pointing guns is very rude among those who hide in the woods, or so I am told."

She was wary. "I will get even with you," she fumed.

Looking at her, Fox Running guessed she was rarely bested at anything. "I expect so," he said, then added with a smile, "But you have to admit it was a good trick."

The trees parted. In a clearing were about a dozen Indians. Most were armed.

"Father!" she called to the older man seated by the fire, her eyes sending a message to Fox Running that no tricks would be tolerated here.

"Greetings, Blue Feather," said Fox Running with enthusiasm for one of the few faces of the past he could recall with joy. He could not help but remember one of the most unforgettable characters of the Northern Cheyenne and Lakota encampments at Fort Robinson in the days years ago when he lived among both peoples. Blue Feather had been known as the Bandit King for his skill in trafficking stolen items without ever seeming to face punishment. "I am filled with joy to see the years have treated you kindly since the Fort Robinson days."

A horse had fallen on Blue Feather's right leg during a Cheyenne raid against the Crow, crushing it. He had survived but could not walk unaided and rode only with great difficulty. At the camp that grew after the Northern Cheyenne and later Crazy Horse's band of Oglala surrendered, he was known as the man who could find or steal anything for any customer — white or Indian. He was tall and well built, now getting heavy from the years of enforced inactivity, with a face that greeted everyone as a friend and hid whatever went on behind the mask. Tiny flecks of gray dotted the hair that framed his weathered face, a face that registered surprise that a young warrior would emerge from the trees calling his name.

Using a stout stick as a crutch, Blue Feather walked closer to inspect Fox Running.

"The scarred child," he said, pointing at Fox Running's face, where the mark of a cavalry saber curved from his hairline to between his eyes. "Yes. I remember you. They said you were marked by the spirits."

"As I recall, it was a soldier's sword," replied Fox Running.

"You were the one . . . the one who saved Crazy Horse that day! Yes!" He turned to the girl. "Why did you not tell me one of your young men was this one?" He looked again at Fox Running. "You are the one! The stories are true?"

"I should like to know what they say."

"You were taken to the land of the white man. You killed them with their guns, and you fight with guns like they do. They gave you a name to take away your soul, and you killed them to reclaim it. You were with the Lakota last year." The recitation trailed off. Fox Running could tell Blue Feather knew more than he wished to say, either from hospitality or innate caution.

Fox Running might argue with the details, but the old thief had it pretty close. "And now I am here."

"To see Cut Sky? Another suitor?" Blue Feather turned to his men. "Every time she goes to Lame Deer there is another one!" They all laughed.

Blue Feather touched Fox Running on the arm and pointed off toward the trees. "Oh! Do you see this ravine behind those trees? It was a mountain until one day she scowled at it. There are ten thousand toads in these hills that once were her admirers who displeased her. And should I tell you what became of the fool who once told her she was wrong? It was a fate too terrible to behold."

"Father!"

The genial thief threw back his head and roared his pleasure as Cut Sky's mouth tightened in disapproval.

"When my leg was crushed, they sang the death song over me, but I stopped them, for I was not ready to die," he said. "That was many years ago, and the spirits have blessed me for refusing to die that day, but nowhere have they blessed me as they have with my daughter. Come and sit. Eat, for we have fresh meat! We must talk!"

Cut Sky moved next to her father so he could throw his arm over her instead of using the stick he held in his other hand, as they walked in what was clearly a long-practiced partnership. For a moment, Fox Running felt a pang of envy. Cut Sky might be hiding from the world in a muddy place and living hand to mouth based on what could be stolen, but she had something Fox Running could barely recall, so long had it been that he was just another Cheyenne boy — a family and a place to belong.

"What did you tell him?" he asked Cut Sky after she walked Blue Feather to the fire where they would eat and then showed him where to leave Coyote Horse.

"Nothing he does not already know," she replied.

"Including what happened to your rifle on our way here?"

"I do not recall anything," she said adamantly as Fox Running grinned, "except that perhaps I should have shot first and spoken later!"

"You would have missed," he replied, "or I would have shot you."

"How did you know about the cave?" she asked intently. "That is my secret place. I do not understand."

"In these lands, there have to be caves and

trees," he said. "I lied and made up something in order to deceive you."

Her outraged expression had him laughing as they sat down for food.

After a meal of stolen beef, a delicacy Fox Running had not eaten in far too long, and conversation about the army, the Cheyenne, Fort Robinson, and any number of things, Blue Feather withdrew to his lodge, along with Cut Sky and Fox Running, proclaiming to those in his camp that this was a suitor who must be set straight!

He waited until they were settled on thick, rich blankets before he let the mask drop. "As much as it would be an interesting world to have the famous Cheyenne Kid courting my daughter, I know that the young man known as Blazing Hands was rejected by the Lakota when he wanted a Lakota wife, but I do not know why. And I know that the Cheyenne called Fox Running works with the army and a white man, and so I am very curious why you are really here," Blue Feather said. "It cannot be to retrace the steps that a boy described as either Lakota or Cheyenne took near Fort Keogh many years ago, when he shot members of his own gang and then, so I am told, forever disappeared. And I can see there is a grim darkness upon you that I did not ever hear of before, and that makes me wonder at your purpose here."

"You are well informed, which I recall was one of your skills," replied Fox Running, seeing Cut Sky hang on every word of her father's summation of his life. He was not surprised that a man who knew everything that happened everywhere had kept track of him over time. "Since you know much, you should know all."

He quickly sketched his life from the time he left the Lakota camp in 1877, after soldiers murdered Crazy Horse. The scars his soul still felt from the massacre at The Pit when the last Cheyenne fleeing from soldiers were killed, or his rejection by the Lakota, were not things to share with strangers. He talked briefly of the Indian School in Boston, and his search for a place to belong after his escape.

"What I heard, I wondered about, for it was like the stories we tell children," said Blue Feather.

"It is a path I never heard before," added Cut Sky.

"It is a path I have walked blind," remarked Fox Running ruefully. "I still often feel blind as I walk, for as much as the spirits of the Cheyenne may be around me, there are Lakota and white voices in me as well. In truth, it can be a babble like the days they give food away at the fort."

"Why are you here?" asked Blue Feather. "It is not just so you and my daughter can point guns at each other and you can best her."

Cut Sky looked daggers at Fox Running. Her father laughed. "He did not say a word, daughter. Your face was the one telling the tale."

Fox Running explained about the murders at the Rawlins farm. "I know the horses were here, because I took them back. No one cares if the cattle were slaughtered and if I just ate some of the meat, or if other horses might have found their way here. The men who killed the farmer and his workers may be trying to stir up more trouble, kill more people, and prevent the Northern Cheyenne from settling and having a reservation here. There are Northern Cheyenne farms and lodges where extra rifles and spare ammunition are being stored for that day when the next battle will rage. If that should happen, between the ranchers who are also preparing for battle and the army, I fear there would be no Cheyenne left this time."

Blue Feather had no response.

"Blue Feather, you and I have seen the

world in many ways. We both know the army and the Cheyenne find it convenient to have no knowledge of some things that exist, which creates a place of refuge for you where no one looks too closely. Your safety — Cut Sky's safety, the safety of every person in your camp — depends upon peace. If there is another war, it would be like a forest fire that burns every acre, including these, for the Breaks would be a hiding place others will find. There will be no safe places, and none will be able to navigate the thin line between worlds. The Cheyenne will kill anyone who is white or works with the army; the whites will kill any Indian on principle. I work with whites and the army to keep this from happening. That is why I followed the horses and why I am here, so that those who killed whites and Cheyenne at the Rawlins farm can be brought to justice and those who call for war against the Cheyenne can be silenced."

Blue Feather's eyes narrowed. "The boy who saved Crazy Horse was all guns and fire. The man I heard of is much the same. This is a different person who speaks to me now."

"There is a time for guns and fire. There is also a time for talk. In the world of these days around us, Blue Feather, both can be weapons."

Blue Feather sat silently. Finally, he said, "I must think. Much is revealed to those who live, as I do, in the shadows where few hide their true faces. You speak of things that I have thought upon, and put light on places where my thoughts have not dwelled. Cut Sky makes a trip to Lame Deer regularly, to be about business that is of little interest to the army or anyone else. I am certain nothing I do would interest the army."

"I am certain much you do would interest them," replied Fox Running with a smile, "but I believe that making life complicated would vex the poor soldiers no end, and I wish to be charitable to them."

Cut Sky saw her father smile as he did when talking to a conspirator who understood how Blue Feather's world operated. How did this Fox Running manage such a feat?

"When next she goes to Lame Deer," he said, "I shall have her find you and speak of my thoughts on this."

Fox Running had never learned the patience of the Cheyenne way, but he knew it was as far as Blue Feather would go this day.

"I do not think my men would be pleased

to know all that transpires. You shall spend time with Cut Sky before you leave, trying to impress her in the fashion of young men, for *that* they understand. Perhaps you can point guns at each other again!" He laughed until a look at his daughter's face forced him to try, unsuccessfully, to stop.

"Show our guest the fish pool," he said to her when the laughing spasm ended. He turned to Fox Running and added, "We shall plan to see you again. I say this so it is clear I have given my blessing that you spend time with my daughter, for someone will ask. Go with the spirits, Fox Running."

"And may the spirits hold you close as well, Blue Feather."

"You have really been to all of those places?" Cut Sky said after he told her, upon her request, the full story of his travels. They sat by the pool where trout and other fish lived. "We moved from Fort Robinson to Pine Ridge, to Fort Keogh and to Missouri and back, and then here after the Cheyenne returned. I thought that was moving often!"

"Why?" asked Fox Running. "Blue Feather is mostly Cheyenne, but he is part Lakota on his grandmother's side, and you are also part Lakota. Why not stay there?"

"What did you just say?"

"I asked . . ."

"About me!"

Fox Running sighed.

"When I floated between the Cheyenne and Lakota camps around Fort Robinson, Blue Feather was a notable character. That was six years ago. He had no wife. He had no daughter. You appear to be older than six, which means he took you in or there is some game being played. I think it is the first. Lakota people speak English with different accents and patterns of speech than do the Northern Cheyenne. You speak that way. Your necklace is styled as a Lakota would make it, yet everything else is Cheyenne, as though you take from each what pleases you and not what you are bound to obey. That means to me that you have parts of both in you, but you belong in neither camp, which means your parents were lost. I am not trying to offend you. I lived as a Lakota, and despite what happened, I will always feel I am part Lakota regardless of my Cheyenne blood. If you tell me anything, please do not lie. If it is not my business, I can accept that as an answer," he said.

She studied the surface of the pond.

"My father was a Northern Cheyenne man. His mother was a Lakota woman who had a white grandfather. My mother was a mix of Lakota, Cheyenne, and, at some time in the past, white. They were visiting Black Kettle's Southern Cheyenne the year I was born, while I was a baby with my father's mother, and both died at Sand Creek. I lived with the Oglala until my mother's mother died, for she had taken me in. The Cheyenne did not want me." Her face reflected bitterness. "My grandmother died near the time of Crazy Horse's death. Blue Feather's wife had died the winter before, the winter of the Custer fight, and he had no children. I had been one of our clan's messengers to him. He liked me, and I liked him. He wanted me to come live with him. No one seemed to care very much what I did, so I became his daughter. It was the happiest day of my life. I am not his blood, but he has called me daughter from that day, and I am blessed."

Her voice caught more than once during her recitation. Fox Running had no idea what to say to a story of someone who had been living without a family almost as much as he had.

"Tell me of your name," he said. "Was it from a vision?"

"My father, on the day I was born, had a vision that, as he was holding me, giant black clouds appeared in a blue sky. There were two of them. As they floated, the sky tore in two. The clouds were drawn into the place where the sky was ripped. The tear grew wider and wider until he could see the stars. He thought he was seeing Seana and taking the long fork to the land of the dead. Then the sky began to heal. Two puffy clouds — the kind I called sky buffaloes when I was a child — emerged from the tear in the sky. They came close until they were over his head. They dropped water on him, and then the sky opened and they vanished," she said. "He believed the dream was a blessing, because water at Sand Creek was so rare, and so they named me Cut Sky."

"It is a beautiful vision."

"It was told to me by those he told of it before he died in the massacre — when the soldiers killed them."

"Do you have any memories of them?" Fox Running's recollections were dim and hazy, but they were real.

"No," she replied. "I do not know more than a few stories and the story of my name. It is as though I had no family."

For a moment, he wondered if her wistful tone was a prelude to a tear, the one thing that could shake him as could no line of men with guns. He needed to find something to say.

"I can shoot the pine cone off that branch hanging from the cliff before you can," he said.

"With what? That little toy at your hip?"

"Afraid to try?"

Chapter Five

June 1883, Lame Deer, Montana

John Dooley labored over the letter. Katherine McGillicuddy had made it abundantly clear she wanted to know everything that transpired in Montana with her new venture and with Fox Running. Dooley was uncertain whether he was there to help or protect the younger man, although at times it was much the same thing.

The woman knew Fox Running. Had she hired them on her own, it would have seemed like charity he would have rejected. To be hired through the army meant he was someone worth hiring, not a charity case. Fox Running also felt beholden to no one. She knew him well.

He tried to gloss over the trough into which the young man fell after the Lakota ended his dreams of marrying Morning Shadow. The truth was, Dooley could not fully understand what drove Fox Running to do what he did, except that he had a deep conception of right and wrong from which he would not budge. He would rather die than do wrong, and woe betide the man who told Fox Running he ever *was* wrong. Dooley wondered how much Katherine McGillicuddy knew of what went on below the surface. The woman had seen something and tried to educate Fox Running to become a lawyer. His education had stuck to him far better than the concept of shoes had. Dooley summarized the Rawlins killings and wrote a hasty closing.

He would walk to the post office in a few moments. He had been glad to return to Lame Deer. Sickles, on the other bank of the Tongue River, struck him as a town where everyone did something that was not quite legal. Not that he disapproved of skirting the letter of the law, for even as a Boston policeman he'd wondered at the perspective of those who outlawed simple things while stealing far more. But when men were hiding something, they also hid things he needed to know in order to avoid a tragic ending to the saga of the Northern Cheyenne.

Dooley saw what Fox Running could not, because he could see without his friend's fierce passion. The army could not help the

Cheyenne openly, or the ranchers and railroad would complain, and the Indians would be fighting the full power of the federal government. Captain Evans wanted peace. The man had risked his career to achieve it. But making peace happen was a delicate dance that would need time without outside intervention before the dancers could learn the steps.

A powerful hand knocked at the door. Dooley, who carried his pistol in his coat pocket, pulled it out and set it on the table in front of him. Only white men knocked; the custom was foreign to the Cheyenne, who would breeze in as though they expected to be welcome at any hour. And who was to blame for that, he asked himself, since he made them welcome, especially the children, who were always a delight.

"Come in," he called.

The door opened to reveal a handsome, tall rancher with a fine silver mustache framing a bold, square face. Dressed in clothes that were neither the odd fashions of the East or the worn clothing of a working ranch, he exuded the attitude of a man who had ridden hard, worked hard, and made his way up from there.

"Ron Sanders," he boomed. "Cattle and Horse Dealers of Texas, Montana, Wyoming, Dakota, and Nebraska."

"A mouthful, that is," replied Dooley. "John Dooley, but I suspect ye already know."

"I do. Is the Indian boy around that works for you?"

"Partners it is we are, since the lad works for no one," Dooley corrected him, glad Fox Running was not around to hear himself referred to as a boy. "No, he is off on an errand and not likely to be here for a day or three, in the casual way they have with time here. How may I help you?"

Sanders moved further in, spied a chair, and settled himself in it. "We represent many of the leading ranchers hereabouts. My home ranch is in Texas, but I don't live there anymore. I own a house in Cheyenne that could fit ten of the shacks where I was born. The boys drive stock up here and sell it, and I keep my hand in; just went back this spring to be sure they remember who the boss is. But now mostly I manage things."

Dooley took in the hand-crafted boots, the rich leather jacket. "Managing must pay well, sir."

"It does, Mr. Dooley. It does. I came out here in '62, a little earlier than many of the men, but later than others. Some of us started with a horse and 160 acres; some not so much. You ever seen Cheyenne, John?"

"The train from Boston that brought me here stopped there," he said. "Gilded and fine were many parts of it, as I recall, although I also seem to recall a preponderance of wet goods establishments!"

"Thirst can be a problem in Cheyenne, but it is easily cured," Sanders said, chuckling in the way of men talking business. "That little city is what we think we can grow here in Montana, up in Miles City."

Dooley knew that Miles City, named for General Nelson Miles, was near Fort Keogh, at the northern end of the Tongue River Valley. "All to cure the thirst of the populace?" he asked.

"All to make life better," replied Sanders. "This part of Montana is perfect for ranching. Now I won't deny some of the farmers their due, but this is ranching country, John. Picture this whole valley raising stock, shipping it East, and you could picture one of the most prosperous places in the entire United States. It would help make this territory a state, which is what we all want."

"Ahh. We do," replied Dooley who was uncertain why more government was a good thing when all ranchers ever did was criticize it.

For a second, Sanders frowned as if detecting a lack of enthusiasm on Dooley's part.

"Ranching needs room and land," he said. "Now I know you and your Injun friend work with the army to keep the peace. Lord knows that's a thankless job. Can't expect those Injuns to go from living wild and stealing everything they could get their hands on to living the proper way good people act. Some of 'em have made amazing strides forward. But you and I know it takes time. While they're out there stumbling around a field to grow a few ears of bad corn, that land could be put to good, productive use by people who can make this country grow. Are you with me, John?"

"Following closely, sir, I am."

"Our . . . well, our position is that all this talk of reservations and all this farming and homesteading is putting the cart before the horse. There's a lot of land in other places where they can go and learn how to plant and harvest. The way I hear it, down in Kansas and Colorado, there are flat fields as far as your eye can see, just for the taking. Scattering the Cheyenne there might make some sense. But putting them here to form a lump in the way of progress, now that's just not right."

"Ronald, me lad, clear as a bell is your thinking, but not why you are sharing this with me."

"We want you to think about your future, John. You are spending your life trying to keep those Indians off the war path when that's the only place they want to be. You can't stop nature from taking its course. Once the army realizes all this talk about land for the Indians is just plain wrong, because they are just not ready, then we can use all the land in these parts as it ought to be used, and we can all be very wealthy. You are exhausting yourself to no purpose. Perhaps if you were to focus on Indian crimes, and you were to ensure that the army makes certain the Indians know the law is enforced up here with no coddling, you might find you have a far more rewarding life financially."

Sanders looked pleased with himself, as though he had finished sharing a message whose delivery he had practiced long and hard.

"And what of the lad I work with?"

"I'm sure we could find something for him to do, John. There are a few good ones who might fit in with a little help. I hear he can read some. That's always good as a first step. We could work that out. What do you say, John? Want to get out of this 'detective' business where no one is your friend and find out what it's like to make some real money?"

Dooley wanted to tell him that he wished Fox Running was there to give Sanders the answer the man deserved, but he temporized. "A wise man thinks before acting, Ronald. 'Tis an interesting notion you present, but too flattering. This wee bit of business we do is not enough to change the world. Trading this in, and the freedom to be lazy, for real work — now, there might be more than meets the eyes here, Ronald."

"Of course you should think on this, John," said Sanders, rising from his chair. "But I wouldn't take too long. There comes a point where all things hang in the balance, and this valley is there now. Think about five thousand dollars, John. Think of what you could do if you had it tomorrow. Think about more where that came from."

He paused, as if gauging Dooley's reaction. "A friend at the right time, no matter how small the gesture may seem, could be of great importance in the future. Many eyes are upon this valley, belonging to many men of high positions in politics and many who, for reasons that date back to the Little

Bighorn, have a purpose that aligns with mine. There are those in the army who understand that only a few years after Custer was slaughtered is not a good time to hand choice land to those who killed him." He walked to the door. "I would think perhaps you might not want to share this conversation with your Indian lad. From what I know, his head for business is not as wise as yours."

If Sanders truly believed Dooley was the kind to turn on his friends, then Dooley figured he'd just been insulted, but he let the remark pass with a genial smile. "And where do I find ye when I wish to talk further of numbers and possibilities, as ye might call them?"

"I shall find you, John. I shall find you." With a slight lift of his hat, the man was gone.

Cut Sky finished loading the wagon she would drive to Lame Deer. She would carry with her Blue Feather's answer to the strange Cheyenne. The wagon was, as always, to be left until other goods filled it up. She would return for it in two weeks or so. She had made the trip often, always so she reached Lame Deer around dawn when most were asleep. The less anyone saw, the less anyone knew. She knew her business well.

She would ask about this Fox Running, for her father's sake and for her own curiosity. Even in their brief time together, she could sense the wildness in him, and yet something very different from the men who talked of exploits more than they ever performed them.

"Cut Sky, it is dangerous on the roads to Lame Deer these days."

Dog Teeth thought of himself as dangerous. He also thought Cut Sky should want him as her man, a notion of which she tried gently to disabuse him, because she knew he had some small role in her father's enterprises.

"Then do not go," she replied curtly.

"Who is this you were with — he who wears two guns?"

Dog Teeth was slightly taller than she was, with long, stringy hair and a dark-brown vest exposing muscled arms. He had a black leather gun belt around his hips, with one gun. He was not ugly, but she believed his features covered a soul that was dark and devious.

"Who I am with is not your concern," she said. "I have told you, I do not wish to keep company with you."

Dog Teeth moved closer. "A Cheyenne woman does as she is told."

"And I am part Lakota. Out of my way." She went to walk past him.

"You will obey, bandit brat," he said. "And I am done with begging."

He grabbed her and tried to wrestle her into the brush. For a moment, his greater strength dragged her into those shadows. Fear rose within her. It gave her strength.

Her right hand chopped down on the hand reaching to grope her as she turned and delivered a kick with her left foot to his groin. As he doubled over, she brought up her right knee and connected with his head.

From the dust, dizzy with pain and filled with rage, he tried to get up.

A rifle cocked.

"You may leave this camp, or I will kill you." Blue Feather held the rifle pointed at Dog Teeth. "If Cut Sky tells me she sees you again, I will speak with those I know — and you should well understand the extent of my friends across this valley, Dog Teeth — and you will find your life at risk. Go!"

For a moment, Cut Sky thought Dog Teeth would reach for his gun. She was ready to pull the knife at her waist. She hoped Dog Teeth would try. She could feel her heart pounding as she waited for some sign that he would resist.

The moment passed. He wilted and held his arms out from his sides.

"Owl Face!" Blue Feather said.

One of Blue Feather's chief lieutenants moved into view.

"Disarm him. Be sure he leaves here on foot. Take him down the trail to Wolf Mountain. If you find a reason to shoot him, any reason at all, do not hesitate."

Blue Feather turned away. Owl Face pulled the gun from Dog Teeth's holster. Cut Sky saw pain, humiliation, and hatred in Dog Teeth's eyes. She wanted to spit in his face. Instead, she held out her hand. Owl Face handed the gun to her. She swiftly raised it and pointed it at Dog Teeth.

"Do you like the way this feels, Dog Teeth? Do you like the way it feels to be helpless? I have heard stories about you. About what you do to girls who are helpless to fight you. Should I summon the girls who have been foolish enough to trust you so they can see you now?" She cocked the hammer. Owl Face watched impassively. Cut Sky held the pose long enough to make sure Dog Teeth thought about it, then let the hammer down slowly.

"I would not stain myself with your blood." She motioned with her head. Owl

Face, larger and stronger than Dog Teeth, grabbed the younger warrior by the left bicep and, with a hunting knife to his back, ordered him to move.

As they left, Cut Sky looked uphill where her father had gone. From the hilltop, he nodded. She nodded back, wondering not for the first time how a man who could not walk unaided always knew to be there for her.

She tied her horse to the wagon and climbed up to the seat. She moved the wagon along the narrow-rutted road as Blue Feather watched.

"She is not of my blood, spirits," he prayed as she left. "But she is of my soul. Watch over her."

Dooley walked through the cabins and lodges that made up Lame Deer. It could well be seen as a squalid, teeming mass of Indians who were trying to be something they were not amid whites who had barely planted the seed of a town. But he knew it was more. The Northern Cheyenne had been almost wiped out. Perhaps anything less would never have made them accept that they had to change. But now, Two Moon and most of the Cheyenne were looking at doing whatever must be done to rebuild their traditions in a new model.

He could see where Sanders would want everything he could grab. Men like him existed throughout the West. Sanders was emphatic about the need for land for horses and cattle to roam, but when Indians wanted the same thing, it had to be taken away. Still, Sanders represented a warning. He knew enough about Dooley and Fox Running to make it clear that someone was watching them. They would never do the man's bidding, but at what cost?

His thoughts were jarred from his head by the impact of a small girl against his legs. "Grasshopper! You must look where you are going!"

"Big Bear, do not call me that in front of our teacher," Spotted Dawn replied.

"Teacher?"

"Miss Mary Ed is going to be here for a few weeks to teach us to read. There she is!"

The little girl pointed back the way she had come. A woman was walking toward them along the dusty thoroughfare. She was taller than everyone around her, with flaming red hair that would have stood out even on the streets of Boston. From her slow gait and her expression, this was one of her first trips through Lame Deer. She reacted with a start when Dooley stepped into her line of sight.

"It takes a wee dram of getting used to," he said. The woman looked younger than he was, likely somewhere in her thirties. "John Dooley. Tongue River Agency. Formerly of Boston."

"Mairead Cullihan of Cambridge," she said. "I . . . well, my friend Annie Campbell encouraged me to come here and teach when I told her I wanted a challenge. She told me to be prepared, but I think I was not. Is it always . . ." She waved her hands, as if struggling to grab the right words.

Dooley smiled. "It is the kind of disorder that would make the good Sisters frown, but there is a beauty in it all the same," he said. "May I walk with you? Spotted Dawn is a very good girl, but isna always informative about the things ye might like to know."

"Yes!" Mairead said with a smile. "I have been the teacher all day, and it would be nice to be off duty so I can ask questions for once."

"Catch up, Big Bear!" Spotted Dawn ran ahead, darting in and out among the adults in a chaotic, laughing snarl of children.

"It is different," he assured his companion, "but it is a joy." He paused. "Perhaps less when it rains."

She laughed. He extended an arm, and they walked through Lame Deer as they might through Boston, but in a world where formality was a stranger, perhaps with broader smiles and a warmer touch.

Fox Running finished looking at Dooley's notes from his conversations with the ranchers near the Rawlins place. The only thing the ranchers and farmers agreed on was that they were visited, and that the blackened teeth followed each visit. Everything else — the number of men, the colors of their horses — changed. Dooley dismissed all the accounts as worthless, but Fox Running wondered if there was something else at work.

"Mr. Dooley, what if there were ten to fifteen men who deliver these warnings? What if it is a large group, like the one that man Sanders represents?"

Dooley was distracted. He was hosting Mairead for supper, the first time in more than ten years he had undertaken a social venture with a woman. Recollections of the debacle his invitation had been were echoing in his head as he alternated between calling himself a fool and recalling the glow of Mairead's smile.

Dooley looked blankly at Fox Running,

who tapped the pages on the table and rose.

"Perhaps I shall ride to see Rides a Crow," Fox Running said, smiling. "Enjoy your evening, and do not overcook the bread!"

Rides a Crow's lodge was near the river, apart from the others. As Coyote Horse poked along at a walk, the horse reacted to something. Fox Running saw movement in the brush. He tensed, then recalled that the Spirit Walker was always guarded. Chiefs and leaders might come and go, but there was only one Spirit Walker.

"Spirit wolf, it is Fox Running. I have come to speak with Rides a Crow." He sensed that his words were understood, but to him the spirit world remained largely behind a curtain that parted only infrequently.

The lodge was noisy with the chatter of children. Rides a Crow had adopted all those who were left without parents when the Northern Cheyenne escaped from Indian Territory to Montana. Wrapped in a Blanket was with her; the young girl, given to Rides a Crow when the child was an infant, rarely left her adopted mother's side.

"I was surprised when I felt your spirit," said Rides a Crow, who was only a few years older than Fox Running. "You are confused?"

"I believe I understand some of what is taking place," he said. "Now that the white men know we intend to stay here, they are trying to start something that will end in fighting, that will force the army to push us from this land. I know the spirits sent you a warning about Two Moon, but I think there are many people doing many things. It is not just one man, but several. I do not know if this is part of the evil that plagued The People on their journey, or if this is the work of men alone. Little was ever said about that, except that there were evil men seeking power with demons."

He looked over his shoulder. The spirit wolf had come up behind him and was listening. Fox Running was certain the animal understood every word. Ordinary wolves could not do that, but perhaps spirit wolves could. He had in the past come upon Rides a Crow when she was speaking with someone but then later found only the wolf was present.

"He protects me," said Rides a Crow, nodding toward the animal. "There were many evil men who worked against The People on our journey, and some still seek my death. They believe if the spirits can be separated from The People, The People will wither and die."

"Is that what happened to Little Wolf?"

The charismatic leader of the Northern Cheyenne had fallen on hard times upon their return, and in 1880 — while the Northern Cheyenne were still clustered around Fort Keogh — had killed a fellow Cheyenne after drinking too much of the white man's whiskey, leading him to separate himself from the rest of The People and depriving them of his leadership.

"Evil can take many forms," she replied. "I have often wondered, but such were those days with so much taking place that I will never know. These times are much like those. For every threat we see, there are five we do not."

"Then what do I do? There are men like Bigelow who want to hunt and kill every Indian, but they are stayed by the law and the army — for now. There are men who ride by night and try to make white ranchers afraid to work with The People. There are those who boast that they can use their money and their power to push us off the land. And there are those who your dream warned us have come to be assassins.

"I cannot stop them all. I cannot kill them all. And there are those among The People who feel betrayed; who want to hunt the way the old stories talk about, who want to push back the white men and the army and take back what was ours for generations. Some speak loosely about Two Moon. Are these words of anger the seeds of action to kill him and blame the white man? Is it the same evil that took hold of Little Wolf? Mr. Dooley and I are given the charge of trying to keep peace, but I do not know what to do, for I fear that solving one problem will make another worse! He chides me for being partial to the Cheyenne, but if The People cannot have a home here, where we belong, there will never be a place for us!"

Rides a Crow and the spirit wolf exchanged glances.

"I cannot give you a simple answer," she said. "It is not like the days when we traveled, when all The People were in one place, all of one mind, and all those who threatened us were outside the circle of The People. Now, we are spread over many miles, and a target for white men who fight using different weapons, as you said. I can only tell you what you already know, what you learned on the Buffalo Spine: that if in your heart you are doing what you believe is justice for both peoples, something that few can understand, then that is what you must do even if it is hard. Especially if it is hard. I, too, struggle because what was done to preserve and protect The People in the years gone by is clear, and that which will protect The People in the future is clouded. I can tell you no more. If you came to me for instructions, I have failed you. If you came seeking to know whether you and I and our spirit friends and all of The People are travelers on a frozen pond in the Moon when the Waters Again Flow, we are. You are not a Spirit Walker, Fox Running, but the spirits know you and seek to guide you. Listen."

He had to be content with that. As he reclaimed his horse at the head of the path that led to the lodge, he saw Coyote Horse standing next to a gleaming black mare, perhaps the most beautiful animal he had ever seen.

"I know you must be Talks to Horses," he said, daring to touch the mare, who allowed it, "and through Rides a Crow, you shared with me this spirit horse that knows my mind even better than I do. I know the loss of this horse means you no longer have as much mischief in your band of spirit horses, but he is a blessing for which I am grateful. Ride gently, spirit horse, and thank you for this gift."

The mare seemed interested in watching Fox Running, who knew a wise and discerning judge was examining him.

He leaped onto Coyote Horse's back. Although the animal wore a bridle, Fox Running rarely sought to control him, knowing the horse could read his mind. "Come, friend, we have far to ride and little time."

He rode to the rocks known as the Buffalo Spine and spent a short while there, attempting to commune with the spirits. Much later, as Fox Running made his way back to Lame Deer, he could not help but reflect on the strangeness of it all. He had gone seeking answers he did not get, yet he felt a sense of calm, as if in all the days to come, the spirits would be there to guide him in ways he might not imagine or ever understand.

Chapter Six

John Dooley had come to accept that, as he neared his fortieth birthday, he would likely spend the rest of his life alone. That realization had been part of his decision to leave Boston. If life would not bring him a home and a family, it could at least provide some adventure. There were many moments along the Tongue River when he would have accepted a smaller share of adventure, but on this evening, he was quite content.

Mairead Cullihan had overlooked the shortfalls of his cooking, admired the cabin he had helped build (although perhaps others had a larger share in the labor than he'd given her to think), and talked about everything from Irish politics to places in and around Boston that were foreign to the Northern Cheyenne. She was, he thought, a kindred soul to the McGillicuddy woman, and when he mentioned Katherine, he was not surprised that they had become acquainted back in Boston while Mairead was teaching orphan children to read. She spoke of Anne Campbell, a writer who had long been one of the Cheyenne's fiercest partisans, and told Dooley she treasured their friendship.

For Mairead's part, she made it clear to Dooley that he was not only a face from a place of familiarity, but a kind and tranquil soul who looked upon life as a time to be happy. Although she had not yet begun formally teaching here, she told him she was starting to understand what a truly foreign world she had come to live in, and what a daunting challenge she faced.

The strictures of Boston meant a schoolteacher did not dine alone with a strange man in his dwelling, but in Lame Deer, everyone knew everyone else's business. The Northern Cheyenne were inveterate gossips, but their observations of one another lacked the venom and spite of the East. Mairead had made Dooley choke and spit his water when she asked him, almost innocently, how many of her students would know how many pieces of bread he ate with dinner.

"All of them, Miss Cullihan," he replied.

"Mairead," she corrected. "Or Mary Ed if you wish to use the children's way of saying it, for then I can call you Big Bear!"

Although she had walked to his cabin in the late afternoon when the sun was out, on the grounds that a white woman could walk unescorted as the many Cheyenne who did so all the time, she accepted his company going back to the lodge where she was staying until the just-begun half-cabin/half-tent school could be finished.

"When they're angry, they can be like fire when it hits kerosene," he told her as they spoke about the ways of the Cheyenne, "but if you are their friend, if they *know* you are their friend, they would die for you."

"Then I'm glad I'm here," she replied, "for no one can have too many friends."

She went back inside with an understanding that there would be more evenings together, but that next time she might tackle the cooking. "For the bread was just a little burned," she said, looking askance at the loud laughter her remark provoked until he explained Fox Running's parting words. Her answer to that was, "Then we shall have to teach you to do better!"

As he walked back to the cabin, Dooley was barely aware of the lodges and the noises around him, until someone grabbed his left arm from behind, so hard that Dooley could not break the grip.

"An offer was extended to you. Do you

have a reply?"

The voice wasn't familiar. Dooley craned his neck as best he could, but the fellow kept well out of view. "Not yet. I've had other things on me mind."

"So I see," said Dooley's captor. "Decide quickly. Decide well." There was a pause. "I hope your new friend knows life among these people can be unexpectedly violent. It'd be a shame for her to find out for herself."

The hand let go, and the man was gone before Dooley could see which path he took. He felt an impulse to go back to Spotted Dawn's family lodge, then checked it. Whoever was watching would be looking for a reaction. He would not give them one.

Sam Rickett's feet were sore. In Texas, a walking man was an item of conversation. Up here, a lone white man on horseback riding through Indian and white lands was more often noticed. The Indians rode when they went off to hunt. White ranchers and cowboys rode in groups. He didn't want to stand out, so he walked.

The lodge of Two Moon was far less prepossessing than he expected. A strong wind could knock it over, although it would have fallen into the neighboring lodge, so closely packed were all of them.

Two Moon himself moved little in the course of a day. He couldn't have if he wanted to, for it seemed his day was filled with visitors. Mostly Cheyenne, a white man here and there, as well as a steady stream of soldiers. At most, there were only three or four times a day when he was alone.

A man in Rickett's line who did his work well spent his time watching and waiting. Some folks never understood that. Firing a gun might take less than a minute, but there was more to a job than pulling the trigger, if a man wanted to live beyond that moment.

The other man had been the real surprise. The first time Rickett saw him across the creek, he was so startled that he'd wasted what might have been a perfect opportunity. The man had seen him, and looked at him with such a lack of concern that Rickett was certain his information had been wrong. Days later, when he found out it wasn't, there was nothing to do but wait for another chance once they gave him the all-clear to go ahead.

Patience. Work done the way they wanted it took patience. Sometimes that meant a job took a little longer, but no one ever complained about the results. As long as they were taking their time picking targets, no one could say he wasn't earning his money.

Howard Porter had heard the stories about the Sickles Massacre, as the murders on the Rawlins farm were called in the local newspaper. Blood rituals meant the Indians had to be involved. He wondered if he was in danger and whether he should buy a pistol. A small one, of course. There were rumors the army was letting an Indian help them catch the killers. He hoped that was wrong. How could anyone think of such a thing! Clearly there was no rational order out here at all.

His thoughts were not whether the Cheyenne should be given land, but who would ever want to live in a land where there was such violence. He kept writing about what he'd heard had taken place. The sooner this report was finished, the better off he would be. He could go back home to Boston and never again have to set foot in a place where violent savages disturbed the proper flow of society.

His employer was right. The Cheyenne were a menace and had to be controlled, not appeased.

■ ■ ■ ■

July 1883, Lame Deer, Montana

Spotted Dawn was, as always, running. The overnight storm had not only cleared the humid air, but it left wonderful splashable puddles, including the one she ran through before slamming into two legs clad in heavy wool cloth.

"Hey, you!" the owner of the legs growled, reaching down to grab the girl. "Look at what you've done!"

Spotted Dawn could see the mud stains that reached to the knees of the man's silly trousers. White men did not like mud. They also wore too many clothes.

"I am sorry," she said, using the words Mary Ed had taught her. She struggled to get free. "Let me go."

"What kind of apology is that? You have ruined these pants. I should make you pay for it, if your family has any money. Or I should beat it out of you!"

Spotted Dawn looked up at the thick mustache above the mouth spewing insults. She wanted to grab the mustache and twist it.

"Let me go." The man did not. She turned her head and bit him hard on the wrist.

With a shout of pain, he threw her to the ground. She landed face first in the puddle, crying out in hurt.

"And who are you to attack Cheyenne children?" came a deadly voice from behind her. Spotted Dawn turned. It was Fox Running, the one who wore guns and was Big Bear's friend. She was scared of him because he almost never smiled.

"This urchin splashed me," the mustached man said. "I am Ben Pierrepont, an agent for the Senate Indian Affairs Committee. I am here —"

"I am Fox Running, and I do not like seeing the children of my people mistreated. You are here to pass judgment upon us, to decide whether we savages should be exiled again."

"Do you call this civilization?" Pierrepont made a sweeping gesture toward their surroundings. "These children run wild!" His angry face was almost purple.

"Should they be working in dark factories for pennies, as your children do in Boston when they are not on the street begging and stealing?" asked Fox Running. "We do not have orphan trains to put children on when we wish to be rid of them. We treasure them. How savage!"

"I do not appreciate your attitude. You

have much to learn about civilization."

Fox Running snorted. "Such as your civilized army that came to kill what you call 'hostiles' because they did not obey your law to leave their land so you could steal it for yourselves?"

"The law is the law."

"Tell me, Ben Pierrepont, is a contract valid when only one person signs it?"

Pierrepont looked wary now, as if suspecting some trick. "Of course not."

"Then when your government decided to move Indians from the Black Hills without their consent, was it legal?"

Pierrepont said nothing.

"We are willing to overlook all that to live in peace, Ben Pierrepont," Fox Running said, "so little Grasshopper here can have a better life than we have."

"Grasshopper!" A gray-haired white man came up to the girl. She knew him — Norbert Downs, who made saddles for a living. "Hello, Fox Running. Is there a problem?"

Pierrepont spoke first, explaining what had happened to his suit.

"Is that true?" Downs asked. Spotted Dawn nodded. "You should watch where you run, little one," he chided kindly, touching her jagged-cut head of glossy black hair.

Then he squatted down to look her in the eyes. "Why are you all over mud?" She explained. He stood. Fox Running kept his hard stare on Pierrepont as Downs rebuked the agent. "So, a man from Washington comes to look down on the Indians and shows them the merits of civilization by throwing a small girl in the mud for committing the sin of being too happy." Downs looked at Fox Running. "Mrs. Downs will clean her dress. We have some pie to share. Unless you need us for anything?"

"Do you want pie, Grasshopper?" Fox Running asked her.

"Oh, yes."

She trotted off with Downs. Fox Running watched her go, her misadventure forgotten now that there was pie. Then he turned to the man from Washington. "Bullying children, Mr. Pierrepont, is wrong. Do it again, and you will find out how much we Cheyenne care for our young. It will be a lesson you will never forget as long as you ever should live."

"You can't threaten me, you heathen! Do you know who I am? I represent the U.S. Senate!" Pierrepont thundered. "I will not be threatened as I walk through this hole!"

Two shots barked. Pierrepont quivered with his hands upraised, far too late to stop the spray from the puddle into which Fox Running had fired both bullets.

Fox Running looked at the man whose coat, shirt, vest, and face were now liberally spattered with mud. "There, good sir. You may now walk past safely. That mud puddle will never threaten anyone again." The filthy vision in front of him made his lips twitch. "There is no need to thank me." He turned away but could not stifle his laughter.

Pierrepont, fuming, watched the young Cheyenne leave. That was bad enough. Then he heard more laughter. He turned and saw the young Cheyenne girl, pointing at him from where she stood with the older white man across the street. The man was joining in the mockery.

He would not take this humiliation without evening the score. His report would show these people who was boss!

"Fox Running!" The commanding voice of Captain Jack Evans could be easily heard over Lame Deer's polyglot din.

Evans and Dooley hurried to reach the young Cheyenne as he walked back to their cabin. "Fox Running, did you shoot at Ben Pierrepont?" Evans asked.

Fox Running's brows knitted. Then the look crept over his face, one Dooley knew from the lad's brushes with authority at the Indian School.

"No," Fox Running said.

"He claims you did. He made a complaint against you before going back East."

"If I had shot at him, he would be dead."

"Laddie?" prompted Dooley.

Fox Running told the story of Spotted Dawn and the puddle. "The puddle was my target, not him."

Dooley was aghast. "A man who has the future of your tribe in his hands comes here and ye do that to him? And ye wonder why they do not love the Indians in Washington? Canna ye learn to bend?"

He turned to Evans for support, but Evans was covering his face with one hand and seemed to be having difficulty speaking.

"You shot . . . you shot a puddle?" he finally stammered out. "My Indians shoot puddles when speaking to men from the Senate! And they wonder why we do the things we do! You really shot a puddle?"

"Twice. I am certain it is now very dead."

"Yes, I can see why one shot wouldn't kill it!" Evans, usually reserved, dissolved in laughter. Tears of mirth came to his eyes, and he pointed at Fox Running. "He shot a puddle! He killed a puddle!" His hand fell back to his side. "From now on, every time some pompous, arrogant windbag from the East comes to the fort to tell us our business, especially from Washington, I shall invite you, and I'll be sure we have plenty of puddles!"

Evans walked off, still laughing as if Fox Running had told him the funniest joke in the world.

"Oh, laddie." Dooley shook his head. "One of these days, you'll push it too far."

"But not today, Mr. Dooley," Fox Running replied with a grin. "And we have made Captain Evans laugh for the first time in weeks. Perhaps all will finally be well now."

CHAPTER SEVEN

July 1883, Tongue River Valley, Montana
The lance sticking out of Amos Greene had two feathers lilting in the wind that softly caressed the corn growing in the fields about five miles southwest of Lame Deer.

Evans and a small group of troopers had been patrolling Lame Deer when the first reports came in. This time, he insisted nothing be disturbed until he arrived, because, back when they were at the Rawlins farm, Dooley — who read everything he could find about how to do the job Evans now had in front of him — had told him that was important.

Dooley soon came to join him. Fox Running was the last to arrive at Greene's farm, which was sandwiched between the lands of Golden Turtle and Flying Sparrow. Both Cheyenne farmers insisted they had no quarrels with their neighbor other than small ones over boundaries, minor crop damage, waste being tossed into one field from the other, and how best to resolve the competition for water.

"He did not like us at first," Flying Sparrow told Evans and Dooley, "but we did not bother him or his family."

"We will harvest his crops so his family can get the money," said Golden Turtle, who acted vastly more agitated than Flying Sparrow. "He had friends who were soldiers, and he was learning that what they said about us was wrong. He would have understood in time."

Snow Hare, Golden Turtle's daughter, was a study in misery as she stood next to her father, befitting her role as his eldest. The girl, who was about fourteen or fifteen, had a wet face. Her shoulders were stooped, her head was down, and she barely responded when Fox Running spoke to her.

"It is the children who suffer," Dooley opined. Fox Running said nothing, frowning as he studied the girl.

Fox Running had remained by the dead man while the others spoke to the Cheyenne farmers. When they returned, Dooley saw to it that the young man's eyes were closed. He wondered if Fox Running was praying or napping, for the young man had remained out all night and had not returned to the cabin after his journey to see Rides a Crow.

"Have you ever thrown a lance, Captain Evans?" Fox Running asked.

"Of course not," the soldier replied, instantly on his guard. "But I have been here long enough to know that this is a Cheyenne lance. You cannot talk your way around that."

"Yes," agreed Fox Running. "A Cheyenne lance. A very fine one. Did you ever see a weapon this fine on any battlefield, Captain?"

Evans looked closer and knew the answer but said nothing.

"See these feathers?" Fox Running continued. "This lance belongs to a member of the Crazy Dogs. We Northern Cheyenne have military societies, groups to which warriors belong. Neither Golden Turtle nor Flying Sparrow are Crazy Dogs, for the members of that society are among those who resist farming. Those men you see patrolling for fear of attack from the soldiers? Many of them are Crazy Dogs. They still act as warriors. This lance must have been stolen from one of their lodges, yet it seems very fine for a warrior's hands to have made. It is too light for any real use."

"I don't understand," Evans replied. "One

of these men here — or some other Cheyenne — likely borrowed a lance. Indians leave things lying around all the time. I know Cheyenne society is complicated, but it makes no difference where they got it."

"No. A lance is not like a rifle." Fox Running was talking out his thoughts, a process Dooley knew brooked no interruptions or contradictions. He wanted to warn Evans, but there was no way he could silence Fox Running long enough to do so.

"This lance was made by hand, was blessed by the spirits for use by one special warrior, I would guess, and is very, very new and well made — finer than most lances I have ever seen, even ceremonial ones. No. I am wrong. It *is* for ceremonies. It has to be. See how the shaft has already cracked from this one use? This is not a lance that would be used for hunting or killing. It was made to be seen. Yet ceremonial lances are usually kept by those who live near Two Moon, and there are no Crazy Dog ceremonies near these farms or anywhere else hereabouts that I know of." He frowned and bit his lip, then looked at Evans as though he had not been aware the man was near. "There is something not right here, Captain."

"This lance was used to kill," Evans

pointed out. "Someone threw it at Amos Greene and killed him. Anyone can see that!"

"It was used to stab," Fox Running corrected him. "Look at it. It stands almost straight. To throw a lance in the air and have it land in this way, a man would need to stand almost next to Mr. Greene, while Mr. Greene lay on the ground and waited for it to strike him. He would have needed to be a very cooperative victim, Captain."

"Greene could have been standing when he was hit. That lance is not a weapon a white man would use, or even know how to find."

Fox Running shook his head. "Captain, why, if I have a rifle, would I use a lance? I have thrown one as a boy but never used one in a fight that mattered. A thrown lance can miss. Look at him! The lance is sticking out of his ribs. If I threw it at him, for it to so perfectly stab him like that, he would have had to remain utterly still in one place. Do you not see?"

Evans was quiet. Dooley was quiet as well, knowing that his wish for Fox Running to stop talking was never going to come true. To a soldier, a lance meant an Indian was involved. Arguing without anything to back that up would not shift Evans one inch.

"May I move him?" Fox Running asked.

Evans agreed. Fox Running bent and slid his arms under the dead man's shoulders. As he and Dooley lifted the corpse off the ground, the tip of the lance's blade was briefly visible, showing that the weapon had passed through Greene's body.

"That takes strength," Fox Running said. "I could not drive a lance through a man of his size, such as Big Bear."

"Thank you, lad," Dooley commented, patting a stomach that was substantial by the standards of the always-hungry Cheyenne but never going to be as round as it had been getting before he left Boston for the leaner world of Tongue River rations.

"Whoever killed the farmer wanted it to look like the work of a Cheyenne. No Cheyenne would use a ceremonial lance in this way unless it was the only weapon around, and there is no one here who would have one! I do not say no Cheyenne would kill. But a Cheyenne would use a gun. Not a lance, or even a bow. When did you last see a Cheyenne carry a bow around Lame Deer?"

Evans admitted that Fox Running made a persuasive case but was not going to give in. "People who kill others don't always do so in ways that make sense."

"And here's life getting complicated," Dooley muttered, with a nod toward a crowd of new arrivals. About a dozen men on horseback, led by Sanders, were approaching.

Fox Running watched the two Cheyenne farmers watching the white men. If the hate flowing between the two groups could ignite, the world would erupt in bright-yellow flames.

The man named Sanders was looking at Dooley for a reason Fox Running could not understand. "We told you soldier boys this would happen," Sanders said as he changed his focus to Evans. "You going to arrest them?" He pointed at Golden Turtle and Flying Sparrow.

"The army needs to investigate," Evans said, looking for any neutral ground he could find. He would argue back at Fox Running when pressed but would fight just as hard against anyone else who wanted justice to be partial to one side or the other.

"Did you kill him because he would not ruin our crops for you?" said Golden Turtle, suddenly belligerent. Dooley saw Fox Running's harsh sideways look at Golden Turtle. Doubt? Skepticism? Something was going on inside the young man, but Dooley was too many steps behind to guess.

"And chase us from our land?" Flying Sparrow added.

"Good man got killed by these Injuns," said a young man behind Sanders. "Army won't act, we will — won't we, boys?"

A loud roar greeted his words.

"Injun lance in a white man," Sanders told Evans. "White man with Injun neighbors. That tells me everything I need to know."

By now, word of Amos Greene's death had spread as though on the wings of the passing crows. A few ranchers and more than a few Cheyenne were gathered. "Stall them," Fox Running said softly to Dooley.

"How?" The Irishman could not understand why this comment amused his partner, who walked calmly toward the Greene farmhouse. Dooley drew in a breath and focused on the group of ranchers. "Mr. Sanders, you and I spoke of the law the other day, and we all know the law can only do what it does when it knows the truth, and so the law and the army cannot do what the law requires without knowing what it is doing, not that it stops the army from being hindside before in other things, and the captain is saying that the law and the army have to do what the law and the army need to do in order to get done what the law and the army —"

"What hogwash is this?" Sanders blurted at Evans, as Dooley prattled on. Evans also tried to defuse the crowd, with little success.

"What is he doing?" said the young rider behind Sanders, pointing.

Fox Running was emerging from the woodlot near the field where Greene lay, carrying two long sticks, each about the size of the lance. As he drew near, they could see the points were freshly sharpened. He handed one stick to Golden Turtle and one to Flying Sparrow.

"Throw," he commanded. He turned to the knot of soldiers and ranchers. "Do not interfere."

Golden Turtle's first throw went five feet, Flying Sparrow's a few feet further. After cajoling and scolding by Fox Running to do better, the men were able to throw the lances about twelve feet, but the throws had little power behind them, and the men looked absurdly awkward as the lances wobbled aloft before clattering to the ground.

Fox Running called out to Evans. "Do you honestly think one of these men threw that lance? Do either of them have that much power?"

"Someone else must have done it!" Sanders exclaimed. "Indians are born knowing how to throw these things."

Fox Running thought of the feeble antics of Cheyenne boys trying to throw a lance and all but laughed out loud.

"Maybe you did it," Sanders sneered at him. "Let me see you throw that stick."

Dooley had a sinking feeling as he watched the younger man's face. Daring Fox Running was never wise.

Fox Running took the sticks from Golden Turtle and Flying Sparrow. Dooley knew what was coming next. "Be ready," he muttered to Evans, who looked back at him blankly. Dooley turned back to look at Fox Running. "Now. Head down, sir!"

The young Cheyenne turned to the line of cowboys and ranchers and threw a sharpened stick in their direction. They all ducked against their horses' necks as it sailed far over their heads. The ranchers were scowling and muttering after they dared straighten back up, and they could see Fox Running leaning against the other stick with a self-satisfied smile on his face.

"Was that what you had in mind?" he asked Sanders.

"Lad," Dooley said involuntarily, gritting his teeth at the stunt.

Fox Running returned to the crowd of

men. He halted within inches of Sanders's horse. "If you look, you can see the stick bounced off the ground, even though its point was carved as sharp as this one." He held out the second stick as though he expected the stockman to look at it. "Someone came up to this man Greene, someone he trusted, who then gutted him. Someone who wanted to blame a Cheyenne. Someone smart enough to have a plan. Someone who thinks he can get away with anything." He locked eyes with Sanders as he drove the stick into the ground. "All the men I know like that are white."

Fox Running turned away. Evans seized the moment to speak to the deflated group. "The army will investigate. I am not listening to allegations against anyone until I can get proof. We have only just arrived to begin our work. Mr. Sanders, I will provide you all the information you might want. Regardless of who the killer is, I am here to keep the peace. My men and I will bring the murderer of Amos Greene to justice."

Sanders nodded, then abruptly looked past Evans. "Hey!" he yelled, as Fox Running drew the lance from Greene's body.

When Evans objected, Fox Running pointed toward the farmhouse, where Greene's wife and children and a few farmhands were emerging. "The widow does not need to see that," Fox Running said.

"Give the poor woman some space, everyone," Dooley called out. He moved nearer to Sanders. "The lady deserves not to suffer more," he hissed at the stockman. "Show some compassion for her."

"You were made an offer because I thought you controlled that savage. Or does he control you?" Sander carped, before turning his horse's head. He clicked his tongue at the animal, and the group of ranchers pounded away.

Camilla Greene had outpaced the rest to reach her husband's body. Golden Turtle broke from the group of Cheyenne to offer his condolences.

She looked at him, her grief-filled face twisted in hate. "If you had stayed in Indian Territory where you belonged, none of this would have happened. I told him no good would come of it. No, he was going to make friends of his enemies. I know! I know! It's your fault!" She dissolved in tears as her two children and a few farmhands finally reached them.

Golden Turtle slunk away toward his land. Snow Hare had run away crying as soon as the widow appeared. Flying Sparrow left as well. The group of Cheyenne farmers and farmhands also dispersed.

"Ken Rikesberry," said one man, who separated himself from the rest of Greene's workers and came up to Evans. "Foreman. You know anything yet? We found him this morning, sent for the army first thing. Been tellin' her she had to wait, but she couldn't wait no more."

Evans asked about Greene's relationship with the Cheyenne. Rikesberry shrugged.

"Good days. Bad days. Simple things them Injuns didn't understand, and Amos and them would yell at each other like the loudest crows you ever heard and get him all bothered, then they'd come by with stew for the family and the next day you'd think they'd been friends all their lives, and then they'd go do something again a few days later. Maybe it was getting better. Hard to say. Boss was tryin' to get to know Golden Turtle's children, have them here to see how he did things and then go over there. Thought that was making things better. That Golden Turtle fella, though. Born farmer. Can't see him doing this, but he's an Injun and you never know with them."

There was little else to learn. Evans said he would stay in Lame Deer for some time, due to the incident, and that troopers would patrol farms and ranches in hopes of either catching someone in the act or at least placating ranchers who wanted to see some protection.

"As for you two," he told Dooley and Fox Running, "you can go places the army cannot. If a Cheyenne did this, I need to arrest him as soon as possible." He held up a hand as Fox Running began to protest. "The same is true for a white man. Amos Greene was a popular farmer who, to all appearances, was killed by a Cheyenne. As the story gets around, and if there is no arrest, it will be nearly impossible to avoid vigilantes attacking Golden Turtle or Flying Sparrow in revenge. The Rawlins murders were one thing. Maybe it was intimidation, maybe not. But this looks very clear."

"Because it is supposed to," groused Fox Running.

"Then find something to tell me what really happened," snapped Evans. "The army doesn't care about theories, Fox Running, we care about results. You know I want to be fair. What you say makes sense if you think about it, but when people get too worked up to think, it won't matter. If vigilantes take action, it will be out of my hands. If you don't like how this appears, find me a more convincing tale to tell when news of this gets to my superiors."

Before they left, Fox Running asked to see the house and outbuildings. Dooley frowned at the request. "The widow needs time," he said. "Becoming a danger to yourself, ye are."

"We don't *have* time," Fox Running replied. "And right now, the danger is that someone is trying to make things worse here to block any hopes of land for the Cheyenne. That is what all of this is about!"

"Sanders expected you to do something. What was it?" Fox Running asked as he and Dooley rode away, back to Lame Deer.

Dooley explained the stockman's visit. "And where were you last night? For all I knew, you had ridden off again."

Fox Running described his visit to Rides a Crow, and that he needed to spend time on the Buffalo Spine.

"I know they are all part of it. I know they all want The People to lose this land," he said. "I can prove nothing. I do not know how they connect or if they connect. There is enough hate for a dozen plots against the Cheyenne. I was hoping Rides a Crow could guide me to one spirit source, or human source, but even her way is not clear. I am tired of talking nicely to those who want to destroy, and who smile to our faces and stab in the back and in the dark, but I truly do not know which is who is what, if that even makes sense." He shook his head and flashed Dooley a rueful smile. "I was hoping the spirits might show some sign that gives them away, but not even the spirits can read the souls of these men."

"Ah, I see, and throwing a stick at yon Sanders was you talking nicely, is it?"

Fox Running grinned as though he was back in detention and they were mocking the teachers. "How was your dinner?"

"Changing the subject, ye are."

"She was married once for a very short time, and her husband died, and she was very lonely," Fox Running said. "It is good for her to have a friend."

Dooley gaped. "How do ye know this?"

"Our little Grasshopper has very good hearing for such hints as her teacher drops," Fox Running replied. "I shall let you know what she tells me about your evening. Tell me, Mr. Dooley, how badly did you truly burn the bread?"

"On wi' ye," Dooley grumbled, blushing.

Fox Running laughed. The ring of hate was drawing tighter around The People, but he had a friend, and he had the spirits. Life often offered less.

■ ■ ■ ■

Dooley and Fox Running split up when they reached Lame Deer. Dooley had plans to meet Mairead at the end of the school day. He wanted to go to his cabin first, to wash off the blood he'd gotten on him from Greene and be fully presentable — or as presentable as anyone was in Lame Deer. Fox Running knew his friend preferred to be alone and that Dooley felt self-conscious when trying to find his cleanest shirt or scrape mud from a coat.

Fox Running wanted to talk to Harry Miller, who ran the general store. Miller knew about working with wood. Fox Running did not. The wood of the lance had a dark color, which meant something was applied to it. Something sticky had been put on it. Perhaps it was something Miller sold, and he might have sold it to someone he would remember. It was worth a minute to ask.

Harry Miller was a crusty man who had fought Indians and was adjusting slowly to the concept of them as his permanent neighbors. The adjustment picked up steam the year before, when Golden Turtle and a few other farmers had asked Miller for credit to buy some essentials. They repaid him in full at harvest time and brought food for his family during the winter as a sign of friendship. Miller might still sit with his old friends and complain about the Indians, but he was often heard to add, "not all of them, now."

The bell above the door rang as Fox Running entered the store. Miller looked up from the neatest area — the part devoted to cloth and thread — and nodded at Fox Running as he continued his conversation with Amethyst Pleasanton, one of Lame Deer's oldest residents. Fox Running waited. Elders deserved respect, and he was not going to rush Mrs. Pleasanton. Fox Running was an infrequent visitor, having little interest in clothes other than something warm to throw over him when it snowed, and no interest at all in the pots, pans, and stray trifles he could not even identify. Not for the first time, he wondered how he would have eaten these past months if Dooley did not like making food.

From the corner of his eye, Fox Running saw Crooked Toe, who was about twelve, silently moving toward the counter, screened from Miller by a table stacked high with bags of flour. The boy's hand reached out, and a hunting knife disappeared from the place where it had been. Crooked Toe turned to leave.

"Stop!" Fox Running called out, startling the boy, who had not seen him. The boy made a dash for the door, but Fox Running was every bit as fast and a lot closer.

"Here now!" Miller said, moving toward them. "What is this?"

"Help me," hissed the boy.

"Crooked Toe has just tried to steal a knife," Fox Running said. He turned to the boy. "Stealing is wrong. Take the knife from under your shirt. Hand it back." The boy started to move, resentment large on his face. "Hand it back properly."

Crooked Toe did as he was told, then clasped his hands across his chest.

"You are not in want," Fox Running said. "Why do you steal?"

Crooked Toe looked from him to Miller, then back at Fox Running. "I am sorry," he said.

"Let me tell your parents," Fox Running said. He glanced at Miller. "I hope you will not turn him over to the army, Mr. Miller. I know stealing is a crime, but I will talk to the family."

"No!" exclaimed Crooked Toe.

"You prefer the army?" asked Miller. "I've had too many things stolen lately, and someone has to be punished!"

"Perhaps you need to explain something to us," Fox Running prompted. "Mr. Miller and I were both young once." He smiled at the store owner. "And I will admit that one of us might have done some things that were mistakes."

Miller made a noise that might have been a chuckle. "Go ahead, son."

The story came out in fragments, but what it amounted to was that Bucky Cunningham had dared a number of boys — Cheyenne and white — to steal knives from the store. The ones with a knife were in some kind of secret club, and those who were without, were not.

"Jed Cunningham had a tough year last year," Miller said. "Some disease killed a lot of his stock. 'Spect there've been hard times. Boy ought to be working with his pa, but I guess Jed's too busy to watch him."

"Mr. Dooley and I can speak to him," Fox Running volunteered.

Miller thought over the offer. "I've known Jed a long time. Better from me." He looked at the Indian boy. "How much you want that knife, son?"

"Mine is very old and dull," Crooked Toe replied.

"Tell you what. You come back here and

help me get all the boxes and crates in that back room of mine in order. My back wouldn't mind the rest. Might be just about enough work for the price of a knife. Maybe one of the good ones I keep behind the counter, way too far for boys to grab! Maybe you can figure out sweeping and cleaning and get a little money here and there. Come by tomorrow if you're of a mind, boy."

Crooked Toe looked skeptical. "Really?"

"I'll give it a try if you will." Miller put out his hand. Crooked Toe, unfamiliar with the custom, looked at it a moment.

"Shake his hand," said Fox Running. "It is how men agree to work together."

Crooked Toe hesitated a moment more, then gripped Miller's hand and shook it once. Then he turned and left the store.

"Thank you," Fox Running said as they watched the boy run off. "He has never been in any trouble...."

"Boys his age," said Miller, "trouble's all they know! Gonna stop me by Jed's place and see. Maybe he'll want his boy to come work for me, too. If I'm going to be an old fool, I might as well go whole hog, son." Miller started to walk away, then halted. "You came in for somethin'. What was it?"

Fox Running asked about substances for

preparing wood. Miller told him any farmer could make varnish, and staining wood was done with extracts from plants. "Not much help. Probably sold a few gallons of that to just about everybody, and probably there are cans of it in barns all up and down the valley."

Fox Running thanked him and then thanked him again for giving Crooked Toe a second chance.

"World changes, son . . . a man has to change with it. Your people want to live here, they want to shop here, they want to raise families here, I'm fine. I got my worries, because I've seen a lot of good intentions wither on the vine, but if peace around here can be bought for a knife, it's worth the price."

Chapter Eight

"The door was open. What kind of white man leaves the door open? Is this his or yours? What smell is that? Did something burn? Well?"

Dooley was certain the door had been closed, but the young Cheyenne woman — or perhaps Lakota, he could never be sure — who had obviously been inspecting the cabin and was not overly concerned about being caught doing so did not appear to be someone who brooked disagreement, since she did not even allow him the chance to speak first.

"And who, lass, did you wish to see and about what?" Manners were always good when talking to a young woman carrying a rifle who looked very comfortable holding the weapon.

"I am Cut Sky," she said, as if this answered all questions.

Dooley's face made it clear he had no idea

who she was. She snorted as she read his face.

"Is this where Fox Running lives?" she asked with a furrowed brow, waving the hand that held the rifle. Dooley watched its muzzle point in his direction.

All over Lame Deer, she had been told this was where the mercurial Cheyenne could be found. She had been intrigued because, although almost all the men and women she talked to knew of him and the white man who was his friend, very few had ever actually spoken to him. Many considered him haunted by spirits; others, a killer like white gunfighters. They all had stories to tell about the white man making friends and becoming part of their lives, but of the Indian with the two guns, there were no such stories of friendship, only stray pieces of the past that did little to illuminate the places Fox Running skimmed over when he gave Cut Sky and her father a summary of his life.

Cut Sky looked at Dooley, who was obviously inspecting her.

"Well, is this where he lives, or does he live some other place?" Her tone reflected the fact that there was no evidence of more than one bed.

"He will na sleep except on the floor. Pure

heathen, I tell him," he added, looking for a reaction.

"As if the Irish way is better," grumbled Fox Running, who barreled through the door without shutting it, as usual half listening to Dooley's mockery. He had been tending to the horses and barely noticed who was in the cabin until he all but bumped into her. "Cut Sky! I . . . I did not expect you."

Dooley smiled at his friend's expression — bewilderment he had never seen before when Fox Running looked at a female.

Cut Sky glanced around the spare cabin. "You burned your bread," she said, looking with disgust at the semi-blackened loaf on the table.

"Tell him that I do, every day, lass, but does he listen? Never!" proclaimed Dooley, gleefully enjoying the sight of his friend embarrassed.

"You are not here to talk of bread," Fox Running said, giving his friend a glare that promised some form of retribution Dooley knew Fox Running would eventually forget. "What message does Blue Feather send?"

"He says you would put him between the anvil and hammer," she said. "You may not know the power of those you seek to find, but he does. You risk only your life, which you value as little. This is clear to everyone. He risks many lives."

"I know there is risk. I have lived with risk for years."

"Do you?" she lashed out. "You live in this fine cabin, with people from far away — white people — who care for you. Will they let you get hurt? Will they let you get killed? If you fail, will they be here for you? Who will be there for us?"

"I will."

"Fine words about the spirits will not stop bullets or feed bellies!" she scoffed. "There is talk that you are justice warriors. There is never justice for those like us, especially army justice!"

Fox Running laid a hand on her arm. She glared at him and sought to shrug it off, but he gripped her harder.

"This is not army justice. This is necessary for the Cheyenne! Think, Cut Sky. If the murders of these men are never solved, and a gang can intimidate good men from hiring Cheyenne, more Cheyenne will go hungry, or feed themselves in ways the army does not like, and there will be war. The People could not survive that. Neither could you! I thought your father understood that this is not just another killing."

"If you want to know what he knows, and

hear what he hears, and understand this valley more than you do, he tells me to tell you to ride with him for one moon. You may come as his daughter's suitor, regardless of my feelings about the matter. Then you may learn what you will learn. If you are so smart, you will learn what you need!"

"Lad, ye canna . . ." Dooley interjected.

"Sickles is not that far a ride."

"And with all of them waiting for Amos Greene's killing to be blamed on yer people, lad, what are ye thinkin' by droppin' it after ye did such a fine job of infuriatin' the ranchers?"

"Amos is dead?" Cut Sky asked. "But he just finished making . . ."

"We just came from it, lass," Dooley said. "He was . . ."

"How is he connected to your father?" Fox Running interrupted, seeing more in her face than another death should cause. He took advantage of her confusion to grab her shoulder and spin her to focus on him as he moved closer and spoke with greater intensity. "Let me say it clearly: what business best hidden from the world did they do together?"

Her eyes darted. She made sounds, but each word was being choked back.

Fox Running was relentless. "Did it also

involve Golden Turtle, and was it the same type of business he had with Rawlins? I know what Rawlins was doing, Cut Sky. I have not yet told anyone because I only just now began to see that this was bigger than a few farmers. Tell me what the Bandit King has been doing, and who he has been doing it with!"

Dooley knew he had been left behind in the conversation, which was now taking place in Lakota and Cheyenne as well as English. He masked his reaction, but the same could not be said of Cut Sky, who was staring open mouthed at Fox Running. Beneath her sun-darkened skin, shame was suffusing her face an even deeper shade.

"You are rude!" she fired back.

"I do not have patience for this," Fox Running snarled. "The truth now, or everyone knows!"

"I for one would like to know something," Dooley interjected, twisting the long whiskers in his sideburns, as the two people yelling at each other in his own cabin seemed willing to ignore him.

"Who . . . How . . ." Cut Sky stammered. "Does anyone else know? Who have you told?"

"I told you. Listen. No one knows. Now I understand why Golden Turtle was so quick to leave for his own land. Did Flying Sparrow know or care?" He tried to read her face and then turned to Dooley. "We need to find out more about that foreman. Whatever his name was. And the nearest lodge. No. Wait!"

He gripped Cut Sky by both shoulders. Hard. Her chin jutted out in defiance. She was trying to regain control.

"Did your father have made what he might call a Crazy Dog lance to sell with the other . . . items?" Fox Running asked.

"How did you . . . What of it if he did? Eastern people buy things without knowing what they mean! They are fools, and smart people take advantage of fools in order to keep eating! Who are you to judge what we do to survive?"

"Ha!" Fox Running released Cut Sky, who glared at him as he leaned back against the table, looking gleeful. He was silent a moment as he studied the young woman, then shifted his gaze to Dooley.

"Bring Captain Evans, please, Mr. Dooley. Do not go too fast. Cut Sky will stay for a few minutes, but no more, before she goes about that extremely unimportant business that has brought her to Lame Deer and that no one needs to know about."

"And when I return, lad, will ye talk in a

language I understand?"

"I am sorry," Fox Running said contritely. "Did I do that again? It is her fault."

"Mine?" Cut Sky said.

"You do not make sense in any language," he said.

Dooley could see the boiling rage on her face slowly coming under control. "Will ye be alive when I return, lad?"

"I have not yet decided," Cut Sky shot back as Fox Running snorted in derision.

With more than a small dose of misgiving, Dooley complied. Fox Running, when he was intent on something known to him and him alone, often failed to notice that he left out almost all the details and explained matters from the middle, bouncing back and forth between the start and end in his own haphazard style.

"Is there anything at Greene's farm that connects Blue Feather to him?" Fox Running said once Dooley was gone. "Anything at all? Tell me now, and do not lie to me, because it will go badly for him if you do. I can hide it when I find it, but if someone else does, it is out of my hands."

"I . . . I do not think so," she said in the meekest tone he had ever heard from her. "They were very careful."

"That is why you wanted the horses? For

your merchandise?"

"I know you must be angry, but it brings us money."

"There is wrong, and there is right, and there is what we do to survive," he told her, waving her words aside with a sweep of his left hand. "Did those who murdered Rawlins give the horses to your father, or did he learn of the death and take them?"

"One of the lookouts on the road where we met saw a steer. The other animals were not far away. My father very likely knows who did this thing, but he is afraid, Fox Running. Not their names, but the gang of men. White men. They are killers. They live not far from us in the Breaks, in a place toward Wolf Mountain, but they do not interfere with us nor we with them. If they should have a reason, they will kill him, because they are more powerful than even you and your white friend. They will kill anyone. They cannot be stopped because they have friends who protect them in ways I do not understand, but I know my father fears. He fears very few, but he is very afraid of them. You do not understand."

"We will see about that," he remarked. "The soldier will be here soon. Captain Evans is a good man. Do not worry. He will not care about things he will be told are not important. He is only worried about who killed Amos Greene and the men at the Rawlins ranch. Do not leave Lame Deer. Not yet. I must find you before the daylight fades so we can meet later after dark in a very obvious attempt not to be seen."

"Why?"

"If I am to be your suitor, we need to spend some time sneaking around behind your father's back so those in Lame Deer he pays to inform him can report back that we are acting badly," he replied, smiling as he enjoyed the dawning of a trick to be played. "Is that not how these things are done?"

"They sold *scalps*?" The captain's voice approached the soprano range.

Evans was in a foul mood when Dooley fetched him. Earlier in the day, one of his troopers had been drunkenly raving about eliminating the Cheyenne from the valley along with anyone who liked them and did so in the presence of Tom Randall, a shopkeeper whose best customers were Cheyenne farmers. Randall had the best of the fight that followed. Because Evans was not in town, his men had waited before taking any action. Evans's troopers wanted Randall charged with a crime for beating up a soldier, but Evans just wanted them all to stop talking about policy matters regarding the Indians that did nothing but make his life more complicated — on the good days.

Evans did not seem to grasp what Fox Running said, which led to the Cheyenne talking louder and faster until Dooley intervened. "Perhaps, lad, starting at the beginning might be simpler instead of starting in the middle again and going both ways at the same time," he suggested, slightly piqued because he had no idea what Fox Running was talking about, either. Indians selling scalps? The lad had been off of his feed for too many days.

Fox Running took a deep breath, which sounded like a sigh to both white men, and explained that everyone knew there was a big business in selling the scalps of Indians, and Indian items taken in wars against the Sioux and Cheyenne.

"Back in Boston, Miss McGillicuddy had friends who collected these things," he told Dooley. "She once took me to a home that had them. They were very embarrassed when they knew they had a real live Indian in their house. It was almost humorous. Almost." He turned to Dooley. "You must have known someone who did."

Dooley shook his head. He had heard

about rich Bostonians who collected items harvested from the dead, but in his circle of friends there was not the time or money for such things, nor much interest. Survival was far more important.

"Several enterprising people out here, both Cheyenne and white, decided to work together," Fox Running said. "The white people in the East who want trophies have no idea what they are really getting, so they are easy to fool."

He then explained how very skilled connivers could fool the rich and powerful. "I had heard of this once before, when I was traveling in Kansas, but never really believed it until now. The ones making scalps would take a mixture of hair from a horse's tail and the long hair women wear, either pulled from the living or cut from the dead, and weave everything together until a supposed scalp that was mostly made of a horse's tail would appear on the outside to be made of Indian hair. By the time they put some kind of varnish or something on it, I guess it is hard to tell. At least it is hard for Eastern people!

"If you can fake scalps, you can fake anything. They also made allegedly genuine weapons, like the lance that killed Greene. I knew when I touched it something was wrong. It was too light. It would not last a day if it were ever used, even in a ceremony. I am amazed it did not shatter when Amos was killed. I am sorry, Captain, I did not fully understand when we were at Mr. Greene's farm. Mr. Dooley has often told me I should not think out loud unless I am thinking straight, and I was not. Greene, Golden Turtle, and others were involved. They have to be, because I cannot imagine anyone riding with something that ungainly and not attracting a lot of attention. Blue Feather, Cut Sky's father, was at the top of the group that was doing the trading, at least on the Indian side. The Bandit King knows how to make money! He would collect what was made, or perhaps he was in charge of ordering what to make, and then he would send their products to someone who would buy them and ship them East."

Dooley waited for a reaction from Evans. The soldier had every right to be angry with Fox Running after the way the Cheyenne had disrespectfully argued with him.

Evans frowned. As apologies went, that one was pretty sketchy, but from what he had heard of Fox Running, that it was offered at all was remarkable. He had a valley to worry about. That came first. "Who was this partner?"

"I am going to find that out soon," said Fox Running in a dark, angry tone.

Dooley stepped toward him. "Now, lad..."

Fox Running held his hands out, palms facing the others. "I am not making war on someone who sold counterfeit items to people in the East. While they were making scalps together, at least no one was taking them from one another! I find it hideous and disgusting that in a world where I was taught I was barely a step above a wild creature, those who are 'civilized' mount souvenirs of the body parts of The People on their ornate parlor walls as testimony to their prowess. I would very much like to see how they would like their hair on the walls of a lodge, but we are not here to debate that. We have to find a killer. We could be looking at anything from someone who did not approve of what they were doing — which would be my people — to someone who wanted to put them out of business, which would probably be your people."

"Fair enough, then," replied Evans. He was still trying to grasp the concept that whites and Indians were doing business in secret while half the valley wanted to kill the other half. He wondered what his superiors would think when they found out all this was going on. Then he wondered why he would ever be so foolish as to tell them. He tried to pay attention again, because Fox Running was pacing, volleying forth words as though the object was to talk as fast as possible rather than to be understood.

"We need to see if the foreman was aware, if he was not receiving money he thought was his, and whether Golden Turtle or Flying Sparrow had a falling out with Greene. I think this is what was going on, not an argument over land or something else. Mr. Dooley, can you ask these questions without the widow being too near, or asking too directly, for I would imagine she does not know? I do not think she would want to talk to me."

Fox Running halted. "We cannot tell anyone what we know, not until we discover who else is involved. I promise, Captain, I will let you decide if this business remains intact when we find out what we need to know. I am not out for vengeance unless people are being killed for scalps, and that was not the case even with the Rawlins ranch. I would not be surprised if the fear of being exposed makes those who are making money off this stop doing it, because I think there is enough shame in this to cover everyone."

Evans nodded. At least Fox Running seemed to be starting with the right intentions. He was uncertain how long they would last, but he could not reasonably hope for more.

"And where do you plan to be, lad?" Dooley said.

"Finding out whether the Rawlins murders were about this same business, for there were traces of human and horse hair in the outbuilding I searched, and something sticky on the floor, as though it had been spilled."

"And this would not happen by chance to be an adventure in the company of the sweet young lass I saw earlier?"

"Cut Sky? I believe she wants to shoot me more than anything else right now. I tell you, Mr. Dooley, I will do anything necessary to solve this crime! Do you really think I am off to enjoy myself?"

Evans remained baffled and wary, but Dooley knew Fox Running would be better used in a place where the army and white men could not go. "I hear the far side of the Tongue River is a dangerous place," he said.

"And there are safe places on this side?" his friend shot back.

■ ■ ■ ■

Cut Sky was waiting where he had told her to wait — on the small cleared part of the wooded land he had bought thinking he would live there with Morning Shadow. For weeks he could not even look at the land without feeling pain. At least now he had no illusions, and there was not likely to be anyone else nearby, since the place was screened from Dooley's cabin by a stout band of trees.

"Did you tell them about my father?" She had tied her horse to a tree. He had dismounted and was holding Coyote Horse.

"Yes," he replied. "They do not care. They know he deals in many things no one wishes to know about. What matters most now is that we speak to the trader who ships the merchandise to the East. He is the one they will discover next, but not soon, for their questions seek to learn who killed Amos Greene."

He sighed.

"We must ride through Lame Deer, perhaps racing and yelling, as we go to Sickles," he said. "We need witnesses to see we were together, since I am pretending to be your suitor."

"I am sorry for the great pain you suffer," she said with great sarcasm, glaring at him.

"I do what I must," he replied with a grin.

"But I must ask about what follows, for I am not aware of these very good plans of yours. Why do you plan to go to Sickles when the answer is much closer and in the other direction?" she asked with exaggerated innocence.

She paused to ensure she had his attention. "I would have told you that when one trades for things, one goes to a trading post, but you were busy telling me what you know and not worrying about all that you do not know!" She smirked in triumph. "I am still waiting to hear more of this plan of yours."

"The Bandit King amazes me again," Fox Running said. "No one would think a man wanting his business done in secret would ever do such a thing." He saw the mockery on her face. "How was I to know he used the trading post?"

"Perhaps you could have asked," Cut Sky remarked. "I shall ride to the trading post in the morning. You may amuse yourself riding to Sickles if you wish. Perhaps it will keep you out of trouble."

Fox Running was uncertain whether the noise Coyote Horse made was a snort of amusement, but there was no question that some very white teeth belonging to Cut Sky were grinning in the moonlight at his expense.

Hawk Larsen's trading post was a small building that had a collection of rough-hewn tables around its walls, each piled with goods. There were furs and pots, some older rifles (Fox Running was certain new ones were hidden from army eyes in the back or kept somewhere else), and stray bits of clothing, some new and some slightly worn.

Larsen knew Cut Sky, but as with all whose business lies in the gray area beyond the rules, he was cautious in his conversation with Fox Running around. Finally, the shallow pool of Fox Running's patience ran dry.

"I need the name of your partner," he said, summarizing what he could guess of the business of selling fake Indian items. "I have spent time in Boston, and I know that without money, nothing happens. You do not have much in the way of money. The railroad will not ship anything for meat or furs or pots. I do not understand all that is going on, but I know that, so far, two members of your partnership are dead. I need to know who your partner is, before even more end up dead, perhaps including you."

Larsen shrugged. "I got no other partners."

"You are lying," Fox Running insisted. "Tell me, or this trading post will be burned to the ground."

"This is someone you call a friend?" Larsen scolded Cut Sky.

"He is trying to impress me that he is tougher than most men," she said, without the least change in the inflection of her voice. "He is desperate to do so, because he has been failing so far in so many ways. He is so desperate to regain my esteem, even though I do not think that is possible, that I am not sure he would not carry out his threat." She paused. "He might try. Whether he would succeed or not, I do not know, based on what I have seen him do so far."

Fox Running set aside the need for a victory in this war of wills and words. "Outside," he told Larsen, pulling his right-hand gun. "I see the kerosene there, and it will do the job. I prefer you not get hurt."

Larsen's existence was built on reading men and their intentions. When he looked at Fox Running's merciless, flat face, he saw no room for talking. "Peter Bigelow."

"What?" Fox Running was certain he had

heard wrong. The man who hated Indians above every other thing on earth was in business with Blue Feather? He took a step toward Larsen with his hands outstretched.

"It's the truth! It's the truth," Larsen wailed.

"Is this so?" Fox Running asked Cut Sky.

She was not sure, because Blue Feather had always worked hard to keep his most dangerous secrets from her. But her uncertainty was not something to share while she was dueling with Fox Running. Instead of an answer, she shrugged as though the question was of no importance.

"Bigelow. The rancher," Larsen interjected. "When I first started putting this together, he had a real scalp. Years old it was when he got it. Strange thing, with him being the way he was and all, but he said it gave him a sick feeling having it on his wall. He was in here, and we got to talking. I sent it back East to a man who said he had customers for that kind of thing. He earned as much off that scalp as selling twenty cows. We have people who place orders, and we fill them. Pete gets a piece of all the profits and pays the shipping costs up front because no one else has the money to do it! Your father knows how it works, Cut Sky, and he knows no one ever gets hurt. Will you tell this lunatic friend of yours? It's just business, I tell you!"

Cut Sky began interrogating Larsen, feeling betrayed that one of the area's most public Indian haters was a business partner of her father. Fox Running felt less emotion over the revelation. White men were always able to separate profits from everything else, and Blue Feather was shrewd enough to know a good opportunity when it was there. Bigelow? Hating Indians while making money off of them. He could almost admire the scheme. No one would ever suspect.

Larsen was saying that Bigelow knew what was shipped and its value. He sold everything to a dealer in the East, who then sold it to the final buyers. Larsen had no idea who that dealer was, nor did he care to know.

"Pete would give me the money. I'd pass it along to everybody, or let them take the things they needed if they didn't want the money," he said. "Nobody ever said nothin' about it, feelings running high the way they do sometimes, and 'specially now with that fella around."

"What fella?" Fox Running broke in.

"You know, they sent some inspector man who talked to everyone about the Indians and the land, about whether there should be a reservation and how big it should be. Rumor says another man come in on the train a few weeks back because the first report didn't come out the way some folks wanted. There's powerful people all mixed up in things here, but this wasn't about land or anything, Cut Sky. You know that, and your friend has got to believe me! Rawlins didn't do nothin' much lately. Mostly he makes me his things in the winter when the ranch is slow. Small spread, but it was good money for him to pay the bills. Got nothin' to do with what happened."

"What did Rawlins do that would make someone murder him?" Fox Running asked.

"You didn't hear this here."

"Cut Sky, are you in the mood for a fire?"

She nodded to play her part. "A big one!"

"All right!" Larsen yelled, putting his hands up and out to stop them from talking. "Way the story goes, ol' Miles, you know, the general that liked the Cheyenne, helped settle 'em, pushing like mad to get them a reservation down here. Lot of folks pushing back."

"We know that," said Fox Running.

"Them folks pushing back want to get the Cheyenne stirred up. Fella come ask me not to trade with 'em fair. Can't do that. Lose my business. Point is: every white man in the Tongue River Valley been warned to leave them Cheyenne alone. Dunno if Amos and Ben got their mouths going when they should have kept quiet. Ben wasn't a man you could give advice to without him gettin' good and mad. Kind of fella would walk over a cliff just to spite you if you gave him directions he didn't like."

"So who are all these 'folks pushing back'?" Fox Running asked. "Are they working together?"

Larsen shook his head. "Far as I know, they ain't. It's not like one of these syndicates — the railroad, ranchers, and such are all out on their own, so if you're square with one you might not be with the other, because nobody knows who they can trust. Way I hear is that the army's involved; not the man Evans, but something unofficial that's big and deep and goes all the way to Washington."

Fox Running let out a slow breath. "When is your next shipment?"

"Sent one a few weeks ago. Won't do another for a while. Maybe one or two before winter if I get anything to sell. Sent Pete word that I want to lay low a while anyhow, since what happened to Ben. Been good money, but good money's no good to a dead man."

■ ■ ■ ■

As they sat on their horses outside the post, Fox Running told Cut Sky to be careful on her way back to her father. "I will be along in a few days," he said.

"You are going to call on Pete Bigelow," she said.

"Might be."

"And I can't go because I am a woman?"

"You should not go because, if you get hurt, I do not believe there is a place I can run to where your father will not find me. Pete Bigelow and I do not get along. The conversation may not be very polite."

"Then you have to make sure I do not get hurt. Wait!" She dismounted and stalked into the post. She was back in a minute, stuffing the contents of a heavy leather sack into the pockets of her jacket.

"I told Hawk it would be a lot easier to keep my mouth shut if I had ammunition for my rifle. Now we can go!"

She started down the road that led west to Bigelow's spread. Fox Running had no choice but to keep up.

Sam Rickett was puzzled. They'd sent him to do a job, but now he was wondering if there were more people doing the job than just him. He watched the army officer who seemed to be the law around here, and the big white man, as they went about their business. They were not stupid men. When it was his time to earn his money, he'd need to move fast to stay out of their way, or make sure they couldn't come up against him in the open. Well, making decisions was up to the men who hired him. His job was to pull the trigger.

Howard Porter finished the telegram to Boston. This ought to be enough. Indians killing a white rancher meant they were on the warpath, or whatever it was called. It was a shame some of them refused to learn their time had passed. Some of the ones he had met around Lame Deer were so very nice, especially the children, who he saw all the time because the school was being built near the boardinghouse where he was staying. Perhaps when those children were grown, it would be time to trust them. That was certainly not the case today.

Chapter Nine

The Circle B was asleep. There were hardly any hands there to begin with. It was summer, and most of them were out on the range. The ranch house was surrounded by cedar trees planted to bring shade for the summer and provide a wind break in winter. Bigelow was there. He had last appeared in the yard around sunset, when he walked into the house from a fire in the ranch yard near its gate, where at least one cowboy stood watch.

The house sat atop a slight slope that gave it a good view of the valley that stretched to the east. To the north and south, the approach to the ranch house was flat. To the west, rock ledges and uneven grasslands were all they could see as they watched from a slight rise that let them spy on the house.

"We will walk the horses near the house, then tie them to the trees behind it," he said. She started to object, but he overrode her.

"Whatever we do short of killing him, Bigelow is going to make noise when we leave. Getting out alive means getting out fast."

She nodded. She was coming to understand that being the daughter of a bandit king in the shelter of the hills was one thing; walking the path of this wild renegade was another; and breaking into a man's house was something about which Fox Running seemed to know the risks.

He stopped her arm when she reached for her canteen to drink. "Not now. We might need it later. You are not thirsty, only nervous."

She wanted to disagree, but he was probably right. She had dumped a pocketful of shells into the pocket of the dark coat she wore over her buckskin shirt. Fox Running wore a dark coat as well over a shirt of thin linen.

It was fully dark now. The guard had been watching nothing happen for long enough to be bored. Fox Running gave Coyote Horse a pat as they began their stealthy approach. "Watch," he told Coyote Horse after they dismounted.

Cut Sky looked askance at him. "You talk to the horse?"

"He does not listen. You do not listen. I treat you the same. Is this a problem?"

She started to argue, then caught a glimpse of teeth in the dimness.

"You can see the doorway," Fox Running whispered as they started forward on foot. "There will be a bedroom on one side or the other. Quickly."

They moved as fast as silence would allow. When they reached the house, Fox Running tried the door. It was not locked.

"If someone challenges you, shoot first," he whispered. "Aim for the legs. Do not kill anyone unless they shoot first. If we are discovered, head for the horses and go. If I am not there, go. Do not wait for me. I will catch up to you and find you. Are you ready?"

Her rifle was cocked. He had a pistol in his right hand. She wanted water. She wanted something to ease the pressure on her chest so she could breathe easily. She breathed in deeply, once, then nodded.

She could barely hear the door latch lift. The darkness inside was deeper than that under the stars. His hand touched her arm. She followed. Her eyes began to adjust. He stopped; his hand pushed against her.

"Wrong way," he whispered. He never lost touch with her as he moved past her to lead the way. His hand was against her stomach. It gripped the buckskin of her shirt. Then she heard a noise. It was outside. Or the wind. The grip relaxed.

Now she could see. They were in a room with a bed. The white bed sheets stood out in the darkness.

"Listen for anyone coming from outside," he said.

She moved to the window, fascinated that it could be so clear. If she had a white man's house, she would have this thing they called *glass* everywhere to let the light in, instead of living the way they did in smoky darkness!

Fox Running lit the candle on the nightstand. Its wavy light cast odd shadows in the room. Fox Running cocked his gun. The sound jarred the sleeping man in the bed. "Whuz . . ."

"Good evening, Mr. Bigelow," Fox Running said with false politeness. "I have some questions that could not wait. My name is Fox Running, in case you have forgotten from our brief but memorable previous acquaintance. I believe we had unfinished business."

"You!" Bigelow's inhale to call for help was followed by the sound of a gun being shoved into his gut.

"I need answers. I did not come here to kill you, as much as I might wish to, but I will if I must, or if I decide you are such a worthless man, I am doing the valley a favor," Fox Running said. "I know you sell scalps that are made of horsehair as well as human hair. I know you sell other fake Indian items to people in the East. Other than Blue Feather, who knows about this?"

"I'm not . . ." Bigelow coughed and choked as the barrel of the gun prodded his gut.

"You partner with that trader Larsen. I know some of your secrets. I need to know the rest. Talk or die."

"Get that out of my stomach."

Fox Running eased the gun back an inch.

Cut Sky saw the brief struggle. A *pop* and a grunt of pain came from the bed. She felt something burn across her scalp, like the bite of a vicious stinging insect. She touched her fingers to her hair. A little wetness. She had suffered far worse. An exclamation followed.

"I should kill you just for that," Fox Running seethed, swatting at Bigelow's hand in the darkness. He heard more than he saw the tiny gun rattle as it skidded along the floor. Bigelow was in such fear of his life, he slept with a derringer under his pillow.

Even in the unsteady light of the candle, Bigelow recognized Cut Sky at the window.

"What does Blue —"

"Ben Rawlins. Why did you kill him? And if you yell, I will kill you."

"I didn't kill Ben," Bigelow snarled. "All the crowd of people thinking he was a saint for hiring your kind. The Indians were so stupid they worked for next to nothing. 'Next best thing to slaves,' he told me. He ought to know. Lived in Georgia before the war."

"He did business with you. I know from Blue Feather what you do. If it would not hurt him, I would tell it to every rancher in the valley so they know what a hypocrite you are!"

Bigelow's eyes took in Cut Sky in the corner. "Man's the only Injun I know with sense. Vision. Not like you, ridin' and whoopin' and poor. Got to have some white man in him somewhere. No Injun is that smart," he blustered.

Cut Sky took a step out of the corner as her rifle moved toward Bigelow. Fox Running held out a hand. She stopped. The movement had made her dizzy. She retreated to the wall and leaned against it.

"Tell me about Ben Rawlins," Fox Running insisted.

"He made these feathered things that would sell for big money. Man had a touch for them. He'd been making them for that bandit Cheyenne, Lakot-ay, whatever he was. Then we expanded the business, you might say. Blue Feather knows a good item, give him that. Sellin' things. No crime. Now get out."

"What about Amos Greene?"

"Amos and that Indian man — Golden Turtle man — they could make things together like no one else. I think I sold ten copies of Sitting Bull's war club. That's why this valley will always belong to me and to the white ranchers. Your kind wait for rations and whine about the days of hunting buffalo. Mine find a way to overcome everything that gets thrown at us. We get a bad harvest, or that beef price dips, we've got other money coming in from the gullible fools in the East. Now get out of my house and leave me alone."

"Who hated Rawlins and Greene? Who knew what was going on and would kill them?"

"Nobody I know of. Think I wanted it known what we was doin'? My own men woulda shot me. Ben was cross-grained, but I never bothered with him. If Amos got killed by some Crazy Dog lance, the way I heard it, it wasn't something he was making for me. That thing was just plain plumb ugly. Back East, they want lots of feathers on everything. I guess they think you people are nothing but birds!"

Fox Running wanted to throttle the man, but his words had the ring of truth.

"You want my thought, Injun, it's that Sanders man and all his stockmen. Some of those Texas men who come here. They want the best land for themselves. We were here first, and I don't care if it's Two Moon or Ronald Sanders — no one gets an inch of my land until the day I die! Sanders made me offers, and I tore them up and threw them in his face. Had the nerve to threaten me, he did! They think they're better'n us, but they're almost as bad as the filth that you people are. Ben might not have been as good at keepin' secrets as he should have been. Talked when he drank. Might have said the wrong word."

Fox Running had gotten what he came for. He lowered his gun slightly, wishing he could rid the world of Bigelow, but he knew he could not murder the man in cold blood.

"Don't think none about tellin' nobody nothin', Injun," Bigelow sneered.

"I will do what I think is right," Fox Running said.

"Know a man named Victor Farleigh, Injun. Rode with the Black Canyon Gang couple years back. Remembers a Lakota called Blazing Hands. Might be my civic duty to report to the army that one of them gang members is at large."

Fox Running felt cold. In his rootless despair after Crazy Horse died, he had roamed the Plains until he fell in with others who were young, wild, and angry. The Black Canyon Gang had a short, violent life in the Powder River Valley and along the Yellowstone at the northern end of the Tongue River Valley. It ended when Fox Running killed two of its members after they tried to rob the army and kill some soldiers. Fox Running had tried to put that behind him when he followed the direction of the spirits and moved to Lame Deer.

"Got a tale to tell. Might have him tell it," Bigelow said. "Or maybe you keep your yap shut, and he'll think a while longer about what to say and who to say it to."

Cut Sky had lost interest in the conversation. The man was a foul and evil liar. She could not imagine why Fox Running thought it was worth asking him anything.

Through the fog of her senses, she remained transfixed with the glass. It was so strong and yet so thin! Her eyes were blurring as they tried to focus on the dancing reflection of the candle. There was a line through one of the tiny panes that went from one corner to the other. It was inside the glass. She wondered how anyone could do that. She pushed against it with her fingers, and it did not give. It should. She pushed and pushed. A little harder. It gave a little. A little harder.

The sound of the small pane shattering was loud in the room. For a second, Fox Running took his eyes off Bigelow to look at her. Then he turned back as Bigelow reached for a pistol that was under his pillow in addition to the derringer. Bigelow pulled back the hammer, swung the pistol towards Fox Running, and fired.

Fox Running swung his own gun from left to right, hitting Bigelow's arm. The bullet sailed into the ceiling. Bigelow's pistol fell from his hand and clattered across the wooden floorboards to rest with the derringer.

Voices sounded from outside.

Cut Sky looked at her left wrist. It was stuck in the window and bleeding profusely from a deep cut inflicted by a large, sharp piece of glass. Another piece remained in her wrist, where blood pumped out around it. She could not understand what had happened. She looked at it with fascination, yet remotely, as if this were happening to someone else.

Fox Running could only see that a dark stain was spreading fast as Cut Sky whimpered. He smelled the blood and heard it drip to the floor. "Cut Sky! What happened?"

She murmured something incoherent.

He grabbed her uninjured arm and pulled. She almost passed out from pain. More shards of glass lodged in her wrist as it came free of the shattered window. "Follow me, Cut Sky. Now!"

Bigelow had rolled off the bed. Fox Running heard a gun cock. He fired two shots in that direction as he pushed Cut Sky through the bedroom doorway and into the hall that would lead to the door of the house. She stumbled and almost fell. He heard the rancher curse.

A rifle fired from inside the room; Bigelow was trying to guess their progress along the hall as bullets flew through the thin mud-and-plaster walls. They barely kept ahead of his shots, the last one covering them with powder.

The horses were at the door.

"Up!" Fox Running called. "Go!"

Cut Sky struggled to mount. Fox Running lifted her to the back of her horse and slapped the animal. It galloped off. He jumped onto Coyote Horse's back. "Still," he told him.

There they were! He could see a few shapes coming around the house. He emptied the rest of one pistol at the figures, then used up the other. He jammed one gun in its holster and started to reload the second. "Go!"

Coyote Horse began to run. Fox Running had time to get three bullets into the cylinder of his revolver. He fired, knowing the house was likely to be all he hit, if that, but it would buy time. He holstered the gun and told Coyote Horse to find Cut Sky.

It took little time to catch up. "How badly are you hurt?" he asked as he reached her. "Can you move your hand? Do you feel your fingers?"

"It bleeds a lot, and it hurts," she said, in an odd, high tone. She did not look at him as she spoke, as her head lolled from side to side. "It was wonderful, and then it broke all apart."

He wondered what she was talking about. "For now, we must get away," he said. "Follow me!"

She tried to keep up, but as they rode, she realized her horse was bouncing way too much and tried to slow it down. Then Fox Running was in front of her, calling her name. Then she tried to move her sticky arm to show him, but it was simply too heavy. Her head hurt from where she had been shot, and the world was rocking from side to side.

Fox Running could see the dark blood that had stained her clothing as well as the blanket on the horse's back. She was bleeding too much. Bigelow must have shattered the glass with a shot. No, she was already bleeding by the time he fired. No matter. That was for later. For now, she had to survive.

They needed to hide. He turned west, hoping the rougher ground would not be the first place Bigelow's men searched.

He stopped at a place where there were at least a few trees and some large rocks that could serve as cover. He pulled Cut Sky from her horse and laid her down by a rocky outcrop that might be enough to hide them in the dark.

"Ride away and come back," he told Coyote Horse, knowing the spirit horse would understand. "Take her horse with you. There is no cover for you here."

The horses galloped off. He reloaded his pistols and set Cut Sky's bloody rifle on the rocks. When pursuers found them, he would be ready. Then he reached for Cut Sky.

■ ■ ■ ■

Harry Washburn was the first to reach the rancher, who was tossing aside his nightshirt as Washburn entered the room.

"What happened, boss?" Washburn said. He pointed to the broken window as he moved to stand next to the ranch owner. It must have been shot out by a bullet. Bigelow, who was rarely alone, was so now. Washburn took a quick look down the hallway. No one. "Somebody try to kill you?"

"The Injun, Fox Running," Bigelow said. "Gonna be Fox Bleeding when I get done with him."

Bigelow gave Washburn a version of events very different from the truth. He could never admit doing business with his bitterest enemies, and the smell of gun smoke in the room made it clear there had been a fight. Maybe if his men could track down that Indian, they could kill him before he spread word of Bigelow's business around. "Almost got him!" Bigelow boasted.

"Looks like he almost got you, too!" Washburn said, nodding at the drip of blood from Bigelow's arm.

Bigelow made a scoffing noise. "He

missed; got the lamp, and a piece of it cut me. Whoever he was with got hurt." He did not name Cut Sky. Nothing could connect him and Blue Feather, not until he got that trader to agree to keep his mouth shut. There would be a price. With that man, there always was.

"Has to be a blood trail we can follow. Get the men ready," Bigelow said. "We can follow that Injun. Thinkin' I had anything to do with this killin'! Gonna tell that Sanders fella, if he gets the Injuns all riled like this, he's gonna answer to me. Musta been Sanders killed Rawlins an' Greene. Tell that army man all about it when we're done with those Injuns."

"You figger the Cheyenne are riled enough to kill, boss?"

"Looks that way to me, Harry. Shame the rest of the valley don't feel the same way about them Injuns. Ready to kill us all, they are. Now let's get after them!"

The single report of a gun echoed in the room. Bigelow stared at Washburn, clutching his chest and swaying. A line of blood dripped from his mouth.

"You were gonna have to go sooner or later, old man," Washburn said without regret. "Least this way, you get to be the first victim when the Cheyenne started a war. Should have worked with us when we wanted you to join us. Been workin' for Sanders since the day I hired on here at your miserable wages. Maybe this is best. They can recall you as a hero 'stead of a miserable old man that hated everything!"

Bigelow dropped to his knees, weaving and swaying.

"Better get the boys so they can see you die," Washburn said. "That Sanders. He sent 'round word that a man who helped you meet your Maker would be looked upon kindly. Your ranch hands were too afraid to try. Not me! Been waitin' for a time when there was no one around. Ought to thank that Injun."

Bigelow made noises, but no words.

Washburn went to the doorway, grinning. "Boys! Boss has been hit! An Injun broke in and done it. Come quick!"

Bigelow heard booted feet running down the hallway. Kneeling was too hard to do any more as he fought to breathe. He put down an arm to brace himself, but it was made of rubber, and he slid to the floor. Looking sideways at the world, he saw boots and heard words. A few faces looked quizzically at him. Then they were gone, and he was wrapped in darkness and silence.

Cut Sky moaned as Fox Running touched her left wrist, fumbling in the darkness. He could feel a piece of something sticking out. It was smooth, with sharp edges, and felt like glass. Blood was steadily oozing around it.

He touched her head. Blood there, too. Not much, but enough to show him that the derringer's tiny bullet must have glanced off her, opening a scalp wound. Now he understood why she had been so wobbly at Bigelow's house. His plan had not worked quite as well as he thought, after all.

Fox Running knew little about treating wounds. His own, he bandaged when there was time, but mostly he let them heal as they would. When he was badly injured last year, a Lakota healer did the work while he slept through it all.

There was blood all over her clothes. If he pulled out the glass, she would bleed again heavily. He found the leather she used to tie back her hair and knotted it around her forearm. Soldiers used tourniquets when they were wounded, but he was not really sure how it was done. He tied the strip of leather tightly. She moaned. He took the cloth off his head, shaking his hair back as the wind sent it flying in his face.

This could kill her. He asked the spirits not to let that happen. He touched the piece of glass. *Breathe in. Breathe out. Pull!*

She would have screamed if she had been fully conscious. As it was, she yelped and tried to pull her hand away. Fox Running wound the cloth around the bloody place and held it as tightly as he could while keeping an eye out for pursuers. He saw no one. *Yet.*

After a few minutes, he touched the spot where the leather thong circled her forearm. Her flesh was pulsing. He untied the knot. He could feel more blood seeping into the cloth and gripped it harder. He could not retie the rawhide without letting go of the cloth, and so he held on.

After a time, the cloth did not appear to be soaking up more blood, and there was no overflow dripping onto his own clothes. He could feel no new wetness from her head, but there was stiff drying blood in her hair.

She did not speak, but she breathed. As he held her arm, his muscles aching, he listened for the sound of anyone coming to find him while scanning the east for the first sign of dawn. He thought of Bigelow's words. *Farleigh.* An image emerged of a young man with greasy hair who preferred to wear nothing but black. Fairleigh had fled after the final fight by the soldiers' campfire, and Fox Running assumed the man had left Montana. He had guessed wrong. Oh, he had been wrong about far too many things.

Coyote Horse and Cut Sky's mount returned shortly before the sun neared the horizon enough for Fox Running to see. Cut Sky's coat and buckskin shirt, along with everything else of hers, were soaked in blood. His coat was sodden where he had held her arm. His arms, face, chest, and vest were daubed in red. She had lost much more blood than he thought. Her breathing was shallow, but not rapid.

He had let go of her arm but left the cloth where it was. They would need to travel soon. He took the rawhide he'd used as a tourniquet and tied it around the cloth that covered her wound, not too tightly but enough to keep the bandage in place. There was nothing else he knew how to do.

"I know you hate blood," he told Coyote Horse. "For now, we are covered in it. Tell her horse to follow and obey. We will ride together on you."

He wished she would wake up, but as long as she breathed, she was alive. She had lost too much blood. He should have tended to her better while he waited for pursuers who never came. Before moving her, he spoke to the spirits.

"If it is to be that her days are over and she is heading for Seana and the stars, send her spirit on its way with no more pain," he said. "If she can live, let it be so. If my words can matter, let her live, for none should die on my account, and if there is wrong to atone for, I must pay the debt, not another."

It was an interesting adventure to put someone on a horse who flopped like a sack. In the end he draped her on Coyote Horse's back, then set her astride after he mounted so she leaned into him. He realized they would be caught in a moment if there was a chase and kept moving west. He had never been to this part of the valley but kept to the rough ground and woodlands. The stench of her blood was strong as the sun shone upon them. Once during the day he heard shots, as though one group of men were signaling to another, but for the rest of it they were alone.

He made an early camp. She still had not awakened. He carried her to a small stream where he rinsed off the blood on her left arm, which was slightly swollen. The water was cold. He drank his fill, as did the horses, and washed off as much of her blood that had caked all over him as he could. He replaced the bandage on her wrist with one made out of a piece of the less-stained sleeve of the shirt he had worn, which he left behind. In the fading light, he could see there was a little red on the cloth, but not much. That was good. She was not bleeding, if there was still blood left in her.

As the last bit of light was fading in the west, he borrowed her rifle and went to find something small to kill for food before full dark fell. Then he saw them. Eight riders at least, maybe as many as twelve. It could be a coincidence, but he had not passed any stock grazing that would call for that many riders. Cowboys pushing hard until almost dark meant they were trying to find someone or something. Him. He was sure Bigelow would not rest until he was caught.

Cut Sky still slept. As the night grew deeper, he lifted her onto her own horse. He tied her hands together under the animal's neck and her feet under its belly. The knots might hold or they might not, but it was what he could do. He knew it would not do her wound any good, but staying where they were would be even worse. He would need both hands to fire his guns, and if she rode next to him on Coyote

Horse, she would be nothing but a target.

Fox Running walked, rifle in hand, leading her horse by the rope tied to the animal's bridle. Coyote Horse wandered along beside him, like a dog. He tried to use the stars to go as far south of the searching men as he could while still moving east. If he was lucky, in the morning the posse would keep moving one way and he the other, and the gap between would keep him safe.

But they were more vigilant than he thought. Although he moved slowly and avoided every open place he could, the trees eventually ended. He could either wait and hope to escape detection in the smaller wooded area where he was, or take a chance by crossing the open ground and seeking refuge in a place he was certain offered a greater chance to lose any pursuit.

"Coyote Horse, if we have to fight, gallop ahead with the other horse. Do not stay with me. If I do not return, guide them."

He could feel a question from the horse, but his purpose was clear. "The spirits bless you," he said to Cut Sky as he touched her leg.

"Halt!" called a military-sounding voice as they were about halfway from the trees to a hill that rose in the darkness.

Fox Running kept moving, but faster.

"I said, halt!" the voice bellowed.

"Do as you were told," Fox Running told the spirit horse. "She is yours to keep alive."

There was no third demand, only a bullet that clipped a branch a few feet above Fox Running's head.

"Over there!" the man called. "I got him!"

A second gun opened up. The flame from the barrel was several feet from the first. The bullet flew well wide of its target. Fox Running thought about trying to run for it, but he could not see where he was.

"Go!" he said. He sighted down the rifle as he let go of the reins. When Coyote Horse's movement sparked another round of fire, Fox Running fired back at the two yellow spots — a little left, a little right, and a little down. He was certain he heard one man groan with the impact of a bullet, but he had little time for rejoicing.

Three new guns joined in. They had his position and fired. Coyote Horse and the limply bounding figure of Cut Sky on her own horse were now well clear. Fox Running moved back the way he had come and fired the last of his rifle bullets. The spare ammunition was still in Cut Sky's coat. Little good it would do him there! He threw the rifle as far as he could into the trees and dove to the ground.

There were now at least four guns firing, and they swept the place where the rifle landed. Fox Running tried to walk bent low. More gunfire sent him crawling on his belly until it ended. Tall grass. He rose and kept moving, a pistol in his hand. The patch of tall grass ended. Back to crawling.

He almost crawled right into one of the pursuers. The man fired his gun, but the shot went wide as Fox Running rose and butted his head into the man's midsection, knocking him over. He heard a howl of anger and fired toward the sound. The bullet hit rocks, striking sparks. The man yelped.

Fox Running heard him calling for help and ran as fast as he could. He reached a slight rise. Behind him, he saw shapes converging and heard boots running. Not caring whether he hit anything or not, he used up four bullets to slow them down and ran uphill, keeping low as best he could to be a poor target.

More trees! Now he went slowly, moving from tree to tree as quietly as possible. Once, he heard a call far to his left. Another answered, far to his right. Either they were very good and knew where he was, or they had split up in hopes that a wide enough net would find him.

He let them go. Then he realized he was not alone. He started to run and leveled his gun to the left, just managing to stop as the shape of Coyote Horse made itself clear. He stumbled on a tree root and rolled over, his shoulder smarting from the impact with the ground and his head hurting from where it hit a rock or something sharp that cut his cheek.

"Do not say a word," he said to Coyote Horse as he reached the two animals. The darkness hid Coyote Horse's expression.

First, he checked the knots that still held Cut Sky, then he tried to orient himself by the stars to confirm which way was east. He mounted Coyote Horse, then reached for the other horse's reins, and they moved at a fast walk to escape.

They kept moving through the night and for most of the next day. Slow and steady. Cut Sky never woke, nor did she bleed. Her injured arm felt hot to the touch. Her sleep was unnaturally restless, with shallow and irregular breathing. He did not think that was good, but for now it would have to wait. He had lifted her back on Coyote Horse once he was sure they had slipped the circle of pursuit, so they could move as fast as possible, which was still slower than he wanted.

The Tongue River was flowing faster than he recalled, but in August it was low enough that they could ford it. "If it was just me, it might be a good joke," he told his mount, having the notion that an animal named Coyote Horse might like to pitch riders in the river. "But Cut Sky is not well."

The horse snorted. Maybe they were communicating. Likely not!

Once they safely reached the east bank of the Tongue, he stopped. It was early evening, but it was light enough to see that Cut Sky's arm had gotten redder and hotter and was now very swollen. As a boy, he saw a healer drain an infected wound, but he had no real idea how it was done. White soldiers heated knives when they dug out bullets. He had to do something.

He built a fire and heated his own blade in it, then laid her on the grass near the river, where it loudly rushed over large, round rocks. The setting sun was just starting to color the west. He wondered if her spirit would feel the beauty of the place, if the spirits around them would ease hers into the next world should all of this go wrong.

He closed his eyes and tried to summon words. "Let me not fail," was all that came to his mind. He grabbed her forearm roughly and sliced into it, drawing a moan that showed she was alive. He squeezed the arm until yellow-colored and clear liquids, along with a little blood, flowed down toward her elbow and into the dirt. He squeezed and squeezed until he could not get out another drop.

He carried her close to the fire. He left the wound uncovered and draped both of their coats over her as he propped her against him. She slept. He looked up at the gathering darkness and the early stars, wondering what was looking down, what the spirits truly made of all that The People did, and whether she would live.

July 1883, Lame Deer, Montana
"He killed Pete Bigelow!"

Evans had thrown open the door to Dooley's cabin without knocking. Dooley was barely awake.

"Whaz?"

"That Cheyenne! Fox Running! He killed Pete Bigelow. Rode into his ranch to kill him. Him and some other Cheyenne! Now there will be a war! What was he thinking? Did you know about this? Get dressed!"

"Captain, could ye line up your thoughts like a train not half off the tracks and explain to me what it is ye are talkin' about? What did he do now to Bigelow?"

"He killed him! The night before last, Fox Running, along with someone else no one can identify, snuck into Pete Bigelow's bedroom and shot him dead!" Evans yelled.

Dooley asked him not to shout. Evans lowered his voice a fraction and continued. "I thought he was trying to find out who killed Amos Greene. Was any of what he told us true? Is that what this has been about all along? Is he the one who killed Greene and Rawlins? Well? What is going on here, Dooley, under my nose? When they told me there was some agency that did not report to the army, I said no good could come of it, and I know you tried, but I think that Indian fooled us both."

Dooley, who had spent much of the earlier evening in the company of a certain teacher, and a fair part of the later evening as time slipped away in conversation that required more than a little wet to address parched throats, was slowly coming to grips with the fact that Fox Running was in deep trouble, or that his hatred for Bigelow had led him to go too far. Only last night, Mairead had warned him the Cheyenne might become a liability if Fox Running was not reined in, and he had objected to her arguments. Apparently, she was a better judge of character than he was!

"Hurry, man!" Evans raved. "The only thing holding back Sanders from starting a full-fledged war is that I said I would investigate. He already has men out searching, and they will kill Fox Running if they find him. You are coming with me."

Dooley grabbed for his clothing. "Tell me everything ye know," he said as he got dressed.

"Fox Running and his partner slipped into Bigelow's ranch house at night. From what the ranch hands say, there was a gunfight in the bedroom. The Indians rode away. There are search parties out now. At least one of the people with Fox Running — or maybe it was him — was wounded, because there was a lot of blood in the bedroom, more than just from Bigelow. You'll see. Hurry!"

"How are they sure it was Fox Running? Didna this happen in the dark?"

"An Indian with two guns on his hips? Even in the darkness, there was enough moonlight to see his profile. Hard to miss that. Only one of those around here, Dooley."

There was. Dooley finished dressing quickly. Evans said the rider who informed him of Bigelow's death had left while search parties were still out. "They may have already found him. If they did, Dooley, there is nothing we can do. Pete Bigelow was a nasty old man. Even Sanders hated him! But, whatever he was thinking, Fox Running was wrong. If they have not found him, the army will have to bring him in. You may have to help me bring him in alive, but I will bring him in one way or the other."

Dooley mumbled a reply. Evans shook his head. "Don't even think of sending telegrams to whoever it is in Boston who's important enough that someone listens. You are not going to be allowed near the telegraph. We are going to catch Fox Running, and then he'll have to pay for what he has done."

The ride to the Circle B was quiet as they rode hard, pushing the horses. Evans brought a squad of eight troopers with him to add to the search, or begin a new one.

Harry Washburn and Reggie Miller, the foreman, were waiting.

"Harry was the one who saw the most," Miller said. "I had him stay behind so you could hear it from him. Last word from the search party was that they found his trail, heading east and a little south of here. I sent word to Ron Sanders to see if he's got some hands to spare. I know the boss didn't like him much, and he didn't like the boss, but I figure we ranchers got to stick together if it's gonna be war like this."

Bigelow's body had been put in the ice house. They would bury him in a day or so, or whenever the hunt for his killer ended. Since he had no wife, there was no family to consider. When the hands were all back, they would look for a will.

"First things first," Miller said. "First we catch them Injuns and hang 'em, then we take care of the boss. That's the way he'd like it."

Dooley asked to see Bigelow. "Ought to pay our respects first," he said solemnly.

"Harry will show you," said Miller. "I'm trying to run the ranch and find those Injuns, so if you need me, someone will find me."

Washburn led them to the ice house. Bigelow's eyes were shut, but his face was frozen in anger. A red hole in the brown leather vest he wore showed where one bullet had killed him. There was a slight black mark on the vest as well, where something had burned it.

"What did you expect to see?" asked Evans. "Your friend killed him."

Dooley had spent the entire ride trying to

think of ways all this could be wrong. Now that he was here, all those explanations felt as thin as the heel of a cowboy's sock.

As they emerged from the ice house, Washburn offered to take them to the room where Bigelow was killed.

In the bedroom, Dooley took in the broken window pane, and the bloodstains on the wall and floor nearby. A bullet had smashed the oil lamp on a table next to the bed. The headboard also showed a recent scar, from the same bullet or another one. Dooley picked up Bigelow's balled-up nightshirt. There was a spattering of blood on it around the edges of a small tear, as though whoever was wearing it had either been nicked by a bullet or cut himself. The blood looked fresh. That puzzled Dooley, because the shirt was found far away from the dark stain on the floor that marked where Bigelow died.

A pistol lay on the floor a few feet from the bed. A derringer was nearby. Dooley picked up each gun and examined it. The six-shot pistol had been fired twice; the derringer had emptied its load. When he looked across the bed toward the door, he saw two holes in the wall. There were larger holes in the wall as well, and a rifle on the floor. After what clearly was a major gun battle inside the room, someone had fired the rifle in a desperate attempt to stop whoever was in the hallway, most likely whoever was running away.

Dooley frowned. Bigelow could not have done that with a chest wound that had all but killed him instantly. Was there someone with Bigelow? There had been a gunfight, but the way Washburn told the story and the way the room itself was telling it were two different things.

As they came out of the ranch house, Miller was gathering every last man in the yard.

"He got around one group down on the trail toward Wolf Mountain," Miller said. "Gonna try to get him before he reaches the Tongue, if that's the way he's heading. He's going back and forth. Tryin' to shake us. Coming, Captain?"

Evans said he was. Dooley pretended he'd dropped his tobacco in the ice house and went back for one last look at the rancher's corpse. He pushed up the left sleeve of Bigelow's shirt. On Bigelow's left arm, there was a cut that matched the bloody mark on the nightshirt.

Dooley let go of the cloth. He had no idea what really happened in the bedroom, but he was holding onto hope that Fox Running had not killed the rancher. Now he had to hope that the ever-growing search party filled with hard-eyed men did not end up as a vigilante hanging.

Chapter Ten

The moan of pain from Cut Sky woke Fox Running, who had drifted in the hours before the sun rose.

"Arm," came out from the sounds she was making. He thought she was speaking Cheyenne. Fox Running listened for more words. He saw her eyelids flutter. He went to the river, cupped water in his hands, carried it back, and tried to help her drink.

Instead, she choked and gagged. Her eyes opened, and she squinted at the early morning light that caught her full in the face. "Where . . ."

"We are at the Tongue River," he told her. "You cut your wrist on the glass in Pete Bigelow's house. You were shot in the head as well. You lost a lot of blood, then your arm grew thick and hot, and there was fluid that drained from it. You were asleep for about two days."

". . . hurts," she said.

"I will be right back," he said.

He went and dipped his hands in the cold river again, then tried to pat her face with water, which he ended up spilling all over her, bringing her wide awake with a start.

"It hurts," she said. By now, the sun was starting to pick out features of the landscape. She tried to sit up and howled in pain as she jarred her left arm. "Tell me . . . tell me what happened . . . tell me again."

He did. In the light, he could see her arm was dark with bruises from elbow to wrist, but it was no longer swollen. She would live.

He used the last of his shirt to rig a crude sling.

"We need to go," he said. "There are men searching for us. I do not know if they will find our trail, because we crossed the rough ground, but I do not want to take the chance. We will follow the river. I shall take you to your father."

"There is a shorter way," she said unsteadily. "It is rough, but there is a trail near here."

He waited until she could stand. He helped her mount, but she wanted to ride on her own. She led the way until they reached the start of the trail.

"You go ahead," he said. "I must see if we are followed. You cannot ride fast. If you hear guns, do not come back."

"Fox Running . . ."

"We shall talk later, Cut Sky. These past days I have asked the spirits to return your life to you and wake you. Now that you have returned, do not be foolish with the gift they have given you. Follow the trail. Get to your father. Offer him my apologies. Perhaps he can talk sense to Bigelow but, for now, stay safe."

He wheeled Coyote Horse around and headed back for the river. Every instinct in Cut Sky said to join him. But she had no gun, no knife, and could not use either in her current condition. She was not even sure how long she could stay on the horse. There was one thing she could do: ride for help.

Fox Running waited. Whoever was searching for him would find him in the end. He wondered why Bigelow was searching so hard. He expected the initial pursuit, but was puzzled that men would keep searching so long. *It must be fear that his secret will be exposed,* he thought.

There was a hat visible above the rocks. Another. He and Coyote Horse were in the shade behind a screen of bushes where they could watch unobserved. He had decided that if the searchers crossed, he would attack them when they came partway. If he could create enough confusion, he could take the trail by the river going north and eventually lose them in the Breaks.

The hats grew heads until six men gathered on the west bank. Fox Running pulled one gun from its holster. There was disagreement among the men. An argument. Then one rider galloped along the trail that led toward Lame Deer. The rest followed, except for one who rode back the way they came.

Fox Running waited, confused. Bigelow must have recognized Cut Sky. He assumed that was why the trackers knew to go this far east. He did not think there was a better crossing farther north, but he would take the river trail and find out.

Dooley waited on the fringe of the crowd of cowboys and soldiers arguing over which way Fox Running had gone. He had almost made a mistake when one of the searchers was explaining why they did not cross to the east bank of the Tongue River. He was near certain the rider with Fox Running was Cut Sky. One or both had been wounded. He was sure they would get to the Tongue River Breaks in the end, but that was knowledge he would not share. At least, not until his own doubts were resolved.

Then he realized Evans had asked him a question.

"Dooley! North or south? Would Fox Running go north or south?"

"To the south, sir, there's not much but the Crow settlements," Dooley said. "He would never go there. I don't know that he'll go to Lame Deer, sir, but it may be best for us to go there if we cannot find him, because, now that he appears to have gotten away, I think we need to go about this in a more orderly fashion."

Evans looked at the collection of ranchers, all hoping for a shot at an Indian.

"I am not saying this because I believe your friend is innocent, Dooley. I am certain he is a killer. But I believe you are right. If we have vigilante justice, it could lead to more Cheyenne thinking the white man's law allows Indians to be hung with impunity. We will go to Lame Deer and begin anew. The army will pursue this investigation, and I shall bring more troops from Fort Keogh." He went back to the group, which received the decision poorly if the volume of noise was any indication.

Dooley felt a little bit of relief. If the cowboys were no longer looking to shoot

Fox Running on sight, there might be a chance to find out what truly happened. He felt like a man buying time without knowing if he was delaying the inevitable. It would do for now. Then he could decide whether his friend had turned a corner from which there was no going back.

Fox Running knew he was being watched. The unseen eyes had first started following him a mile or more ago. He hoped this meant Cut Sky had reached Blue Feather's camp. It would take time for one of the watchers to get to Blue Feather and ride back with instructions. He rode slowly. There was no need to tire anyone out. As he rode, he wondered how he would explain to Blue Feather that the daughter who was whole when she came to Lame Deer was coming back with an arm that might never be usable again, and a head wound that had caused unknown damage. And he was supposed to be pretending to be her suitor!

"It really was a good plan," he explained to Coyote Horse. "Until it wasn't."

As the path turned, he could see three men ahead. They were blocking the way only if he allowed them to do so, but he was not there to fight.

"Blue Feather wishes to see you," said the

middle one. There was no friendliness in the command.

"And I him," replied Fox Running, thinking to himself that at least no one had shot at him. Yet.

There was not even the pretense of a welcome for a supposed suitor. There was barely an acknowledgement of his presence.

"Play nice with the other horses," he told Coyote Horse as he dismounted. "And come when I call you, you contrary animal, for we may need to leave here in a hurry!"

One of the three men led him through the camp to Blue Feather's lodge. The other two walked behind. Fox Running felt the impulse to draw his guns to see whether they would shoot or run, but he was becoming tired of this game.

"Inside," said the one leading him when they reached the lodge. He went in and found it empty. He sat on the ground and waited. He waited a while, in an unspoken message about his importance to the one who had deigned to meet with him. He rose out of respect when Blue Feather entered.

"I will hear from you all that happened. Leave out nothing," the older man commanded, leaning on his stick. His face was a thundercloud.

"I will not do that," Fox Running replied.

"You are here in my camp, surrounded by men with guns, and you defy me?"

"Yes. I will see Cut Sky. Then I will decide what to tell you."

"Demands? You make demands?"

"Would you like them to know you dealt with Pete Bigelow? Would you like them to know what you sold?" Fox Running hissed in reply. "I can speak very loudly."

"Perhaps you should be a suitor for my daughter, since you bargain hard."

"Perhaps."

Blue Feather strode out of the lodge, pounding the stick he used as a crutch as he limped and lurched across the camp to another lodge filled with women, who scattered as his growling presence entered. Fox Running followed.

Cut Sky was lying on a dark blanket, wearing a linen shirt and a dark skirt. She looked pale, with dark ridges under eyes that looked more alive than the rest of her. Her left arm was neatly bandaged and, from the aroma in the lodge, coated with salve. Her hair had been trimmed by skillful hands, making him grateful he had decided against hacking away the blood-matted clump.

Her eyes were wide open as she watched Fox Running and Blue Feather.

"A good Cheyenne woman would have a proper meal waiting instead of this," Fox Running waved his hand in a dismissive motion, "silliness."

"My horse has a hoof infection that can only be seen by putting your face right up to his left hind foot," she replied. "Tend to it."

Fox Running knelt by her pallet. Their eyes met, filling in places where words were shallow and empty. He took her right hand in his left one, held it as he closed his eyes for a long moment when only the spirits heard his words.

"Father," Cut Sky said.

"Yes, Daughter."

"Find Fox Running something to eat to stop this endless whining I hear, and find me a true warrior who thinks of something other than his stomach."

"A good Lakota woman would not fill the air with the stench of salve when a man must eat," Fox Running chided her.

"And a good Lakota man would not beg others for food he has been too lazy to hunt for himself," she said with a slight smirk.

Fox Running smoothed the hair that was now neatly parted and braided, neither congealed with blood nor stinking as it had during their flight from their pursuers. He stood and turned to her father. "Now we can talk."

Blue Feather turned to leave.

"No, stay," Cut Sky said.

"The women were clear," said Blue Feather, in the tone of a man who has learned that advice from wise women is not to be taken lightly. "You need to rest."

"I will rest when he bores me to sleep," she said. "Until then, I must listen to see how many times he inflates his own importance."

"I shall have food brought." Blue Feather left the lodge. From outside, they heard him giving commands.

"And you?" Fox Running asked Cut Sky.

"I will live. I may only have one arm to swat my husband, whoever I might choose from my suitors, but I will live."

"Then all is well."

Blue Feather returned. Despite his best efforts, he kept returning his focus to the spot between Fox Running and Cut Sky where their hands were tightly joined.

Fox Running went through most of the story. He left out how the window at Bigelow's was shattered, and Larsen's belief that a federal inspector had come to make a report. He did not want Blue Feather interfering in that. He also omitted Bigelow's threat about Farleigh, and any mention of the Black Canyon Gang.

Noise erupted outside. Voices, urgency.

Blue Feather left without a word and was back within moments. "You have lied to me," he accused Fox Running. "You will leave my daughter's side this moment and leave this camp."

"Father!"

He glared at her. "You did not know? You did not see?"

"See what, Father?"

"This man killed Bigelow during your adventure, and now the army and ranchers are seeking him to hang him. How could you not tell me this?"

Cut Sky argued, both of them talking in a stream of multilingual outrage, until Blue Feather finally yelled for silence.

"He was alive, Father. I do not remember much, but he was alive when we left," Cut Sky insisted.

"He was trying to shoot through his own walls to kill us," said Fox Running, who had risen to his feet. "Can you imagine a man so full of hate he destroys his own house to kill? How do they say I killed him?"

"You shot him," Blue Feather said. "They do not know who you were with. Another Cheyenne."

"I will tell them . . ." Cut Sky began.

"You will not!" Blue Feather commanded. "They are not looking for the truth. They are looking for someone to hang!"

"Who is looking?" asked Fox Running.

"The army. Your friend rides with them. Ranchers were searching, and although the army said it will find you, they still search for you to kill you."

Fox Running's right hand had drifted to his gun, and he idly drummed his fingers against it. "Why?"

"They want to kill you because you killed Bigelow!" Blue Feather raged. "You will lead them here. You must go."

"This is a safe place. He must stay," countered Cut Sky. "We killed no one, Father!"

"I did not kill him, Blue Feather. He was a foul, evil man, but I did not kill him," Fox Running said absently, without heat, as if the matter was an unimportant detail. "Did he have family? Did someone want his ranch?"

"White men always want someone else's land," Blue Feather responded sarcastically. "He had no family. No one liked him, but everyone feared him. That rancher Sanders, I was told, offered him twice what the land was worth, but Bigelow spit on his offer.

The one who carried the tale said this was a literal act."

"How often did you see him?" Fox Running asked. "Bigelow, I mean."

"As little as possible. It was in the summer. Very early. He had a grievance against the men from Texas and Wyoming. The big man who talks loudly . . . the one who says he represents them. I do not know what their differences were. It may have been the land. Bigelow was one of the first white men to settle here and took far more land than he would ever use. He always believed he needed more. I do not want to make more of this than I should. He always had a grievance against someone."

Fox Running nodded.

"The trader. Larsen. He and my good friend John Dooley are the only ones who knew Cut Sky was with me. Mr. Dooley will not say anything, at least for now. He will need to know what happened before he talks. Cut Sky may need to speak with him, for in this case he may not take my word. Someone needs to tell Larsen not to speak of her. It may not be this day, but in time he will be asked, because everyone knows that traders are often able to pick up stray information others do not possess."

"He shall be spoken to," said Blue Feather.

Fox Running knelt by Cut Sky and took her right hand again. She gripped his tightly.

"I must prove this thing false," he said. "I do not know how to do it, but I must. I will be back when I can."

"Warriors," she said in mock distress. "You can tell when there is real work to do because that is when warriors ride away to go hunt for imaginary buffalo."

Blue Feather cleared his throat. "I shall wait outside for you, Fox Running."

"There are trails that lead from here," she said urgently after Blue Feather had left. "We can be gone beyond their reach in a few hours."

"We may yet need them," he replied. "But first, I must find my friend and let him know I did not do this. Then, we shall see what to do. The ones trying to deny The People their land will use this against the Cheyenne. I cannot allow that to happen. I have made promises that I cannot break. I will fight this."

"I do not know what good Lakota women or good Cheyenne women do, Fox Running," she said, "but daughters who have a man like Blue Feather as their father know how to fight, and if you fight them without me, I will haunt your spirit until the days are no more. And that is my promise."

"Then I must be back soon with a robe from my imaginary buffalo." He released her hand and stood up. "The white men have hunted me before. They will never catch me. I will be back."

He strode from the lodge as her eyes, misting, followed him.

Dooley had insisted that Evans set up temporary headquarters at the Lame Deer cabin where Dooley lived. Not only did it show he was supporting the army, it ensured that any bits of information that came to Evans would also come to him. Dooley knew Fox Running would not set out to murder Bigelow. But Fox Running hated the man, and he knew his friend could flare beyond all reason.

As he told Mairead in the moments of solace he found with her, he was troubled that Fox Running had run away. Guilty men ran. The longer he hid, the worse it would be.

He had already begun thinking about what to do when Fox Running was captured, because, unless Fox Running had left the valley behind — something Dooley could not imagine — sooner or later, the searchers would find him. They would need to bring him to Fort Keogh, to stand trial and be kept in the prison there. Otherwise, there was no building stout enough to resist vigilantes. And if Fox Running was hung, or shot by vigilantes, it would not be long before all of the valley was aflame.

One of the first things Evans did after establishing his headquarters in Lame Deer was telegraph Fort Keogh that Fox Running was being sought. Word soon flew from fort to fort, and across the territories so that if the suspected killer tried to get away, the army could catch him.

The telegram was soon received in Fort Riley, Kansas, where Carson McAllister had drifted after losing his last two jobs for drinking too much and writing too little. Everyone at the Cavalryman saloon knew his tale — how the story of his life had been taken out of his hands when some Boston woman took over the newspapers that ran his articles about the Cheyenne Kid. That was why a boy was dispatched to find him as soon as the telegram arrived and drag him, regardless of how drunk, to the fort.

McAllister was certain at first that this was a drunken dream. The telegraph operator said there was no mistake. McAllister fired off a telegram of his own to Frank Howard in St. Louis, a friend from better days:

CHEYKID NOW KILLER MY STORY GIVE EXCLUSIV.

He waited in the telegraph room, sober now.

The reply wasn't long in coming. WRITE NOW GO THERE PAY FARE OLD RATES WELCOME BACK.

McAllister chortled. This time, he would win the fame he'd been denied. This time, that Indian had gone too far to escape justice. And McAllister would be there for the hanging, a sad moralistic last chapter to the adventures of the Cheyenne Kid.

The next morning found McAllister once again bleary eyed, but not from a night on the town. This time, it was from writing a story that the army was kindly telegraphing to the offices of *Western Territories News,* a growing rival to the paper that had fired him, which would print it the next day in its weekly edition and have it delivered by train across the territories of Dakota, Wyoming, and Montana within a week.

"You can hide, but I will find you," McAllister said to himself as he boarded the train for a date with his destiny.

The story told readers, "Army Hunts Killer It Sheltered," with the sub-headline adding, "Cheyenne Kid Murders Rancher in Tongue River Depredations."

As the train lurched, McAllister took a deep pull from his silver flask. It was good to be back.

News that Fox Running was wanted for killing a rancher was received differently along the Tongue River Valley and beyond it.

Rides a Crow began talking to the spirits when she heard, while asking her spirit wolf and the spirit horses to find Fox Running before anyone else could. She knew Fox Running had almost untold depths of anger within him, could be quicker to act than think, and would stop at nothing to remove obstacles to the Cheyenne having the Tongue River Valley as their reservation. She did not believe he would kill without provocation, but focused as she and the spirit wolf had been on protecting Two Moon, she could not be sure Fox Running had not caused the violence that always lurked on the edges of her consciousness.

Both her spirit animals told her they could only sense Coyote Horse's determination to get away and could sense no hint that Fox Running had killed anyone. Instead, they said, he had been begging the spirits to save a life.

Sam Rickett heard the news with impassive silence as he ate a meal in Sickles. Half the talk was that the Injun had done the world a favor; the rest, that this proved Indians were always waiting to kill white men. Then the talk went to the weather, and the army, with equally passionate disagreement. Was it possible the Indian had changed sides? Everything was possible in this place. Maybe someone would remember Rickett and let him know something? He would have asked the ones who hired him, but he had no way to communicate with them. All he could do was wait and wonder. He would be glad to get back to Texas.

Howard Porter had telegraphed Boston again and received the same stern reply to stay through the summer. Porter was aware that the Cheyenne believed the whites were out to arrest Fox Running because he stood up for them. One little girl with a lovely face and the worst raggedy haircut he had ever seen told endless stories about him. Even the white landlady at Porter's boardinghouse said that if Fox Running had killed the rancher, he had done the world a favor. Porter tried to understand, but they all told him he would never know what was really going on because he was from the East.

In Boston, Katherine McGillicuddy learned about the manhunt after Annie

Campbell at Fort Keogh sent the news. The telegram arrived on the same day as a letter from two weeks ago saying that the experiment of having Dooley and Fox Running there to fix problems was working well, according to Paul Collins, Annie's husband. Katherine was glad the money she was using to support them came through an organization that was funded by another organization that was attached to yet another organization she controlled. She had learned the hard way that being publicly associated with Indians could hurt her business. It felt like hypocrisy. It *was* hypocrisy. But if she wanted to win the game, she had to play by the rules, not whine about them. And, to her, supporting the Indians when all the moneyed interests around her were against them was a game she was not going to lose, unless they left her no choice.

Now she had no weapons. She could rave with impunity about it, but in the end, the only thing to do was what she had done — walk to the church where she told her most private thoughts. Fox Running called God "the spirits," but she knew it would not matter what words were used, only whether there were good intentions.

In Denver, Colonel Franklin Shepard, who had overall command of the forts in

Colorado, Wyoming, and Montana, received the wire in addition to others that came from Washington by way of St. Louis. Other communications came to him as well from friends who had ridden with the Seventh Cavalry and those who were friends of the army — especially the latter.

He wired Evans, making it clear that Evans would be expected to bring Fox Running to justice, dead or alive. He also made it clear that from the War Department's perspective and that of the army's high command and the men who would determine promotions, there was little interest in the second option.

"You the army?" the man in the doorway called in at Evans.

Evans wondered if a denial might work, because the young man looked like any number of shiftless men drifting. The kind that might want to ride in a posse only if it paid.

He sighed. "Yes, I am Captain Jack Evans. Can I help you?"

"Vic Farleigh," said the man. "I hear Fox Running killed Pete Bigelow. That true?"

"That is a possibility," Evans said. "Bigelow is dead, and Fox Running was there. The army is investigating, and we want to speak with Fox Running. Do you have information about him?"

"Oh, I got information," said Farleigh. "I got real good information."

Even though Dooley expected it every night, the hand that came down over his mouth and the voice whispering "shhhh" in his ear were total surprises. Evans was snoring nearby in a rough-made bed that Hard Morning, a Cheyenne who was good at carpentry, had slapped together.

"My land," Fox Running whispered before he took his hand away and moved through the opened cabin door.

Dooley, who slept fully dressed nowadays, put on his shoes and emerged into the moonlit night. The Cheyenne's land was a short walk from Dooley's cabin. He had only cleared a small amount when he learned he would no longer be marrying Morning Shadow.

"Were you followed?" The whisper came from the dark between two trees.

"There was a wee cat who showed interest until he realized I did not plan to feed him."

"I did not kill that man."

"A powerful case they have, so can ye prove it? Ye broke into a man's home, and ye had a gunfight with him. Those are crimes, lad! The man had the law on his side, and ye did not. What possessed ye?"

"He was the one selling phony scalps and the other things we talked about along with Blue Feather," Fox Running said. "Secret partners. The items went to the trading post, then from Larsen to Bigelow, then from Bigelow to the East. Blue Feather coordinated making everything. I went to Bigelow to talk about who killed Greene and Rawlins, and then . . ." He did not want to discuss Cut Sky's role. "He fired first."

"Can ye prove it? Can ye prove any of it? They know ye were not alone. Who else was there? Do you have proof you did not kill the man?"

"No. The only one with me was Cut Sky. She was hurt, and since she does not recall anything and would be nothing more than an Indian trying to get another Indian off, I would not even sic the army on her."

"Tell me all of it," said Dooley. "From the moment you got to his house."

Fox Running did.

"You're sure he was in a nightshirt?"

"Of course I am sure," said Fox Running. "It was almost comical, that this man in his big long floppy shirt with his big fat floppy belly had guns hidden all over his room. He was expecting someone to try to kill him. That is what he knew his crew thought of him. Do you know he shot through his own wall to kill us when we left?"

"He was dressed when we found him. There was one shot to his chest. The bullet went through his vest. I was curious, because I found a nightshirt with blood on it in his bedroom, and there was a cut on his arm but no corresponding cut in the shirt he had on."

"He was not dressed when we left. Someone killed him afterward. I can understand why someone would hate him, but I do not understand why he was shot to death. Perhaps if we were in a court of law in Boston, we might have a case?"

"Out here, lad, I don't see how that helps. They want ye dead before ye ever get to a courtroom. Do not even tell me where ye are hiding; I don't want to give something away."

"I have two other things to tell you. One is that there may be someone sent here from Washington — not the man we all knew about who came through this summer, but someone else whose job it is to file a report against a reservation. There also may be hard feelings between Bigelow and Sanders. I think Sanders realized that Bigelow didn't just hate the Cheyenne — he hated everyone and would not let Sanders get a foothold any more than he would the Northern Cheyenne. But Bigelow was an old man with no family. Time was on Sanders's side."

"I have met Sanders, and you have not. The man is pushy." Dooley began to wonder. If Fox Running did not kill the rancher, the number of people who could have was very small. "Look at it like this: ye want Bigelow out of the way. An Indian attacks Bigelow. If ye have a man in his crew, a man who rides with Bigelow but is paid by Sanders to do Sanders's bidding, it's an opportunity to get rid of Bigelow and let the blame fall on the Indian — if there was such a man, which there probably was."

"And how do we prove that?"

"I don't know, lad, but maybe if you put those Indian skills of yours to work, you can find Sanders's man among those who ride for Circle B. Find him. Follow him. Maybe get him to tell who killed Bigelow."

"Even if he did it?"

"I don't know!" Dooley snarled. "Think ye should, though, lad, before whatever ye do next." It was all too complex and convoluted for his taste.

Fox Running knew his friend's anger was not entirely misplaced. That made it worse.

They both kept silent.

"You have been gone too long," Fox Running said finally. "If you need me, leave sticks in the shape of a square by this tree. Be careful, Mr. Dooley. I do not trust anyone."

"You're learning, lad. Took a while, but you're learning."

Dooley waited for a response, but silence convinced him Fox Running had gone through the woods to wherever he was hiding, if in fact he was not hiding on that plot of land in the middle of everyone.

He walked for a while, checking to see if he was followed, and then returned to the cabin.

"Did I hear you go out last night?" Evans casually asked the next morning.

"All of this!" Dooley remarked. "Sleep, I could not. I tried counting sheep and then someone came along to rustle them!"

Evans laughed. He had a vague memory of another voice, but after the past few days, anything was possible, even that a voice he was certain belonged to Fox Running was speaking to him in his dreams. He had spoken to no one about the information Farleigh had given him. The years between the Custer fight and the return of the

Cheyenne were filled with so many gangs, most of which were nothing more than lost young men. During the time Farleigh talked about, Evans had been endlessly patrolling for the remnants of the Northern Cheyenne. He had a vague memory of the gang's name but had sent a courier to the fort for Sergeant Garrett Jones, the fort's living encyclopedia.

Evans told Dooley that his soldiers would start a search from Lame Deer to the river. Some Circle B riders would be helping; others were riding with Sanders and his men, hoping to find Fox Running first.

"If you know where he is, John, I hope you will tell me," Evans said. "His choices are simple: if I find him, he might live. If they do, he will certainly die."

"I thought you might come," said Rides a Crow, as she stroked the neck of the magnificent black mare that was often by her lodge.

"I did not kill him," Fox Running said.

"I know," she said, lightly patting the spirit horse. "Coyote Horse is faithful to his clan. He told his leader, and she told me. I must know more. I . . ."

The rusted wolf, which always looked gaunt, walked into the lodge and sat at her feet.

"Now that our very tardy spirit friend has finally consented to join us, we may begin," she said. "Whatever you have told your white friend, here you must tell everything. I cannot help you if I do not understand."

When he was done with all of it, including Bigelow's claim that a member of the Black Canyon Gang was alive and could harm Fox Running, she had questions, but not for him.

"Are these men so filled with hate?" she asked the wolf aloud. "Could it be that one evil white man held back the power of more evil white men? Will the evil be such that you can find him?"

A few moments of silence fell. Fox Running knew the wolf was communicating to Rides a Crow, but he did not know how. "And if you do not, then what?" she said angrily to the wolf, speaking again out loud. "This is no less a threat than what we faced on the way from Darlington! I was not afraid then, and I am not afraid now!"

After a long silence when they looked at each other, the wolf made a noise and left.

"Hunter and I speak by spirit talk," she said. "You may have felt it, for you have some spirit gifts. He will go find the man who conspired with Sanders to kill Bigelow. I do not know how we will convince anyone that he committed this crime, but once we know who it is, perhaps we can think of a way. When that is done, we can worry about how to deal with what you did when you were even more foolish than you are today. And now you must do that which is hard."

"What? I will do anything."

"That is why it is hard. You must do nothing. Hunter will return to me in a few days. He can find the evil men. They would kill you before you came close, and they will not show themselves in front of others as they would in front of him. Until then, find a place where none can find you. Go across the Tongue River to Blue Feather, for I am certain Cut Sky would welcome you."

She paused, trying to find words that would soak in and not ignite Fox Running.

"White men are not like us, Fox Running. You know that from your time among them. They are quick to kill and take revenge, and then, when it is too late, they weep and mourn and beg to be forgiven. If they cannot find you, they cannot kill you only to regret it later when they know you are innocent. For now, hiding is the only way you can be safe. Now, before you go, eat. Take bread with you, for, just as your spirit must be strong, so must all of you for the trials ahead."

Fox Running ate and then packed meat and bread in a sack. He mounted Coyote Horse, who waited at the head of the path to Rides a Crow's lodge. Then he turned and slowly rode away, looking for all the world like a dawdling Indian with nothing at all on his mind but time to kill on a warm August day.

But, as he rode off, Sam Rickett, who had been watching Rides a Crow's pathway, pulled at his mustache. Bits of information no one thought mattered were always what mattered the most. Sooner or later, everyone was vulnerable. Everyone.

"Sir!"

A trooper in front of the cabin opened the door, thrusting inside a man who clearly did not want to be there. "Hawk Larsen, sir. Runs a trading post. One of the Cheyenne farmers nearby told one of our scouts he saw two Cheyenne there recently. One sounded like that Fox Running character we been chasing, sir. Turns out it *was* him, along with some other Indian from the other side of the Tongue River, sir."

"Tell us about this, Larsen," said Evans. "Fox Running is not a trader, so what was his business with you?"

"Um, sir, I can't do that."

Evans stalked over to Larsen and grabbed the older, rounder man by his coat collar, crinkling his nose at the smell of him. "This valley is about ready to erupt because Fox Running killed Pete Bigelow. Whatever you think you can or cannot do, let me tell you one thing: if you do not answer my questions, I will lock you up in Fort Keogh and burn your trading post to the ground! Or maybe I shall burn it with you in it!"

"I think he means it," Dooley chimed in. " 'Tis well you should talk."

Larsen paled. "I'll talk to you, but it cannot leave this building. I would be as good as dead."

"If you don't talk, ensuring your death is among my options," growled Evans. "Why was Fox Running at your trading post, and who was he with?"

With a moan and a sigh, Larsen told Evans about the secret business in fake scalps and Indian artifacts that connected Rawlins, Greene, Blue Feather, and Peter Bigelow. He admitted Blue Feather's daughter was with Fox Running.

"I know it don't sound right when you just say it, sir, but it was good money! Nothin' illegal, 'ceptin' most of the Cheyenne don't like it much. But it was them making fools of the whites, and they liked that, knowing that back East a man with a horse tail on his wall was bragging about it being an Indian scalp."

"Think carefully, Larsen. When you told Fox Running that Bigelow was involved, what was his reaction? Was he one of those who was angry at this?"

"Of course not."

"Why do you say that?"

"He was traveling with Cut Sky." The name meant nothing to Evans. "She's Blue Feather's daughter, like I said. He was part of this deal from the beginning. Might be her father never told her which white man was helping to make them money, but she had to know it was one of them. No, sir, Captain Evans, sir, he didn't look upset or angry or anything like that at all. He looked like a cat just given a box of mice to play with. Pleased, like. Don't know why. Now can you please swear to me you won't tell a soul? The Cheyenne learn about it and there's going to be revenge not only on me, but on Golden Turtle!"

Evans sighed. "I'll take your request under consideration." He waved the man out of the cabin and then turned to Dooley. "You know Fox Running. You know what I told you two to do. What was he up to, and who is Cut Sky?"

"She's a lass with whom he is . . . um . . . dallying, should we say, Captain," Dooley responded. "They met in some Indian fashion that I dinna recall."

"Recently?"

"Aye, sir. A bit too wild for her own good is the lass — flint and tinder, they are together, sir — but a charming couple they made, sir."

"Yes, I can see that. Attacking Pete Bigelow in his home and killing the man. Very charming."

"Sir, I know ye will think I'm speaking from friendship, but I dinna think they went to that foul man's house to kill him."

"Dooley!" Evans threw up his hands in exasperation. "It does not matter if they went there to plant flowers. While they were there, they killed him! I did not know until it was just pointed out to me that Fox Running was also known as the Cheyenne Kid! A gunfighter! When a gunfighter breaks into a house, it is not to make tea and have conversation!"

Dooley was as unmoved by the outburst as he had been by any number of more violent ones from Fox Running when his friend was a boy at the Indian School of Boston and gifted with a rare ability to rave for hours. "You dinna know him, sir. I do.

Set everything else aside and forget Fox Running."

"I wish I could!"

"Think about Bigelow a moment, sir. Killing him is nowhere near as bad a punishment as it would be to let out that the man was working hand in glove with Indians to market phony scalps. He would be humiliated. Fox Running wants this land for the Northern Cheyenne, sir. He's a mite fixed on that idea. He would not risk it to kill one wee man. He could have done that in the spring, had he wanted."

"But you saw the room, Dooley. There was a gunfight in there."

"But riddle me this, sir. If Fox Running snuck into the house and killed the man, who fired through the wall? Saw ye the holes, the same as I did. If no one else was in the room, there was no one else to fire at someone leaving, and if Bigelow fired at them coming in, they would have left. We could see the holes were fresh, sir. There was plaster dust all over."

Dooley could see Evans was turning over the idea. Now or never.

"Two things happened in that room, sir. There was a scrap between Bigelow and those Indians, because there were fired guns left behind and marks all over the room.

But Bigelow had a burn mark on his vest near where the bullet that killed him went in. That only happens . . ."

". . . when a gun is very near the person being shot," Evans finished. "Yes. We had a case when I was in Minnesota where a soldier killed someone at close range and tried to lie his way out of it."

"And, sir, that nightshirt Bigelow wore had blood on it that matches a small cut on his left arm. His shirt — the one his dead body was dressed in, sir — had no blood there. The cut had stopped bleeding by the time the shirt went on him."

Dooley stopped, hoping Evans would come to the conclusion himself.

"So, you are trying to say Bigelow was surprised in his nightshirt, some chaotic fight took place, Fox Running fled, Bigelow got dressed, and then someone killed him?"

"I think that is what happened, sir. That's the only thing that could have happened, unless the man was dressing and undressing like a madman!"

Evans could not fully suppress a smile. Dooley had that effect on people.

"But who? Why?"

"That I dinna know, sir. I know Fox Running has a temper and a reputation, and if there were four dead men in a gunfight I would say it might be his work, but to walk up to a man this way and kill him is not like him, sir. Not at all. From the guns in his room, it's clear Bigelow expected *someone* to try to kill him, and I dinna think it was Fox Running. We need to think who he was afraid of."

Evans frowned as he considered Dooley's words.

"You may very well be correct, John. I hope Fox Running will surrender himself and tell us his side of the story. For now, regardless of what you just said, I have orders — orders, John, that do not allow me to speculate on what may have happened, orders that must be obeyed — to bring him in. I am a soldier. I must obey. Whatever this started out as, it has grown into something far bigger. I do not know how long I can contain it."

Evans looked out the cabin's window. "I will not ask if you have heard from him, because, if you have, I do not want you to be in a position to either betray a friend or lie to me. But if you do hear from him, tell him he must either surrender to me and take his chances, or live as an outlaw until they catch him and kill him." Evans turned back from looking outside. "Has he ever mentioned the Black Canyon Gang to you?"

Dooley shook his head. Evans explained. Dooley let out a sigh. "He told me once, sir, that Hat Creek changed his life — he was there when those Cheyenne were killed who had fled Fort Robinson — and that he was ashamed of himself for wasting the time after Crazy Horse died. I assumed he went sowing wild oats, but I never asked for the details."

"I am told outlaws hide in the rough country near Sickles," Evans said. "My men and I ride there today. I would like you to ride with me, John."

"So I don't send word to him?"

Evans smiled thinly. "Perhaps that, a little. Also, John, if we find him, you may be the only man who can talk him into taking the only chance he has to come out of this alive. Shall we go?"

Most of the Circle B riders had gone back to the ranch. Bigelow had been a hard man to work for, and although the fact that the Indian had killed him meant they wanted to see the Indian dead, a few days of riding the high plains looking for a man who had gone to ground or was halfway to some Indian reservation made them reconsider how much time they wanted to spend in the hunt.

Sanders had sent riders to stay in touch with the army. If by chance they blundered into the Indian first, he wanted to be there to finish things off the right way. Fox Running was far too slick for his own good and might talk his way around what Sanders had planned for him. Sanders had been surprised at Washburn's fast thinking. At first, he had been elated. Then, as Fox Running eluded pursuit, he began to wonder.

Washburn had sought out Sanders immediately after Bigelow's death to get his reward, but the stockman had told him brusquely that their business should be handled later, when conversation between a cowhand and the head of the alliance of ranchers might not seem unusual. "Don't generally carry much gold on me, Harry," he said at the time.

Now, as the number of hands was dwindling to those who truly wanted to kill an Indian, Washburn was hoping Sanders would find the time.

In part he was unnerved by the brown-gray wolf that had wandered into their camp over the night. Wolves were always around, but rarely this close. One of the riders commented on it, and another wanted to shoot the critter when it would not go away. The wolf had stared intently at the riders as if the animal knew what they were talking about, and their conversation ebbed.

The wolf had remained near Washburn throughout the morning, without scrounging for food at the camp like the other animals. Then it was gone. Washburn saw it later, about fifty feet behind Sanders. Something about the animal was unnerving Sanders as well, because he pointed at it, and two men starting riding towards the wolf, who easily darted away.

Sanders watched the animal and then made eye contact with Washburn. He nodded at the cowhand. Good! That had to mean Sanders would meet with him soon. Washburn wanted to get his money and leave Montana behind. Secrets paid well, but they had a habit of leaking out along with a man's blood if a man stayed in one place too long.

Evans had about twenty-five soldiers and another twenty cowboys with him as he left Sickles behind and moved into the Tongue River Breaks. Dooley could only think that this expedition reminded him of the War Between the States. One side dug in and hidden, the other walking into a trap. He could tell from the faces of the soldiers and cowboys that he was not the only one expecting a fusillade of rifle fire with every step their horses took along the twisting paths.

Smoke! Evans signaled for a halt. There was no question someone was camped out up ahead.

"All of you, be ready to fire. Have your rifles ready," Evans commanded. "Don't start a fight, but if they start one, finish it!"

Dooley could tell from the light beyond the trees that they were nearing a clearing. The smoke was getting thicker.

Evans and two other soldiers burst into the clearing, only to find no one there. On top of a stump was a piece of paper, held down by a rock, corners flapping in the wind.

Evans ordered soldiers to dismount and keep their rifles trained on the woods. Dooley dismounted as well and walked over to the stump with Evans.

I am innocent of killing Peter Bigelow, the note said, in Fox Running's scrawled handwriting. *I will prove this. Until I do, please leave my friends alone.* There was a postscript. *My friends do not like coffee, but there is some on the fire for you, Captain Evans, because you have been a fair and good man to our peoples, and I know you are doing your duty. Until we meet in happier times.* The letter had a flowing signature and a drawing of a running fox.

As the soldiers and cowboys looked at the camp, they could see it had once held several lodges, all of which had vanished.

"How did they know?" Evans asked Dooley. "How?"

"If someone knows Larsen talked to you, sir, they may have known what he would say. Keeping secrets out here, sir, isna easy."

"Search for anything of importance," Evans said. He took a pencil from his saddlebag, turned over the paper, and left his own message, putting the paper back under the rock as the soldiers turned to leave. *Give yourself up while you still can,* Evans's message said.

Dooley read it as the captain wrote it, wondering where in the trees and broken ground Fox Running and Blue Feather were hiding. For he knew they were there, and he knew it would take only one misstep for Evans's failed raid to turn into a shooting scrape.

"They are leaving," said Blue Feather, watching Evans through field glasses.

"I do not think they will be back," said Fox Running. "The captain is doing his duty, but I think his heart is not in this."

"We will change our camp to be safe," said Blue Feather. "The chicken bones from this one were building into a mountain, and it is time to move when that happens."

"We should post guards, Father," added Cut Sky, who seemed to have bounced back faster than Fox Running could have hoped. "The trader's warning came with plenty of time, but we may not be so fortunate the next time. And until they finally post a reward that makes it worth turning this one in, I suppose we must continue to feed another idle warrior and keep him safe?"

"I am open to offers, daughter," replied Blue Feather. "After all, what other suitor of yours has brought us this much entertainment?"

The men with Blue Feather laughed. They had been sharing with Fox Running the predicaments of those who came to claim Cut Sky and found they were no match for her will. He was learning.

Chapter Eleven

Fox Running heard the thud of an object hitting the dust. Again. Again. He took a gun from his holster and moved out of the lodge where he was staying. Softly. Quietly. The fire had long burned itself into oblivion. Not even a glimmer of red showed.

A sliver of crescent moon was low in the western sky. *Thunk!*

Fox Running slowly moved toward the sound with his thumb on the hammer of his gun and his finger on the trigger.

"I smell gun smoke and horse sweat; it must be Fox Running," laughed Blue Feather, whose broad silhouette was visible against the star-filled night sky. "Come and join me. Put the gun someplace where it will not go off and injure someone, particularly me! You do not need it here."

"How do you know I have it? It is so dark here."

"You are awake. You will have a gun. It is

that simple," the older man said. "Set it aside a few moments, and I will teach you a new game. But you must hurry."

Intrigued, Fox Running went back to his lodge, set down the gun, and returned to the small cleared area where Blue Feather was standing, throwing something. *Clang!* Metal on metal. Horseshoes?

"It is a simple game, Fox Running," said Blue Feather. "You throw the horseshoe, and if you throw well, it will hook itself on one of the points of the moon."

Blue Feather pointed in the dimness to the sky, where a tiny sliver of moon still hung over the horizon.

For a moment, Fox Running was unsure what to say. Did Blue Feather really believe he could do this? His thoughts were interrupted by laughter.

"No, I am not crazy. It is an amusement. Try."

Fox Running tossed one of the horseshoes. Again. If one passed by the moon at all he could not see it.

Blue Feather gathered the metal shoes. "It can be done. See?"

He softly tossed a horseshoe at the fading, dipping thin curve in the sky. Fox Running could see it cross the moon on the way up, and cover the tip of it on the way down.

"It began as a way to pass the time on nights when I cannot sleep," said Blue Feather. "I have done this since my leg was injured, and the pain would not let me rest. Now it is what I do when my mind wishes to talk to me, for there is often too much taking place in the day to allow me to think. It is the time when what I do entertains the spirits so much that they come and talk to me and help me with my troubles."

"What troubles you tonight?"

"You."

Fox Running was uncertain how to respond. Blue Feather did not wait for a comment but settled himself on the ground, grunting as he landed without aid of a stick to help him down. Fox Running followed him.

"Cut Sky would sooner douse a warrior with stew than cook it, yet every night she spends hours making food that is the best it can be with what we have; she argues against anyone who tries to tell her what to do, yet you order her, and she obeys; she is freer than the wildest spirit horse, and she follows you willingly. Anyone who says anything about you faces bared teeth. There is something in you she sees that she needs. What is it you see in her?"

Fox Running tried to put in words something that he could feel but not explain.

"Long ago, I expected I would ride the road of my father and other warriors. That was the path I sought when I asked to marry Morning Shadow of the Lakota, for she was a wife who would fit in that world. I no longer believe that. A lodge, a home, a family — all those may wait someplace, but they well may not. It was not my will, but that of the spirits. I have learned this."

Fox Running watched the low moon for a moment.

"I have come to accept that every day I rise may be the last one. I do not ask the spirits for that which they will not give. I ask only that I not ride alone, and that one person have my back even if that means risking everything, for it has been a lonely road, Blue Feather. Until I met Cut Sky, I did not think a person like that existed. She does, and she is your daughter. I have lost many people in my life, Blue Feather. Almost all the people I ever cared for have gone. I do not want to lose her."

"You took her to a place where her life was in danger."

"We are Cheyenne, Blue Feather. Our lives are in danger every day. I think I can stop her from taking the risks she wishes to take by stopping her from breathing, but I do not know if even that would work. She understands this, as do I. We were put here to do something the spirits created us to do. One day that work will end, and so will we. Until then, we shall face down each new morning and celebrate each evening. And we will not surrender, Blue Feather, not this day or our last day, no matter what it costs."

The older man sighed a deep, long breath.

"After my leg was injured, I learned to see the world differently. I had to be smarter, think faster, be shrewder than others, for I could not survive any other way. My brain, and not a gun or bow, was my weapon. Like you, I lived outside the rules and ways of others for most of my life. I have learned more about the white man's way than many. I know when they are threatened, they are ruthless and brutal, and when they are not, they can be kind and generous. You threaten them. This reservation you want threatens them. As long as you pursue it, you risk your life beyond all measure. By doing so, you would risk her life."

"Yes."

One point of the moon was now all that gleamed above the far mountains. They watched in silence as it slowly inched lower and lower until it was gone.

"There are very evil men in these hills,

Fox Running. Do not think you can defeat evil, for it is deeper and vaster and mightier than one man, even one man with my daughter at his back." He started to rise. Fox Running helped him to his feet. "Evil corrupts. Even those who are good can be turned to evil purposes when they know not what they do. I know the spirits guard and protect you, Fox Running, but with so much evil all around, you must be careful. For her sake, if not for yours."

"I do not plan to be a martyr, Blue Feather."

The older man placed a heavy hand on Fox Running's shoulder.

"No one ever does, Fox Running," he said softly in the darkness. "No one ever does."

With that, the Bandit King limped to his lodge.

For generations, the spirit horses of the Northern Cheyenne had ridden the Plains. Legend said that these animals, descendants of the horses given to The People by the spirits, could appear to Spirit Walkers as humans, could warn humans of storms and enemies, and would roam the land as long as The People endured. They were few now, as the ring of settlements by the white man reduced their land and carved it with railroad steel. They spent much of their time to the north, where there were fewer settlers. Talks to Horses, who led them, would go north for weeks to feel the freedom of the wind in her mane, but she always returned, because since the days of The People's return to the Tongue River Valley, she knew that as endangered as were the spirit horses, the Northern Cheyenne were even more so.

She had gone with the spirit wolf to find the evil that was trying once again to steal hope from The People. So much land. So much room. So much evil. If the men who sought to kill The People were not so brutal, they could be pitied, for they rarely saw the beauty of the land, only what it could bring them in money — something of which they never had enough.

On this night, Talks to Horses was galloping as fast as she could, with the thin crescent moon barely above the horizon. It was this — the stillness of the sleeping earth, the distant and seemingly fragile pattern of the stars, the freedom of running fast — that made life worth living. That, and the fact that she was helping Rides a Crow, the Spirit Walker who was their friend, and Hunter, the spirit wolf who growled and bit at everyone and would happily lay down his life for The People.

She steered clear of places where humans gathered. As the wheel of stars above let her know she was nearing her destination, she galloped faster. Rides a Crow would not be the only one who needed to be told.

"It is your horse," Blue Feather told Fox Running after calling out that he was entering the lodge where the young man was staying. He knew Fox Running had a hair trigger and did not want to provoke him. "There is something wrong. He was quiet all night but is restive now. No one else can come near him. You must come."

Coyote Horse was trying to batter his way out of the fenced area that held all the horses. Usually, Blue Feather's men let the horses loose, but this was a new place, and they did not want them going back to the old camp.

"Coyote Horse!"

The horse stopped and glared at Fox Running. Fox Running could not explain how it was, but he suddenly realized that someone had found the man who killed Bigelow, and he was being summoned to confront him.

"I must go," he told Blue Feather. "This is a message from the spirits."

"Your spirits are almost as noisy as you

are," Cut Sky chimed in, arriving out of breath. "Where do we go?"

He pointed at the bandage she still wore on her left wrist. "You are not going anywhere."

"Then go," she said, "but I am the only one in camp who knows where I hid your guns."

"Cut Sky. Give them to me. We do not have time for games."

"I started this. The evil man shot at me. I am not going to make stew and wait."

"The practice might help."

"You have entered my life, and in my life we play by my rules!"

"You are complicating *my* life, and there is work to be done that matters even more than your temper."

Blue Feather watched as will crashed against will like two resounding clubs. He was half expecting them to come to blows when she turned and stalked away. He was certain she was smiling.

"They are in your lodge. I never touched them," she called out over her shoulder. "I need to dress properly as befits a nurse in charge of an infant warrior. Leave without me, and I will shoot you myself."

As Fox Running started to tell Blue Feather he would do his best to protect her, the older man held up a hand.

"The spirits will do as they do, my friend," he said, marveling that this was what passed for conversation between them. "Those of us in whom the fire has burned out cannot feel the heat of it as do those for whom it still burns. We shall count the days until the two of you return. We shall pack you meat and bread for your journey."

"And bullets," replied Fox Running. "For those I shall need most of all."

Long before he started his career as a Boston police officer, a career cut short by an injury from the War Between the States that left him unable to walk very far or very long, John Dooley had been apprenticed as a carpenter, a job he approached with more resignation than enthusiasm.

Since coming west, his lessons had served him well, to help build the cabin where he lived and the rough furniture within. Now, he was doing perhaps his hardest job — making benches for the Indian school while Mairead Cullihan watched.

Evans had been summoned to Fort Keogh to report on the hunt for Fox Running, who everyone agreed could well now be anywhere. The army, as indicated by telegrams that came regularly from Colonel Shepard in Denver, was losing patience.

Dooley had so many things to do that all seemed pointless, that he threw them aside to make good on his promise to turn long slabs of pine into benches for Mairead's students. It was not a vast chore. She hoped, at most, for twenty students. He planed and smoothed and carved, until there were six benches that would sit four children apiece.

"I hope some of the parents will come, too," she said, "or perhaps we will have more students than I think."

Dooley enjoyed hearing her optimism. He had confided in her many of the problems that were surrounding him, and she had offered a solution. He admired her wisdom and was beginning to hope there was another perspective to the valley's future than the combat envisioned by Fox Running.

Using the cooking pot that belonged to Spotted Dawn's family, and what she initially advertised as an old family recipe but later admitted was what she could recall and what she thought she forgot, Mairead had stew bubbling outside the cabin that would serve as her home as well as the school. Dooley was talking about her prospective students. "They will be ill-disciplined, they will not listen, they will . . ."

". . . be children, John. They will learn

something. I do not know what lies ahead for them, but they need to learn to read and write and count, or others will take advantage of them. I suppose I may offer them poetry and books, but I mostly want them to be able to know what they must. I cannot imagine the world they will grow into, if their reservation becomes permanent. Many of their parents never knew about white men, and now these children will live to see a whole new century. Do you know that the newspapers I saw in Boston when I left were talking about the invention of carriages pulled without horses? I do not know how their legends and stories and spirits will coexist with a world of machines, John, but I think the world would lose something very precious if that should happen. Yet I know they must change or be ground under." For a moment, he thought he heard a hard edge in her tone. "Do you know what I am doing?"

"Becoming a Cheyenne more and more every day?"

"No! Every time the children talk about one of their legends, I try to write it down. Annie Campbell was telling me she thought I should publish them someday, to show people that the Cheyenne have a culture that is much more complex than men riding around making noises and shooting arrows. John, why are you smiling?"

"I think the Cheyenne are very lucky to have you, Mairead." He swallowed. Might as well get it out. "And I am lucky, as well."

"And I, John," she said. For a few moments, reservations, wars, and guns were far away as he held her in his arms.

After the embrace ended, they talked until well after dark. When Dooley walked home, his head beyond the clouds, he was so intent on the memories of the evening he did not notice the note delivered by one of Blue Feather's men that lay on the ground by the door.

"Circle B hand, aren't you?" Sanders said, meeting Washburn in the morning as the men searching for Fox Running lined up for their food.

Washburn acknowledged it.

"Like a man wants to see justice done. I do that," he said. "I figure we have about one more day of hunting for that Injun before we give it up. My spread is about five miles north of Bigelow's. Box S. Not sure what happens to your outfit, but come and see me about a change, if you think you want one. I'm sure we can find something to make it worth your while. Hundreds of reasons I can think of."

"I think a change might be just the thing I need," Washburn replied.

"Then ride with me when we finish. Look for me. I don't wait for anyone."

Washburn barely tasted the beans. His reward for doing the work Sanders had offered to any number of men on Bigelow's crew was coming soon. He could hardly wait.

Even if John Dooley did not know who she was, the presence Rides a Crow exuded would have told him she was not just anyone.

"I am surprised you are here," she said as she entered his cabin with the bearing of someone who knew exactly what she was about. "I thought you would be with him. Did he not ask your help?"

"Who?"

"Fox Running," she replied.

She chose what came next carefully, seeing Evans in the background. She knew as a soldier he had a duty to follow, and he was unswerving in that duty, even with all his good intentions. He had smiled in greeting, for the two of them could never meet without recalling the day when Little Wolf entrusted Evans with the Northern Cheyenne who had come with him from Indian Territory and stopped running from the army.

"The real killer of the evil man has been found," she told Dooley. "Did no one tell you? Did no one send a message?"

Dooley explained that he was not at the cabin for most of the past day.

"There was a piece of paper among the trees," she said. "It may be important."

She knew it was but also knew Dooley needed to find it in his own way, or he would not believe it.

"Do you know more than this?" Dooley said from the doorway when he returned with the bedraggled paper in his hand.

"I do not," she replied, knowing only that she had felt it was needed to visit Dooley and Evans. "The spirit wolf and spirit horse will know, and they will find you and guide you."

"Dooley!" Evans's tone was sharp. "If this is about Fox Running, you have to tell me where he is."

Dooley showed him the paper. It said, *The man who killed Bigelow rides with Sanders. I am off to find him.* It bore Fox Running's signature and his trademark drawing of a fox.

The paper had obviously been left outdoors for hours. The message was clear that Fox Running expected them to join him. Evans looked from Rides a Crow to Dooley.

"Go ahead of me, Dooley. Ride by the camp where my men are staying. Have them saddled and ready to move out in one hour. No. Get them riding as fast as they can mount! Start toward the Sanders spread. Take that road."

"Sir!" Dooley was gone.

"If you did not come to see him, you came to see me," Evans said after Dooley left.

"Your wisdom does you credit," Rides a Crow mocked gently. "Many days it has been since we met when you welcomed Little Wolf home."

"Many days," he agreed, sighing deeply as he leaned against the table. "It was easier to end war than to build peace."

"You are wise, Captain," Rides a Crow said. "These years have tested us. They have tested you. You are a man caught between what your orders say and what your heart says; what your duty demands and what your soul requires; what those around you tell you as their words worm into your mind and seek to enter your soul like a weasel in the night, and what you know to be right."

"How do you know . . ."

"After so many years, Captain, you ask?"

Evans flushed.

"I do not know the truth in all things, Captain, but I know Fox Running did not kill that man. To kill in war, or to save one's own life, these deaths do not stain the soul. To murder, to kill for pleasure, to kill for profit, these darken the soul until it no longer can find the light. Fox Running has killed many men. None darken his soul. What the men say whose newspaper articles your generals read; what the men say who want The People scattered to the winds so others can possess the land; all this is false. You know this. Within your soul, where your deepest secrets are kept, you know this. When others pour poison in your ears, you still know this.

"When we met, I knew you were a white man who would do right. You cannot live as anything else. Doing what is right is filled with danger. You know I have lost my dearest friends because they would not stray from this course. Yet for you, for me, for them, there is no other. Some covet riches, some length of days. We, who will have neither, are called to do something harder — that which is right. I came to say this because the soldier I met near Fort Keogh will always be a hero to The People, an example of honor to generations, and my friend. You were born to be a Justice Warrior, Captain, as was Fox Running, even if you two cannot ever agree on how the job is to be done."

She smiled warmly at him before continuing, "And no matter what you are ordered to do, you can never live with yourself as anything else. I am here because your soul called me to come before you go and meet Fox Running."

She had spoken for barely a minute. And, in that time, Evans realized that more than anyone else, she had cut to the heart of it all.

The joy he had felt that March day of 1879 when he offered peace to Little Wolf was not because he had ended war, but because he had answered the voice within that demanded something more than duty.

"I must go," she said, moving for the doorway. "You must go. Until the end of days, your name will be among those listed when I and those closest to me ask the spirits to watch over our friends."

"Rides a Crow." She stopped. "Thank you. I think perhaps I had lost my way."

"It is easy to do so when others offer you help," she replied. "Go with the spirits, Captain."

She was gone, leaving Evans — for the

first time in weeks — aware not only of what the army should do, but what he must do. It was time to ride!

The Box S was a grim, foreboding place. Sanders had constructed a low stone wall that ran from one barn about twenty yards to the left of his house to another barn about fifteen yards to the right. The wall had a roughly ten-foot-wide gap. On either side of the gap, armed men stood guard. Small huts had been built to provide shelter in bad weather. For just a moment, Washburn felt the intimidation that had been Sanders's goal.

"Coming?" Sanders asked as he and the rest of the crew moved ahead.

Washburn rode on, feeling silly for letting the look of the place put him in awe. Still, he would be glad to get his money and go. Sanders had said on the way that he never kept much with him. "Too many robbers. I keep what is mine where no one can get it!"

Washburn dismounted. Sanders had his horse taken to the ranch's stable.

"Too late to ride anywhere tonight," he told Washburn. "Been hard work trackin' that Injun. I bet he's somewhere hiding with somebody's help. They all protect their own, no matter what. He's probably in Lame

Deer in that nest of 'em. Find him when we clean it out. Time to go over this Evans fella's head. I know the men who have the real power; get some real action. Men like Evans need to be moved aside, and I know the men to do it. Done good work. Bunk with the boys. Settle up in the morning."

Washburn followed the grim hands, who talked little as they settled into their places. Sanders had pushed a hard pace, and they had nothing to show. One of the men showed Washburn where to put his bedroll. There was little talk and less humor. In time, the bunkhouse went quiet. Outside of it, a rust-colored wolf lowered his head to his paws and drifted with the sounds of the night as he waited.

"Do you know where we are going?" Cut Sky asked as they stopped for a brief rest. They had ridden through the day and into the night. The tiny creek trickling through the meadow would give the horses water.

"No," Fox Running replied. "Coyote Horse does, and that is all that is important."

"How does the horse know more than the rider?" she asked.

He looked back in silence.

"No. Do not tell me! I am riding in the

dark with a man who knows less than a horse he has named after the Trickster! I must have been wounded in my head and not my wrist."

"I believe you demanded to join this adventure," said Fox Running.

"That was when I thought you were smarter than your horse!"

"At least now you know better, so this trip has not been a total waste of your time," he said placidly.

"What are we going to do when we get to wherever it is your horse is going?" she asked. "Or has he not yet told you?"

"If we are fortunate, we will find the man who killed Pete Bigelow and take him so he can tell the truth to the army."

"Do you think he will just give up?"

"I almost hope he does not."

She searched his face to see whether he was serious. He was. "It is time to ride."

Cut Sky mounted. She was certain Fox Running would be as happy to kill the man as bring him in. And how would that help? This adventure would end in more death, and the chill of it made her shiver. She tightened the coat around her, even as she knew her feelings had nothing to do with the pre-dawn cold.

■ ■ ■ ■

Light was breaking in the east as the first round of birds began their songs.

Talks to Horses had few equals and fewer friends. As a spirit wolf, Hunter had long been one of each. They waited in the small woodlot near the ranch house. *<Did you sleep all night, lazy one?>* the black mare sent in spirit talk.

<I tried, but some horse kept shaking the ground,> the spirit wolf sent back.

<What do we do, clever scheming one, if none of those we have summoned appear?>

<What we always do, my friend. Do their work for them. After all, did not the spirits create the Northern Cheyenne so that the likes of us would have an occupation in constantly saving them?>

"You sure you don't want to stay here?" Sanders said as he handed Washburn a small, heavy cloth bag. Washburn wanted to see if there were really gold coins in there, but Sanders's presence intimidated him. The stockman had asked him to stay behind when the hands ate breakfast and went to their chores.

"Montana winters," Washburn joked.

"If you pass this way again, stop by," Sanders said. "If you look for work just about anywhere between here and Texas, they all know me. Mention my name."

"Might do that," Washburn replied. Sanders had only obliquely referred to killing Bigelow, thanking Washburn for "that bit of business."

"Guess you got miles to cover, and I got a ranch to run," Sanders said. "Take the trail easy."

"I will. Thank you."

"Don't mention it. Man does a job, man deserves his reward." Sanders walked out of the bunkhouse's dining room. Washburn finished his coffee as he heard Sanders issuing orders to his hands.

Sanders was a hard man, Washburn mused as he saddled his horse and mounted. A yard full of hands had all been sent to work here and there. Even with all that, a few hands seemed to have the time to watch Washburn. Some seemed to watch very closely.

For a minute, Washburn felt a flicker of fear, then set that aside. Ranching was a hard business when one bad cattle drive could put a man behind, or if the price in the East fell. It took a brutal man like Sanders, or one like Bigelow, to make it pay.

He'd put some miles behind him and decide where to go. Colorado was a little less raw; a lot more ranches. Horse ranches. No more cows. They might pay better. And no one would be around to remind him of what Sanders had just paid for. A fresh slate.

Talks to Horses and Hunter were on the move as soon as Washburn left the ranch yard. Talks to Horses could sense that Coyote Horse and his rider were near. Washburn started heading east. Riding easily, as though he had all the time in the world.

The wolf clambered up and over the rock ledges as Talks to Horses stayed on the trail. They could not lose the evil man until he confessed, for even if Washburn could fool humans, the mark of murder was on him, and the spirit animals had no doubts what he had done.

Cut Sky realized they were moving faster. Fox Running had started to leave her behind, so she kicked her horse to a canter. Fox Running held a pistol in his right hand. She was not sure what would happen next, but she held her rifle tightly with her good hand. She might not shoot well from the back of a horse with one arm bandaged, but she was certain she would soon find out.

Washburn was sure he was being followed. The few times he tried to look back, there was nothing on the trail. He kept his pace. If there was someone there, he might need to save the horse's speed for an emergency.

Evans caught up with Dooley and about a dozen men he knew he could rely on about three miles out of Lame Deer. They stopped twice to rest and water the horses and were closing in on the Sanders ranch as daylight broke. Evans and Dooley had spoken little. Unsaid between them was the fear that if the man who killed Bigelow rode with Sanders, they could be fighting Sanders's hard-bitten riders in a contest where the army might not have the upper hand.

Washburn reached a split in the trail. He could move east to the Tongue River, or south to leave the valley behind and reach Wyoming. North toward Lame Deer was out of the question. East would be safest, because the trail was dotted with farms and ranches. South would be the fastest way to leave Montana, even though there would be some rough country. He still had the sense of being observed, although he scanned the rocks and tall grass in vain for anyone following. Foolishness makes a man see things that are not there, he told himself. He would head south. In two days, he would be far from Montana, and he could start spending that money!

Cut Sky's mouth fell open as she and Fox Running reached the place where the trails crossed. Standing there was a black mare that was clearly more than simply another wild animal. Fox Running's horse acted as if he knew the mare, a glossy animal with her head held high.

Fox Running began to dismount, for he could see there were recent tracks. Coyote Horse would not hold still to let him.

Fox Running looked at Talks to Horses, who was pointing with her head to the south. Fox Running stopped trying to dismount, and Coyote Horse stopped misbehaving.

"Thank you," Fox Running said in a reverent tone, looking at the sleek black mare with wonder and awe. "I am honored."

He turned to Cut Sky. "He is not far," Fox Running called, guessing at the meaning of the horses' conduct. "We must hurry. We are not the only ones following him!"

Cut Sky did not want to go. She wanted to look more at this incredible horse, to touch it and feel the spirit within it. The spirits were real, and they were in front of her in this horse. For a moment, she was certain the spirits told her she could go, for she would see the black mare again. Fox Running had galloped ahead alone. She must catch up!

The first gunshot sounded at the far edge of Dooley's hearing, but the ensuing round of fire was clear. Just south.

Evans pointed forward to move the squad faster as the troopers reached into scabbards for their rifles. The soldiers soon galloped up to and past Dooley, as the big man, not used to riding more than short distances, urged his horse to keep the pace.

"Bugle!" screamed Evans as more gunshots erupted. "Let whoever it is know we are coming."

They rounded a corner of the trail. Fox Running and Cut Sky were standing over a fallen man. Cut Sky — identifiable to Dooley by her long, flapping braids — was firing a rifle at an unseen target, Fox Running, his pistol as a wolf dragged the wounded man behind the cover of some rocks.

Fox Running saw the soldiers and leaped up the nearest rocky ledge, Cut Sky barely a step behind. Then they were gone as the gunfire intensified.

Dooley rushed to Washburn. Bigelow's ranch hand had been shot four times, once in the leg, once in the chest, and twice in the right arm. A shot near the wrist had shattered a white bone that stuck through his skin; the other had struck near the shoulder.

More gunfire.

"The lad and his lady are fighting someone, Captain," Dooley called.

"After them!" called Evans, pointing. His men followed Fox Running and Cut Sky.

Evans hurried over to Dooley and Washburn. "How is he?"

"I know some men live with wounds like these, sir, but many do not," replied Dooley. "There is a lot of blood, sir."

"Sanders," whispered Washburn. "Double cross. Get him. Man . . . Bigelow dead."

"Sanders? What does he have to do with this?" asked Evans.

"Fooled you." Washburn grinned through the pain. "Fooled you. No! Don't let him take me!"

The exclamation came as the spirit wolf looked down on Washburn from the ledge above him.

"No one is going to take you," said Dooley. He knew a wolf was a companion of Rides a Crow, but for all his time around the Cheyenne, he could not fully understand where their legends left off and reality began.

The wolf continued to glare. Washburn swallowed hard. He could feel death and judgment near. It was the second that scared him, for the first was assured.

"Paper," he gasped. "Write it."

"Write what?" asked Evans, telling Dooley to find paper and a pencil in his saddlebags.

"Sanders. Sanders done it. Old miserable coot. Got him."

"You killed Sanders?"

Washburn spit blood and grinned through red-stained teeth.

"Fooled all of you," he said. "Bigelow. Sanders wanted . . . paid . . . two hundred dollars. Old man hated everyone. Cheated me. Sanders . . . all the boys . . . fools. Easy money. Waitin' was hard."

"You killed Bigelow?" asked Evans.

"Dead," he replied loosely. "Perfect. Indians did . . . favor . . . bustin' in . . . take blame. Shoulda known . . . Sanders never pay. Get him for me. Get him. Got it written?" His focus drifted to the wolf, who still looked down. "See! I ain't no bad man. They're bad men. Rich men, rich friends . . . Custer stuff."

"Custer?"

"Little club. Hates Indians. Got that writ yet?"

Dooley shoved a paper in front of Washburn.

"Can't read it," he said. "Lemme sign."

Washburn tried to hold the pencil in his blood-slick hand. It slipped.

"Hold that paper still!" he complained. With the blood that dripped down his right arm, he scrawled something that looked like an *H* followed by a line and a *W* with more of the same scrawl after it.

"Now go get him," Washburn said. "Cheated me." He coughed red. "Don't let that thing get me." He was pointing to the ledge, but the wolf had soundlessly left its perch.

As if to remind them, three shots rang out.

"I'll stay," said Dooley. "See to your men."

Evans moved away from the dying Washburn. He lifted himself up the rocks.

Five of his men were clustered behind three boulders that provided natural cover. The sixth held a rag to his face.

Corporal Andrew Powers rushed to meet him. "Stewart was wounded when a bullet hit the rocks here, sir," he said. "Sprayed his face. Think it missed his eyes."

"What's going on out there?"

"There were about a dozen men, sir, we think. Looks to me that they shot the man who was wounded, because the Injuns didn't shoot at him at all. Ever."

"What was all the shooting, then, Corporal?"

"Those men took cover behind some rocks. They laid down rifle fire, sir, too heavy and too hot for us. The two Indians moved like nothing I ever saw, sir. Flanked 'em, one each side. Wild, crazy thing to do — as if they thought they couldn't be shot. We kept the men pinned down, but it would have been death to attack them in front. The last shots came from beyond those rocks." He pointed far the left. "The men may have made a run for it."

"Let us go see, Corporal," Evans said.

No one fired on the soldiers as they left their cover. They crossed the ground to the line of rocks behind which their opponents had retreated.

Seven men lay there, either dead already or in their final moments of life. Evans went down the line. Two had been hit from the front, through the head, and they fell straight back. The others were hit through the body. They had been taken from the side.

More shots.

"Go, Corporal!"

"Follow me!"

The soldiers ran toward the sound. Evans saw them stop, pointing their guns at someone. Powers called to whoever it was to surrender but received a combative reply. "No!"

Evans saw one Indian who had circled behind his men lifting a rifle. The Indian's braids were waving. Powers ordered the soldiers to lower their guns in response to something Evans could not hear.

Evans drew his cavalry pistol as he strode toward the Indian, who demanded that he lower his weapon.

"The fight is over, Captain," Cut Sky called out with a smile. "Even the army must be able to know when the dead no longer need killing."

She pointed at three more dead men. Evans wondered if his eyes were fooling him. The Indian who had created this carnage was a woman? He took in the bandage on her arm. A wounded one? And she was with Fox Running. What had Dooley called them, a "charming couple"?

"Is that Evans?" called the other Indian. Evans knew the voice. Fox Running.

"How should I know?" replied Cut Sky. "White men all look the same in their uniforms. These are your playmates, Cheyenne, not mine!"

"Tell your men not to think about anything foolish," Fox Running called as he walked toward Evans, holstering his right-hand pistol as though five armed soldiers were not behind him with their guns in their hands. "They are all dead except for two who got away. Did the other man die? We needed him to live."

"He died," called Dooley. "He had a tale that he killed Bigelow."

Fox Running drew his guns and swiftly turned to cover the soldiers.

"Cut Sky, keep your rifle on the captain."

"What are you doing?" called Dooley. "Stop this."

"I did not kill Bigelow, but if the man who did kill him is dead, there is no one to say I did not do this. I will not be arrested, Captain. I will not sit in a jail until someone breaks me out to hang me."

"He confessed," said Evans, taking a step forward.

"One more and you are dead," said Cut Sky. "Ask these men who have seen my work if I can shoot."

Evans stopped. He lifted his hands.

"He confessed," Evans repeated. "Washburn confessed. I will not arrest you. He signed it in his blood. You have my word. I accept the confession. Do not run off. Do not shoot. I will not arrest you. My word was good enough for Little Wolf. You know that. I am telling the truth."

Fox Running knew the story. Evans had never lied.

"Laddie, put the gun down; the Captain tells you the truth. Lass, you, too," added Dooley.

"Cut Sky?"

"Everyone knows Big Bear is honest," she said. "The captain did not damage our home when he came calling. The Spirit Walker has said he is a friend. Trust him."

Fox Running holstered his pistol again. Cut Sky lowered her rifle and began to join the men.

"Powers!"

"Sir!"

"See about the rest of these cowboys."

"Sir!"

"Whose men were these?" Evans asked.

"Harry Washburn had ridden with Sanders, and he said Sanders paid him to kill Bigelow, so I would guess they are Sanders's men," said Dooley.

Fox Running and Cut Sky were sitting on

a rock together as the soldiers examined the scene. He was reloading both pistols with swift efficiency as he spoke to her about a rock outcrop he thought looked like a white man's nose. After he finished, his hand, which did not shake, had sought hers, which did. His reeked of smoke and metal. She took it.

"There are stories about you," she began, trying to put into words what she had just seen. "I did not think they could have been true."

"They probably are not," he said. "There was one gunfight, and then there was a man who wrote for a newspaper and cared nothing about the damage he would do, and then there were stories upon stories."

"Do you know how many men you just killed?"

"Together, we killed ten of them. The only one that matters is the one who was trying to get behind me. I am particularly partial to that shot, and it was yours." He turned and smiled, as though they were talking about something of no consequence. "Your bandage has blood on it. Your father will give me a scolding."

"You are very calm about this."

"Cut Sky, I have fired guns at men since the Custer fight. I know what death is, and

I have come close to sharing in it. This cannot be your first fight."

"They have never been so close," she said. "There were times when my father . . . when we needed to leave one place quickly. Sometimes there were men with guns. I did not look back. This time, I could see their faces."

"They rode for an evil man who would like to scatter The People and kill Indians, whether they are Cheyenne or Lakota," he said. "Do not let their faces haunt you, Cut Sky. They came to kill, to murder. It is not to be mourned that what they sought to give, they received instead. It is justice."

"And you are a Justice Warrior," she said.

"I am a man who is trying not to be hung for a murder I did not commit," he reminded her. "I need to have justice for The People. I . . . I cannot explain it fully, Cut Sky, for this land has nothing about it that is different from many other places. The rocks, the trees, the way the grass moves endlessly when the breeze awakes — it is all beautiful, but there are beautiful places in many locations. This . . . this is ours. Mine. It is Northern Cheyenne land. I lived for years as a boy with no home. I am not even fully sure I know what home means. But for The People, *this* is home, and until I go to my rest, Cut Sky, I will fight whoever comes to try to take it from us. Anyone. Everyone, if I must."

"Even me?"

He made a face. "Not without reinforcements."

"There are times when you are wiser than you appear," she said loftily. "At least the army man heard what the dead cowboy had to say and accepts it. You are no longer forced to hide."

"I will no longer be hunted by the army," he said, "but whatever Washburn said, his words on paper are only words on paper. There is nothing that can prove Sanders ordered him to kill Bigelow, unless Sanders were to admit it. I do not believe he would do that. He will not pay for his crime."

"Why would one white rancher kill another?"

"Bigelow would join with no one. He hated everyone. He was only out for himself," Fox Running said. "It may be that Sanders coveted the land Bigelow owned. It may be that Sanders wanted him dead to accuse the Cheyenne of the murder, as happened. We will never know the full reason, because there is nothing in the white man's law that can convict Sanders of plotting murders, but there is one thing we do know."

"What is that?"

"That Sanders will not stop, and there are more like him."

Evans waited as long as he could before approaching Fox Running. Cut Sky had gone to speak with Dooley. The Cheyenne measured Evans as the soldier walked closer. Evans could see Fox Running tense.

"A man tells a tale about the Black Canyon Gang," Evans said. "Do you have one to tell? I would like to hear it."

Fox Running looked at the man who might be the best, and the only, soldier ally the Cheyenne had. He began to talk.

Cut Sky observed their conversation and went to join them. Dooley touched her, jumping back as she swiftly turned to face him.

"Easy, lass," he said. " 'Tis a talk they need to have by themselves."

CHAPTER TWELVE

August 1, 1883, Lame Deer, Montana

Fox Running, Dooley, and Cut Sky returned to Lame Deer while Evans went to ask Sanders about Washburn's claim and inform the rancher where he could collect the bodies of several of his men. They brought Washburn's body with them to bury. Dooley had removed the money from Washburn's coat. He was unsure how to dispose of it. He would not give it back to Sanders. Some of it would pay for a box to bury Washburn. The rest he would hide. There would be a need.

The sight of Fox Running riding openly into Lame Deer caused a minor stir. When the army left, he had been a wanted man. He did not act so now. Washburn's body was left with Len Trenholm, who would build the box. There was a plot of ground where whites and Indians who had no family were buried. It would do.

Dooley watched Fox Running closely. The Cheyenne gunfighter's mood had steadily worsened throughout the ride. Cut Sky was aware of it and looked at Dooley more than once. Big Bear knew Fox Running better than anyone. He should know what to do! Dooley, who had no idea how much of his past Fox Running had shared, did not.

"Um . . . while you were on vacation, as it were, the captain was staying here," Dooley explained as they entered the cabin.

"Oh, John!"

Fox Running reached for a gun. Cut Sky stopped him just as Mairead Cullihan ran into the cabin and into Dooley's arms.

"It was all over town that you were riding to catch a murderer. I . . ." Mairead stopped short when her eyes lit on Fox Running. Something almost tangible passed between them and was gone.

"We did," Fox Running declared, with an edge to his tone. "But it was not me. I will allow you two to talk in private. Cut Sky, let me escort you back to your father."

"Wait," Dooley said. "Mairead, these are my friends, Fox Running and Cut Sky."

"You are the teacher," said Cut Sky, filling in the silence when Fox Running said nothing.

"Yes," Mairead answered. "Classes will

start next month. If you know of any children who would like to learn to read, please send them to the school. It is near Spotted Dawn's lodge."

Cut Sky exchanged a few more words with Mairead and then, aware that Fox Running planned to say nothing, agreed with Fox Running that it was time to go home.

"That young man is even more dangerous than I suspected," Mairead said after the Indians had left. "Not to mention rude. I can see why the army worries about him and why the newspapers write those things."

Dooley thought of trying to explain that a day spent killing men was likely to lead to rudeness but decided that being in the arms of a good woman was more important than dragging the reality of his world into hers.

"You are the rudest man in the world," Cut Sky scolded as they walked to their horses. "Your friend's woman comes to see him and you want to shoot her?"

"I did not know who she was. He never introduced us." Cut Sky could hear wounded pride or something like that in his tone. For his part, Fox Running could not explain what he had seen in the woman's glance, but he knew he did not like her.

"I would have enjoyed hearing that," she

said. " 'Here is my friend Fox Running, who has not really broken as many laws or killed as many people as everyone says.' She is a teacher and spends her day hearing stories. You could have welcomed her to your cabin instead of scowling."

"It is not mine, now that the soldier is living there with Mr. Dooley."

"Oh, Fox Running," Cut Sky cooed. "Poor Fox Running! Now that he is no longer a wanted killer, no one cares about him! Oh, the poor man! Perhaps, if what I saw earlier was your true ability, you may want to practice shooting instead of having a temper tantrum. I will not always be there to save your life, the way I did today. At least five times. Perhaps more. I shall let you know for certain how many times I saved you when I tell Father how much you owe for putting his daughter in danger. He will be angry!"

Fox Running looked into her wickedly mocking eyes. He tried to fight the smile but lost. "Then I shall tell him how his daughter hid under a cedar branch while I did all the work, like a true warrior."

"Yes, a true warrior. Do little, talk much!" They had reached the horses. "Now, if you are good on the ride, I shall let you eat more stolen beef!"

"And if I am not?"

"Cedar bark stew is fit for warriors who talk more than fight," she teased, "and for those who cannot win a race against a woman. Coyote Horse, go!"

She slapped Fox Running's horse before mounting her own, laughing loudly as Fox Running chased the mischievous animal.

Howard Porter sat in his room and looked out at Lame Deer. He did not understand. Every Cheyenne he met was walking taller and prouder as though they had won a victory, just because the wild one known as Fox Running had been exonerated of murder, even though he had killed men who had killed the man who killed Bigelow. Those he had come to know talked about "Justice Warriors." One related the story of a boy forced to apologize after being caught stealing when Bigelow wanted him killed. So many of the Cheyenne were so involved in their farming or trading that they seemed to have little time for anything else. Most apparently wanted to live in peace, or at least they said so. He had also noticed a pattern that he omitted from the writings he was compiling to make the case against the Cheyenne.

The white farmers, shopkeepers, ranchers, and others who had spent a lot of time with the Cheyenne were those who liked them the best. Those who never had met one to talk to, hated them the most. Porter was convinced that the Indians were not vastly changed from the days when they roamed the Plains, but also that, even when they did things that were clearly violations of how proper people should behave, they did not act out of hate or malice. It was a sobering thought, to realize that the people fighting for civilization might be the cause of many problems.

That was not a thought he planned to write down.

Sam Rickett heard the story fifth-hand over breakfast. Now he was certain there were other men around the valley who were being paid to do the same job he was, probably with different paymasters. He had not worried a lot about someone getting the drop on him, but now he would need to be even more cautious, in case whoever hired him also hired someone to make sure he was silenced, and no one would ever know what was done.

After hearing the tale, he went back to his room and pulled the well-thumbed sketches from his bag. He looked at one for a long time and wondered if it might be best not to wait for instructions and just get the job done now, for there was no question in his mind it was a job that needed doing.

Needed doing badly.

August 3, 1883, Tongue River Breaks, Montana

"I have heard of this of which you speak," said Blue Feather, who made no secret of his pride in his daughter for sharing in the attack on Sanders's men.

"When we were at Fort Robinson, there was talk that men from far beyond the fort had ordered the murder of Crazy Horse," he said. "There were soldiers who had some secret handshake and words, who believed that not enough had been done to punish the Indians for defeating Custer. There was once a powerful man in Colorado who led them, but after he died and many in the East demanded the army no longer hunt Indians to kill them, I heard little about these people. Since we came to the Tongue River Valley, I have heard talk that this 'secret society' may now exist again among the whites, because they want to stop the Great White Father from giving the Northern Cheyenne a reservation. But all of this is only talk. I cannot tell you what is real and what is as insubstantial as the smoke of this fire."

"Does it matter?" asked Cut Sky. "There are white men who will hate us until the stars all fall. We knew this from the day we were born. What of it?"

"Many white men — even those that most people would call good men — believe anything they do is fair when they are fighting to take Indian land," Fox Running replied. "I have seen this. That is why a man like Bigelow was tolerated. As much as many people hated him, as long as he would hate the Indians, he was useful."

"Will this ever end?" Cut Sky asked.

"I do not know," Blue Feather replied. "I believe that when there is a reservation, it will be hard for the white man to ever take this valley for themselves. The more they think it is likely there will be one, the harder they will fight to prevent it." He drew in a breath. "We have talked of war and death enough for one night. Cut Sky, I shall see you in our lodge, for I am tired and need my rest."

Little was said as Fox Running and Cut Sky sat looking into the fire, while it slowly burned down. Their hands had joined in the shadow between them.

"White people know many fine words," Fox Running said at last. "I have come to despise those words because, when they coat their tongues with compliments, they sharpen knives for the backs of those they flatter. What I know is that today you fought with me, and I was safe because you did. I do not know, Cut Sky, what will happen next. You spoke earlier of guns, of killing. Until the path our people walk is clear, I cannot turn aside from what I must do. It is not a path I can ask anyone to walk."

"Nor should you," she replied. "For those who will not walk it of their own free will are destined to leave it one day." She looked into the red-orange flames and up beyond into the star-filled sky.

"We have lived here and lived there, Fox Running. I know some call my father the Bandit King, but we steal less than it might seem, and he lives more by his wits in trading than he does by stealing. He enjoys the title, so do you not ever hint he is more honest than most! There is no piece of dirt and rocks and trees that I would die for; my home is where I am standing. Yet this that rages around me is my fight. The white men who would grind us into the mud as they do the gardens of the Cheyenne when they drive their cattle over Cheyenne homesteads do not care if I am welcome in the circle of the Lakota or the Cheyenne, or if generations ago my grandfather may have known theirs. I understand this now. And I say this: they may hate me until the river runs backward, but I will stand with whoever will have me and fight with them until I die."

His hand squeezed hers.

"Then we shall fight them, Cut Sky."

"And never surrender," she replied.

And the fire glowed a fierce red in its final spasm of burning before it faded to black, leaving Fox Running and Cut Sky alone beneath stars that had shone upon generations of warriors as they, too, made their vows they would keep until death.

August 3, 1883, Lame Deer, Montana

Evans rode in late and briefly voiced his disgust to Dooley. As they sat over the food that Spotted Dawn's family provided, on the grounds that Mairead Cullihan believed Dooley would kill himself with his own cooking, he explained the situation.

"Sanders insisted he had no idea his men knew he paid Washburn money and said he was shocked they ambushed him. Said the man was a good cowboy who informed him about the Indians while working for Bigelow. Washburn wanted to start a ranch, and Sanders thought it would be a good investment. Said he was sorry Washburn said those things while he was dying. Said he will make sure his men never go around killing people again, and the hands who did it, did so without his blessing."

Evans balled up a piece of paper and threw it into the fire.

"I know he's lying. He doesn't care that I know he's lying. There is nothing I have that can challenge him. His word against a dead man. Maybe some slick lawyer back East in some fancy courtroom could talk a judge and jury into convicting Sanders of being responsible, but it would never play out here. Sanders said he was pleased to know Fox Running was not a murderer and said you, John, should sleep better at night knowing you do not share a cabin with a killer."

"He paid me a visit once and wanted me to change sides," Dooley said. "I think he has had his answer."

"I am glad for you that Fox Running is no longer suspected of killing Bigelow, but we are no closer to learning who killed Amos Greene, and Rawlins and his men. I do not want to make known any of their dealings in phony scalps."

"Thinkin' of this I was, sir. Never did learn, did we, what Golden Turtle knows about all this. It could be Greene's murder was nothing more than someone trying to implicate an Indian in the killing of a white man who hasn't been hostile to them and stir trouble. Greene and Rawlins might both have been picked not out of spite, but because killing them might cause a reaction. The lad, Fox Running, has told me a thousand times if he's said it once that all the evil in the Tongue River Valley is aimed at stopping the Cheyenne from getting a reservation. Perhaps he is right."

"It is an unpleasant thought, Dooley, that we live in times where people are killed to advance someone's political program."

"Only if you are not Irish, sir. For us, that's our history."

As they rode to question Golden Turtle, Dooley asked Evans whether there was some secret society that revolved around Custer.

Evans stared at Dooley a long time before answering. Dooley looked straight ahead.

"Custer was a controversial man in the army, long before his death," Evans began. "Many men liked him. There were some who utterly despised him. He mixed politics with being a solider, and that is always bound to cause trouble."

Dooley looked over to see if Evans had

more to say. The captain was picking his words carefully.

"After the Little Bighorn, avenging him became a rallying cry among some of the officers. That was to be expected, since, from a military perspective, there was a war on, and the enemy had dealt us a major defeat. But many people in power seemed to have made avenging Custer a pretext for wiping out the Indians and taking every bit of land in Montana and the Dakotas that could be taken. The army was sent out here to subdue the Indians, forge peace, and enforce that peace. We succeeded with the first two, but I think there are many powerful interests who've decided that — by any means possible — the Indians should be utterly broken. As a soldier, I oppose that. The war was to make the West safe. We won. We have made treaties with them. We have made promises. If these men who work behind the scenes can instigate a final Indian war, which I do think some people want, it will be wrong, because all those who die will be people like Greene or Rawlins who wanted nothing more than to live in peace."

Dooley asked about the Black Canyon Gang. Evans said he had to meet again with the man who made claims against Fox Running but had not been able to find him. "As Fox Running tells it, he helped steal as part of the gang, but he never shot anyone except the gang members who shot a soldier. A sergeant who knows everything that ever happened is coming down. He will tell me the truth."

"Foxy doesna lie."

"But if a white man comes forward with a tale that can be believed, it will not matter, John," Evans said grimly. "It will not matter."

When they reached his farm, Golden Turtle did not want to speak. Dooley informed him they knew all about his trade with Bigelow and were not intending to make that public but would if Golden Turtle was not forthcoming with the truth.

"Amos made that lance," Golden Turtle confessed. "We could not find the right wood, but the whites in the East do not care. He had found some paint that would dry to the color of blood, and he was going to paint the blade with it. That is why I came to his farm that day, to find out if it was ready. Then I saw him. I . . . I was scared. My family is scared. One of us has stayed awake all night with a gun since this happened."

His eyes went back and forth between

Dooley and Evans, to see if they understood and accepted his words. Flying Sparrow knew there was more than farming going on, he added, but as long as some money came his way, he was happy not to know more. To help keep their business a secret, Golden Turtle told them he and Greene staged fights in public.

"Amos knew many people did not like it that some of us who are Cheyenne know the Earth better than they do. It was important they not think he was helping me. If anyone watched us long enough, they would have known we were not enemies, but if we were watched, I never saw anyone."

August 4, 1883, Sickles, Montana
Once again, Fox Running was staring at the ground where Rawlins and his men had been killed.

"Do the worms talk to you?" Cut Sky asked.

She had refused multiple requests and commands to remain behind. Blue Feather's face had registered his satisfaction in hearing someone else try, and fail, to bend his daughter's will to anything else but her own plans.

"Yes. They ask me not to dump your stew here, for they have done nothing to face such poison!"

"Then they shall go as hungry as you will!"

He did not answer. She walked closer to where he was on his hands and knees, swiping dust this way and that.

"Babies play like that," she suggested. "I did not know it was a game for warriors."

It had not rained. There should have been blood. There was not.

"Do you have your rifle?" he asked.

"Are the ants now making war?"

"I want to look in all the buildings," he said. "The bodies were here. You can see the dark places where some of their blood flowed out. Remember the fight with Sanders's men?"

She did. Blood was everywhere.

"Yet here there are several dead men and very little stain of blood."

"What does that mean?"

"They were killed elsewhere. The bodies were hacked to look like the work of angry Cheyenne, with the scalps left as a sign of contempt."

"Does it matter?"

"I do not know. I do not know why someone would arrange the dead in this fashion if they were not killed here, but I know if it was done, perhaps Mr. Dooley, who was a police officer in Boston, can help determine why."

"I will look in the buildings this way," she offered.

"If you need me, fire once," he said.

She wanted to tell him she was not a child, but there was about the ranch house a sense of something wrong that made her leave off her teasing. Not evil, but it had been deserted since Rawlins and his men were killed. She felt the chill of death. She walked into the house. It had four rooms. She had been in settlers' houses before and wondered why they needed so much room. The rooms were dusty and dirty but free of any blood.

Behind the house was a heavy door that led down to a root cellar, where vegetables would be kept to preserve them. She opened the door. The cellar was musty, dank. It smelled of something that had died. Above all, it was dark. She swallowed. She closed her eyes and waited, knowing that, when she opened them, she could better navigate the darkness.

Then she saw it and fired her rifle.

Fox Running dragged the corpse to the surface. Cut Sky was not a white woman who would faint when the wind changed direction but neither had she lived her life wallowing in death. Perhaps in later times he would ask her which was louder, her scream or the gunshot. He looked at her face as she stared beyond the hills at whatever she was seeing in her mind and let her remain there.

The corpse was a white man. He had been dead for some time and was unpleasant to behold, as well as to smell. Fox Running thought he looked like a soldier, though he did not wear a uniform. Although cowboys had wind-roughened, sun-reddened faces like this man's, soldiers often had haircuts identical to the corpse's and were usually bigger through the body than the lean, hard men who rode the range. This man was older than most cowboys.

He had been killed by two shots through his chest. Two other wounds, one on his right arm and one on his left leg, would have made it hard for him to carry on a gunfight.

His coat was old and battered, but the .45 he wore at his right hip was new. Fox Running examined the weapon. It had not been fired. It was worth taking as a prize, but whoever killed this man had left the gun behind. The coat held one other surprise. Four teeth. Not human. Taken from a dead cow. Painted black.

Fox Running had been squatting over the man, but the discovery of the teeth rocked him back on his heels. It made the most sense that this man had been killed by Rawlins or the men who rode with Rawlins, because the cellar was behind the house and would only be known to someone who knew the ranch. Hiding the body in the dark cellar meant they did not want it found if someone searched the barns.

Someone at the Rawlins ranch had killed the stranger. If the teeth he carried meant what Fox Running thought they meant, perhaps the man was part of the gang threatening Rawlins. If the gang this man rode with knew he had been sent but never returned, it could explain the savagery in the attack on Rawlins, and why all the rancher's workers — Cheyenne and white — had been treated the same. He had noticed in his first search that the hay in the stable was disturbed but had thought nothing of it. Perhaps what he sought was hidden there.

Before he did anything else, he would need Dooley's help.

Cut Sky stiffened at his touch. He stroked her hair, which she had worn loose and long this day instead of in braids. For a second, his hand lingered at the spot where her hair was thinner from her scalp wound.

"Who was he?" she asked.

"I do not know." He told her his theory. "I need Mr. Dooley. I will not ask you to stay here alone. Can you ride to Lame Deer to fetch him? I can ride to your father for an escort for you if you do not wish to ride alone."

She did not look at him for what seemed like an eternity.

"Everything you touch is death," she said finally, with wet eyes.

It was sad, but the truth. There was nothing to say.

"I will ride to Lame Deer," she told him, flicking back her hair to show a face that was proud despite the shock she had suffered. "And then I will ride to my father's camp. There is much I must think about alone."

She rode down the path toward Sickles and then to Lame Deer. Fox Running remained behind with the dead and wondered if he would ever see her again.

Sam Rickett was good at his trade. He had found good places to take care of all the names on his list. Except for two, who always seemed to be moving, he knew when and where they went just about every day. That was good enough for now.

They had told him that, when he was ready, he should send a telegram from Sickles to a man named McGillicuddy in Boston saying so. Just the one word, "Ready." Strange ways, but so were the ones who hired him. The gold double eagles were good, though. Now all he had to do was wait for a reply. He hoped it would come soon. Something told him that when the weather turned cold, this Tongue River Valley was no place for a Texas boy.

August 5, 1883, Sickles, Montana
"She said her piece and left," Dooley said as he eyed the body of the unidentified corpse. He looked at Fox Running for a meaning, but the Cheyenne's face was unreadable. "It can be a wee bit much, lad."

"If he was part of a group making threats, the ranchers and farmers here might know him," Fox Running said, changing the subject to safer ground. "If we put him in the wagon, would you haul him around to see? I know he is not much to look at, but maybe someone will recognize him."

"Do ye really think so?"

"I think they might recall having seen him. I think he could be recognized as if he were alive. I don't know if they will be able to tell us who he is, but I cannot think of anything else to do. Can you?"

Dooley had read that in a murder case in Boston, the police had taken a picture of a murdered man and showed it to people. But the nearest photographer was in Cheyenne, and from the looks of the corpse, it would not keep for another week while someone made the journey to Wyoming and back. "And what will you be doing?"

"After Cut Sky left to find you, I searched the ranch more thoroughly. I discovered what looked like a place where money might have been hidden; at least a heavy box was stored under the hay. I can tell it was heavy from how it dented the wood. The box is not there now, so whatever it held was important to someone. The men were not killed at this ranch. They were left here to be noticed. Think about it, Mr. Dooley. It is August, you are hauling dead bodies, men who can never give evidence against you. Even if you wore some kind of mask during the killing, do you keep your mask on, or does it become too hot?"

"Perhaps I should ask the ranchers if they saw a group of men with a wagon in the past few weeks?" Dooley said.

"While you do that, I am going to look for

where it happened. I cannot say why, but I think this is important."

"Lad."

Fox Running turned to look at him. Dooley knew that, after losing Morning Shadow, Fox Running would be expecting the worst. Cut Sky might be brave, but even bravery could be worn down by the lives they led. "She'll be back."

The Cheyenne turned away and mounted.

August 5, 1883, Lame Deer, Montana
In a world where frontier officers often used their absolute power over their soldiers to become tyrants, Captain Jack Evans was noted as one of the most even-tempered commanders a trooper could serve under. It was therefore with surprise that Sergeant Greer Cassidy witnessed the spectacle of his commander stomping into Greer's tent at the Lame Deer camp and throwing a handful of papers in his direction.

"Sir?"

"Read those!"

"Sir?"

"Read them, I said!" Evans yelled.

Cassidy smoothed out the crumpled pages of the *Western Territories News* to read a highly fictionalized version of the encounter between Fox Running and the men who killed Washburn.

"Balderdash, sir," replied Cassidy. "Nothing different than what that man usually writes. The men once reported they found something true in that rag, sir, but in the end, it was just another falsity. It is all prattle without anything true in it."

"Yes, there is," snapped Evans. "I recall my report that I sent to Fort Keogh. Whoever wrote that story had read my report! All those details that are changed slightly are close to my report. They are all changed just a little, as if whoever wrote this had the report to copy from as they scrawled their fiction."

Cassidy inhaled sharply. So that was the problem.

"Did you give my report to anyone, Cassidy? Did you write an extra copy for someone? If you did it for extra money and did not know how it would be used, you can tell me. I will not be angry."

"You are very angry, sir."

"Because my report has been twisted by some scribbler who was given it by someone between here and Fort Keogh!" Evans growled.

"No, sir, I did not make a copy, other than the one for the fort and the other to have here, sir . . . but it was curious, sir."

"*What* was curious? What does that mean, Cassidy?"

"There was a new courier the fort sent after we set up camp here, sir. Man's name was Dietrich. Must not have been very good, sir. There was a telegram from Denver yesterday that the colonel had not received a report from you in days, and we had been sending them right along. This morning I received a reply that this Dietrich I told them about had not reported there, ever, but that he was not our courier. Wilson Cormac was. Now why a man would ride from the fort to here and back and then vanish is a mystery to me. I know some of the men meet women, sir, and use their duty as couriers to have some time with them, but they usually return."

"So my report went somewhere, but not to the fort?"

"So it seems, sir. A few reports, I believe, sir, if you want the full truth of it, sir. Two of the men have gone to ride the route to the fort, to see if he met with foul play, sir."

Evans tapped his foot, the pace rising and falling in tandem with his thoughts. "Keep me informed, Sergeant."

"Yes, sir!"

"And Sergeant?"

"Sir?"

"All future reports will only go by men you know and trust. I must go to Sickles. If anyone from that rag of a publication shows himself, put him in irons if the men can't seem to shoot straight." Evans paused. "I do trust you, Sergeant."

"Yes, sir." Cassidy smiled inwardly. In a world where officers never apologized, it was as close as he would ever get and far more than most would offer.

"Oh, sir?"

Evans turned.

"Sergeant Jones arrived this morning, sir."

"Thank you, Cassidy. Find him and send him to me."

August 5, 1883, Sickles, Montana
There was a small pen near a pond in a swale behind the Rawlins ranch house. From its size and location, Fox Running guessed it was for sickly new calves and their mothers, or other stock that Rawlins wanted to keep a close watch on. The pen was all but hidden from view as the land dipped down after rising from the house and then rising again to a mix of woods and meadows that gave way to the open plains.

One fence rail had been hit with bullets over and over. At a glance, it looked chewed by giant teeth. When he walked over to it, he could see blood still staining the grass in a couple of places. The bullet-wrecked fence was about ten feet long — about what it might take if the men who were shot were lined up. He walked back, away from the fence. Five feet. Nothing. Ten. Nothing. There! A rifle shell in the mud. He stood by it and looked to his right and left. It was not exactly a line, but there were a lot of rifle shells in this one place. It looked like someone had lined up a firing squad and executed Rawlins and his men. Indians killed quickly, efficiently, sometimes in a frenzy, but never in straight lines. White men killed in many ways, but there was only one group of people that killed in this fashion. Soldiers.

Cut Sky sat idly by the fire. Whatever her father was doing, it had meant a stream of Indian and white visitors throughout the day — men who looked from side to side when leaving his lodge and who melted into the woods when they were gone rather than taking a trail. She guessed that, after saying he had stopped his business in phony scalps, he was starting it up again, or that he was up to something else he knew her expanded knowledge of the world might make her disapprove of. As if that would ever really matter.

"Do you make stew from air?" Blue Feather said as he emerged. He studied his daughter. "What makes you so miserable?"

She told him about the corpse she'd found, and how every step Fox Running took seemed bounded by death.

"I do not ask for an easy way, Father," she said. "I do not know if this path he walks is one where I belong. I do not know if I am strong enough. I do not know that I want to be strong enough if it means looking at death as he does, as something that no longer matters."

Blue Feather leaned hard on the stick he used as a crutch as he lowered himself to one of the logs around the fire. She knew with his leg this was not easy. He exhaled from the effort as he sat.

"The spirits give us puzzles, Child, and not answers. I recall the raid when my horse fell upon me. My life as a warrior ended. My life as an object of pity began. Then came the hard times for the Lakota and the Northern Cheyenne. No longer did it matter that I could not sit a horse. I had spent years watching men. Now I learned how to manage them. I learned that what one wanted, another could provide, even if it meant stealing, and that in arranging these things there was a life to be made that never could have been if I was a warrior on horseback. I learned that if enough whites and enough Indians did business with me, none wanted their secrets known, and I was safe to be a bandit king or whatever they wished to call me as long as I did not flaunt this. I could help my people in a way that made no sense, but it continues. If horses disappeared here and reappeared there, or cattle, or goods, or guns, there were enough men making a profit that — in a fashion far different from what any treaty would expect — made us all dependent upon one another. Yet I know the day could come tomorrow when the army might tell one of its officers to 'clean out that den of thieves,' and it would happen. Peace may come to the Tongue River Valley one day, Child, but that day is far from this one."

He touched the white spot on her face.

"When we fought off the Shoshone that day, when your rifle exploded and your face was forever marked, I thought about the life I lived, about whether it would be the death of you, who, if not my blood, are my daughter in all things. I came then to understand that this scar you bear, like mine, is a reminder from the spirits that we own not our destinies, and also that if death was to be our lot, it could have been given to us. I say this, Child, because if the spirits want us to live, then live we shall, and live boldly we must. You think about Fox Running. I ask you this, child of mine: is what you are feeling nothing more than what you feel when you go to a high place and look down? For is not the spirit telling you to walk boldly forward with your proud head high, and your fears screaming back that this is a thing you cannot do, when inside you know they are wrong?"

She was silent. After a few moments, she said, "I have a very wise father."

"I have a very brave daughter."

They sat in companionable silence as thin blue swirls rose from the tiny fire, until a current of air took hold and tossed them until they were gone.

"But I do wish," he said after a time, "that this stewpot you cannot see held something more substantial."

Cut Sky rose and embraced her father.

"The stew is cooking behind the lodge," she said. "For if I left it here where you sit, the Bandit King would steal it!"

And for one moment in a valley of fear and fire, despair was banished.

■ ■ ■ ■

"I believe I may know him," Evans said as he looked into the wagon bed at the dead man. "There was a group of soldiers who came to Fort Keogh in the spring. They stayed a few days and left. They were supposed to be scouting for someone. It might have been requested by the railroad. I do not recall clearly. They had orders signed by everyone who needed to sign them and did not report to anyone at the fort. In fact, they were very arrogant that they were beyond my command.

"I think this man was among them, but I do not know his name or what became of those men. I could be wrong. Many soldiers pass through the fort, and I do not recall them all clearly." Evans made a face. "He is also, well, starting to become truly repulsive. He should be buried, and soon."

Dooley had spent two days hauling the corpse around the east bank of the Tongue River. No one knew the man's name. There were riders passing through from time to time, was all anyone would say. Ranchers who were afraid from their warnings were hesitant to cooperate.

"You come and go," said one. "Those men

are always here."

Fox Running had said little.

"You are not thinking loudly enough for me to hear, lad," said Dooley.

"Let us say Rawlins and his men were killed because they killed someone from this group of men. They were killed very privately, because why? Did it take time to find them all? Did the murderers not want the sound to carry? But they wanted the bodies seen afterward, and they wanted to show their power. These men seek to intimidate. Amos Greene was killed in a very different way. Did anyone ask about men like these coming to intimidate him?"

Dooley had to admit that they did not, so quick were the condemnations that an Indian had killed Greene.

"Can you spend another day in the company of our dead man to see if anyone near Greene's ranch knew him? If this is all connected, it will be easier to find who did these killings. It is still possible Greene was killed for another reason."

He looked at Dooley, who was regarding him with suspicion, for he knew Fox Running was too prone to hiding secrets if it would help a fellow Cheyenne. "I do not know," Fox Running said. "I have a guess, my friend, but I cannot be wrong when I voice it. There are too many lives at stake, and the army cannot be put in a position where it is in the middle."

"Aye," grumped Dooley. " 'Tis our job!"

Evans and Dooley agreed to haul the dead man to Greene's farm, which was only a short journey past the burying place. "Where will you be?" asked Dooley.

"I shall be along tomorrow," Fox Running replied.

Evans frowned, but Dooley knew he could tell the captain on the way that Fox Running needed to find Cut Sky and would dally in the Tongue River Breaks for a reason even an army officer could understand.

Chapter Thirteen

The bullet whistled through the trees from the unseen sniper's position on the hill, sending bits of wood flying and leaves floating to the ground.

"When I wanted acorns, I did not shoot them off the trees," remarked Fox Running as he kept plodding up the path on Coyote Horse. "There are strange ways practiced by those who live here, Cut Sky."

Silence.

"You are infuriating!" She strode down the slope, rifle in hand. He noticed the bandage was gone from her wrist.

He dismounted. "Of all the people I know who might wish to kill me, only you would try to kill me with acorns!"

"If I wanted to kill you . . ."

". . . you have had many opportunities," he finished.

They stood in the path like friends who once were deeply bonded but had grown awkward. He asked about her arm; she about the dead man.

"Did you find the answer you were seeking?" he asked at length.

"I did," she replied.

"Do you plan to share this?" he asked, seeing a slight break in the impassive wall she showed him.

She answered with, "Why did you come?"

"For you. It is not just that I need someone who watches my back when I hunt men who have killed. I need to know that, in all of this world, one person will be there, even if the rest leave. I do not promise ease and peace. I can only promise . . ."

"No," she said. "I have spoken to my father. This is not a time for promises people often make to one another. This is a time to walk where we are afraid and trust in the spirits. I am afraid, and I cannot promise not to be, but I can promise I will not walk away from you and back into a place that is safe. I can pledge that."

"And I."

She grinned. "Good! Then come to the camp of my father the Bandit King and explain how you will pay the bride-price he will demand for his daughter, who he —"

Whatever she meant to say ended as she found two arms clutching her tightly.

"I would embrace you in return, Fool Running, if you would allow me to put down my rifle so it does not go off by accident and take off your head," she said, feeling inside the strength of spirit to walk ahead without looking down.

Sergeant Garrett Jones shook his head as Evans mentioned the Black Canyon Gang.

"Mostly they stole to eat, sir, and you know how those young men eat!" he said. "They were unusual, though. There were Indians and some white men. The Indians were mostly just wild, but the white men — they were older; they were pretty hard. The one who led them, Buff Walker, was dangerous."

Jones outlined the attack on some army wagons that left one soldier wounded.

"One of 'em, Lakota kid as I recall, said they should take the food they needed and go. So's the soldier told me. Two of 'em wanted to kill the soldiers. Walker shot at a soldier and hit him, then the Lakota kid killed Walker and one other. The rest of the gang took off. That Lakota kid did what he knew to bandage our soldier. It wasn't much, but he tried, and then he took off. Never heard from them ever again. Lakota kid saved them."

Evans listened. He had investigated. Victor Farleigh could go tell his tale to anyone he wanted or just go back into whatever hole he'd crawled out of. The army was not going to bite.

Howard Porter had lost the habit of writing a daily summation condemning the possibility of a Tongue River reservation. Rumors had begun to circulate — rumors that whites and Cheyenne both accepted as fact — that some band of army zealots devoted to Custer was going around killing Cheyenne and anyone who helped them. He had taken a journey to the smaller town of Sickles and heard stories there of bandits and outlaws in the wild country, of mysterious groups of riders and of this person they called Fox Running, who seemed to be inflated into something like a Robin Hood, or at least mixed up with a bandit family. There was also clear hesitancy to say anything good about the Cheyenne, and a lot of fear.

The loudest complaint about the Cheyenne was that they existed at all, a complaint voiced by men who frequented the town's saloon and who acted to Porter much like the soldiers he had seen when he passed through Fort Keogh. These men had no interest in a peaceful future for the Tongue River Valley. They wanted a war. For a moment, Porter wondered if his report was supposed to serve as pretext to start one. That thought chilled him.

Right and wrong were turning muddy, and Howard Porter did not like this. His Boston benefactor would not like this. He needed to close his eyes to what he saw, hold his nose to what he read of his work, and write.

August 8, 1883, Sickles, Montana
Sam Rickett read the message. This was not how they had told him all this would play out, but nothing ever went according to plan. It must be important for them to break all the silly rules they'd laid down to be sure no one could identify anyone else, and he could never say who hired him if it all went bust.

Time to get to work. First, he would clean the gun. Then he would use it.

August 10, 1883, Lame Deer, Montana
Mairead Cullihan was reading a book as she sat in a chair by the window of John Dooley's cabin. It was pleasant. And quiet!

The only noise came from Evans across the room scratching with a pen as he wrote out a report. He had returned from Fort

Keogh that day after delivering the Miles City newspaper some information about the gang terrorizing ranchers and farmers. He used the cabin when he wanted a quiet place to write the endless reports the army required.

"These gangs operate in secrecy and live off of fear," Evans had told John before he left. "Once we tell everyone in the Tongue River Valley not to be afraid because the army will get the gangs sooner or later, they will no longer be able to scare people."

Now Evans was writing something for a commander in Denver. He had told her it was important — something that needed to be put in writing.

John had gone out. Ruffled Hawk had come to tell him about a boundary dispute with his neighbor, and that they wanted John to resolve it. She had thought there were maps for that sort of thing, but he said it was better that both the neighbor, who was white, and Ruffled Hawk wanted to find an agreement in person instead of fighting over a piece of paper. She had told him not to worry about leaving her. She told him she was pleased he was so often called upon to arbitrate. She told him it was a sign of the respect everyone had for him.

Fox Running had been very mysterious of

late. He had gone away. He was more secretive in his movements lately. His dislike of her was growing obvious, and becoming a subject of concern.

She could hear footsteps walking confidently up to the door. The latch lifted.

"Oh, come in," she called, not looking up from the book. "John is not here, but he'll be back soon. Captain Evans is here!"

The latch stopped.

"Come on in; it's all right," she said, watching Evans write as though no one was speaking. "Do come in."

The latch lifted. The door slowly opened. Evans looked up as the light from the doorway hit his eyes. He started to rise and was drawing breath to speak when the first blast from the gun struck him. The impact of the bullet sent him back into the chair. Three more shots followed. The officer slumped over the table.

Mairead waited soundlessly behind the door, frozen in place. She stared at the slab of timber. Then she heard the feet moving quickly away as the door slowly swung shut.

She swallowed hard at the ghastly sight of Evans dead in his chair, telling herself that silly women only scream in novels and not in real life. A few quiet words escaped her: "Do hurry home, John."

■ ■ ■ ■

August 10, 1883, along Rosebud Creek

The August night was warm. Rides a Crow slept under the stars with Wrapped in a Blanket at her right hip.

"I was enjoying peace," she told her visitor.

"What is that?" asked Fox Running.

"I have been told you know what you seek. In time, you will find them, or they will stop for fear of being caught."

"And find other ways to stop The People." She sighed.

"It will be true for many years," she said. "The end of this war — for if it is not a war as our fathers fought, it remains a contest for survival — is so far distant it cannot be seen. Yet the wind that blows to flatten all before it still blows, Fox Running. We are nothing more than sticks tossed in that storm. I know you are troubled by something more than this, for their hate is the clay that molds our world. I can feel your concern. Tell me."

"Golden Turtle has lied to us. If I am to bring justice, I must act. All must face justice. Yet I fear that taking justice the way we are told it must be done would be worse than allowing a murderer to live."

"How do you know this?"

Fox Running sat on Rides a Crow's left, so as not to disturb the child. "I threatened him with the destruction of his family, those he walked from Indian Territory to save."

"You can be a hard man, Fox Running."

"Justice is a hard calling. The man Greene, who had his own wife, was paying attention to Golden Turtle's oldest daughter, who helped them fashion things to sell in the East. In a bad way, not a good one. A very bad way."

"The lance."

"It was not until I saw a man at work putting on some type of substance to preserve a piece of wood that I realized this had been done to the lance and done soon before it was found in Greene's body. Once I knew more than they suspected, they all admitted what took place. Snow Hare was the one who applied the substance, her father admitted, because her touch was light. On the day we found Greene, her hands had flakes of this substance on them. I did not know what it was at the time; I thought she had been cooking. They had been working in Greene's barn. He acted in a way that was wrong toward her, and not for the first time, and she ran, holding the lance. He chased her. She stabbed at him, and he ran full upon the lance.

"She ran home then. She confessed all to her father, who was enraged that a man he thought of as a friend would do that. I do not know if he could have saved Greene, but he did not even try. He walked to where the man lay dying and sang a death song to curse his spirit," Fox Running said. "He left the body there because he had no idea what else to do with it.

"Snow Hare has said nothing to me, and I have not spoken to her. She does not know I know of the man's actions. Golden Turtle did not want her shamed, for she hopes to marry next year. I ask you: what is justice? Should a girl of sixteen who was foolish be sent to the white man's prison? For that is what will happen if the full truth is told. Should her father be jailed for lying, when he is the one all the other Cheyenne look up to for the way he farms his land? If he cannot help them, and their farms fail, will that not hurt The People? If the army comes to arrest Snow Hare, I know Golden Turtle will say he killed the man, and there will be no justice done. Should Greene's family learn that their father and husband was wicked and evil in ways they did not know? I think these things, and then I say that a person who commits murder cannot go unpunished."

"As you know."

"Yes, as I know," he said, recalling the exile his family endured when his father, Red Eagle, killed a fellow warrior, creating a blood feud that ended only when Cheyenne leaders ordered all blood feuds ended because The People were already too few.

"Why are you here?" she said. "You have already decided."

"I need to know if I did right by the spirits. The white man's family was wronged. Golden Turtle must work their land for them and let them share in the profits from his farm as well. He will tell them he is doing this because of his fear of the men who ride in the night. I have spoken to the Greene family. They will tell the army they were ashamed of what Amos was doing by working with Blue Feather and will blame men riding in the night for killing Amos Greene. Once the army is convinced, they will look away and not want to know more. I believe his widow may know more of his conduct than I thought at first, but I know his children do not."

"And what of the white men who ride with you?"

"I will also tell them the gang that killed

Rawlins killed Greene, and that Golden Turtle, who made phony things for Blue Feather to sell, was afraid. Mr. Dooley will guess at some of this, for he is very clever. Captain Evans will wonder what lies below the surface but not ask, because he has learned that army justice is not always the justice of the spirits. He is a very good man. Also, once the family tells him the same lie I do, and begs him not to make life worse for them, he will not go farther."

"How do you know the family will do what you want? I have heard that they were very angry with the Cheyenne."

"The man who is the foreman there knew more than he told us. He does not want the widow to know the truth about her husband's bad conduct. He likes her. He will tell her that if others learn of Green's part in making false relics, the family will have no friends."

Wrapped in a Blanket stirred. Rides a Crow touched her head gently.

"Why do you doubt yourself?"

"Because the punishment for a death has long been banishment, if not death for death in a blood feud. I cannot banish Cheyenne children as I was once banished. I cannot."

"But you dare not tell your friends?"

"They would feel bound by their laws to

act in ways that those laws require, no matter what they feel."

"Then you are in a place where justice is like balancing a needle in the wind; in whatever manner you have achieved this, you have succeeded. It is late. You are tired from this. If the spirits think Golden Turtle or Snow Hare deserves more punishment, it will come to them. Fear not. The justice of the spirits may often be slow, but it never fails."

Night sounds enveloped them before Rides a Crow asked her final question.

"Will not these men you fight claim they are innocent of the Greene man's murder?"

When the cricket was finished, Fox Running spoke.

"I do not plan to leave them alive to do so."

August 11, 1883, Lame Deer, Montana
As he approached the cabin, Fox Running knew something terribly wrong had happened. Cheyenne and soldiers were gathered together. He heard talk of a dead man and pushed his way through.

The cabin was a ruin. Blood had spattered one wall and the table Dooley had built. A dark stain covered a large space of the floor. Dooley was sitting with Mairead on the bed by the far wall.

"They killed Evans," Dooley said. "He was here with Mairead. I was called away to a silly argument that was all over nothing. Someone came, shot him, and left."

"Is she hurt?"

"Scared, lad. Not shot, though. Whoever it was must have known Evans was here and come for him."

"It was no secret he was living here," Fox Running replied. "It had to be Sanders or the men we have been chasing."

He walked further into the cabin. He wondered why anyone would kill the soldier and not the witness. It made no sense. He voiced that thought and was abruptly told by Dooley that Mairead would not have been visible because she was sitting against the front wall of the cabin by the window and never saw the killer's face. The assassin had never even entered the cabin and must not have known she was there, he said.

Fox Running stopped at the table, noting the bloodstained papers on it. "Is that what he was writing when he was shot?" he asked. "What was it? He was just at the fort when he went to Miles City."

"I don't know, lad. Whatever it was, there's so much blood on it, it's ruined. Some report for the army, I guess."

"Where is Evans's body now?"

"After he was shot, someone came and called the army. They took him to their camp. I know he had family somewhere in the East, but I don't think they were close. This place had been his life."

"And his death."

Fox Running had known Evans was pulled both by his desire to bring peace in the manner of the white man to the Tongue River Valley, and by the brotherhood of soldiers who wanted the Cheyenne wiped out before they could possess the valley as a reservation. He had done what was right and paid the price.

Now others would pay.

August 13, 1883, Lame Deer, Montana
The army confirmed that Captain Evans had family in the East but had given instructions that if he died in Montana, he wanted to be buried in the Tongue River Valley. Rides a Crow, whom few could brook when she was determined, decreed that he would be buried on a hill overlooking Lame Deer, not far from where Dull Knife had been laid to rest earlier in the year.

An army chaplain from Fort Keogh had read a service over him. Then Rides a Crow walked through the crowd of soldiers, small ranchers, and Cheyenne — the latter breathless to see the fabled Spirit Walker, who almost never emerged in public.

"When the world called for war, this man worked for peace. When white men turned hard faces at The People and wanted us dead and dispersed, he welcomed us at the end of our journey with a hand that was open and a heart that was true, because he believed in peace among peoples," she said. "When our people wanted to break that peace, we could tell them that one man among the whites was a man of honor, and we could not let him be dishonored. He would never abandon his honor; he helped us learn to live by rules that have been a heavy yoke at times but have helped us endure.

"Captain Evans was killed by those who want to divide our two peoples, by those who want the Tongue River Valley to be a place where they can say The People who possessed it once are no more; by those who hate everyone, of all skin colors. The spirits will not rest . . ." She started to cry, then checked her tears. "They will not rest until the one who did this deed has been caught and punished. The wind that never ceases to blow away everything that blocks The People from having this land as their home will not stop because one man died, and if we all die it will raise warriors from the stones to take our places!"

She looked down at the rough box in which Evans's body lay.

"When The People had no friends, he was our friend," she said. "And when we take our journey to Seana, when we join those who walked before us, we shall see our friend, and he shall embrace us in a place where there is no pain and sorrow and war and hate, and we shall know joy. He bought us hope with his life, my people. Let us not squander what he gave."

Howard Porter heard the pure sincerity flowing from the young woman's soul. He had heard tales of her — they called her a Spirit Walker and said she was the link between the Northern Cheyenne and their spirits and was protected by them. He had wanted to speak with Evans. He wondered if this woman, for she seemed literate, might be worth speaking to after all.

When Rides a Crow finished, she stood by Evans's coffin a moment, then left, her face wet. A man who had waited in the woods, apart from the hundreds of mourners, came to stand by the casket. Porter heard the crowd gasping that this was Little Wolf, who had left his self-imposed exile to say his goodbye. The man knelt, touching the box, and then kissed it. There was absolute silence on the hilltop except for the wind. The Indians were deeply moved. A few whispered Little Wolf's name. Little Wolf never spoke. He rose and looked over the crowd. He nodded his head in a sign of respect, then walked away alone. After he was out of sight, as Annie Campbell's pencil flew in her efforts to sketch Little Wolf's surprise visit to the soldier who had welcomed him home, what seemed to Porter like every Cheyenne for miles around came to pass by the box and leave carvings and other gifts as their way to honor Evans.

As the line came to an end, Fox Running approached Dooley, who had been silent and thoughtful since Evans was killed. Fox Running knew Dooley must have been wondering if Evans was the real target, and whether all of this was worth dying for.

"There is an old Lakota saying, or perhaps a Cheyenne one. Or perhaps it was Irish. 'If snakes keep coming to the rock you sit upon, you must clean out their den.'"

"But how do we know where that is?" asked Dooley.

"We ask the biggest snake."

"The daughter of the Bandit King has

scruples about breaking the law?"

Cut Sky had come to Lame Deer to pay Blue Feather's respects to Evans and now confronted Fox Running. "The daughter of the Bandit King does not wish to be killed in a foolish scheme. The last time you tried this, it did not produce the results you wanted."

"Does Blue Feather not know what a magpie I seek to take from his camp? That his lodge will no longer ring with the scolding of a jay?"

"He understands that a man who kills his daughter on a foolish raid will be hunted until the far side of tomorrow," she replied. "Do you have a better plan than the last time?"

He grinned. "Of course."

She knew the grin meant trouble. She was right.

Chapter Fourteen

Sanders's imposing ranch now lay before Fox Running. The stockman could not have replaced all the hands lost when the ambush against Washburn failed, but Fox Running was certain he would face more than enough men who were hired for their ability with guns and not their willingness to herd cattle.

He lifted each pistol out of its holster, checked to be sure they were fully loaded, spun the cylinders, and lightly set them back in place. He waited until, like the building of a strong wind, it was time to let loose the storm within him.

Two men stood at the gate, by the edge of the fence. They had rifles in their hands as they watched Fox Running walk Coyote Horse closer. If they did not know who he was, they would make a guess soon. One of the books he had read in the Indian School in Boston quoted some general as claiming that all success came from doing the unexpected. He was doing it.

"Far enough," one guard said as the young Cheyenne advanced within hearing range, after a duel of stares in which Fox Running refused to yield. The rising sun was warm on his neck, and perspiration dripped down the faces of the men opposing him.

"Sanders here?" he asked.

"Not to you," the guard replied.

"Not very hospitable," Fox Running said.

"Don't care."

"Git," said the other guard.

Fox Running let the silence hang. "Tell him I came to talk," he said finally, averting his gaze. He squeezed gently with his legs, pressuring Coyote Horse to turn. The animal obeyed. One man drummed his fingers on the barrel of his rifle; the other began lowering his.

Fox Running had a gun in each hand before either guard could react. The men held their rifles away from their bodies to show they were not trying to fire on him.

"I can kill you, but I really do want to talk to your boss," Fox Running said. "Call him."

They did. Seconds later, Sanders emerged, rifle in hand.

"I can put you down before you get off a shot," he said. "Nothing to say to you."

Fox Running waited silently.

Sanders cocked the rifle and put it to his shoulder.

From the woodlot to the right of Fox Running, a rifle fired, kicking up dust by Sanders's left foot.

"Put your rifle down; tell your men to do the same," Fox Running said. "The next shot will not miss."

The scene froze as the wind whipped a dust devil across the ranch yard. Fox Running pulled back the hammers of his pistols. "I am here to talk to you," he repeated. "Otherwise . . ."

This time, the rifle kicked up dust just behind Sanders.

"She does get impatient."

"Drop 'em, boys," Sanders called, putting down the rifle and stepping away from it.

"Stand by the fence," Fox Running demanded. "Drop the pistols, too." They complied.

Fox Running knew the gunshots would draw a crowd sooner or later. He would have to make this quick.

"I know that you know who killed Ben Rawlins. I know you would like to brag that it was you, but it was not. You can tell me who did it or I will kill you."

"Don't know what you're talking about."

Fox Running fired. Sanders's hat flew off

and sailed along the ground. Fox Running wanted to grin. Shooting at a hat was a huge risk, because a miss high would have made him look stupid, and a miss low meant he would never get an answer.

Sanders took a step back. "Thought you were this justice warrior. Kill a man in cold blood, and you got the army after you."

"Killing a man who helped to kill a friend is justice. Last chance."

Sanders did not seem the least diminished. In fact, he gave a slight smile as he shook his head.

"Talking about Evans? Army's a nest of spiders, boy. You know what, boy? I'm going to give you what you want. And I'm gonna tell you why. Ever see one of those machines that mows down the wheat? You think the wheat stands a chance against that machine? But you want to go ahead, Son, go ahead. Because when you're all done killing and being killed, I'm going to ranch this valley right. That Bigelow. Not saying nothing, but he wanted land just to have it, to be sure no one else had it. When I get that land, it'll be run proper. You and those army men, all you see is ground to kill for. Go ahead! When you're done, I'll be rich, and you'll be forgotten."

"I want an answer."

"Over near Wolf Mountain. Place they had a fight a few years ago. Some old ranch buildings where these army men live. All high and noble about some secret society to avenge Custer. Full of it. They just want to kill all of you — every last brave, every last squaw. Tried telling them once that your kind are like the Pony Express when the railroads came — doomed. They got no patience. So you go and kill everyone you want, boy. Make the valley burn and bleed. Then one day, while you distract everyone with your fighting, everybody will wake up and find out who really owns it."

Fox Running tried to judge the words. The contempt was real. So, too, might be the information — except for the fact that Sanders would be sure to tell them Fox Running was coming and that they should prepare an ambush.

Two quick shots from the hillside drew three returning shots from near the bunkhouse. Yelling came from Fox Running's right, briefly claiming his attention. Sanders bent down to retrieve his rifle.

"I would like you to pick up that gun," said Fox Running. The stockman froze, then rose with his empty hands high.

"You. Your people. Your spirits. I will bury them all," Sanders said. "And I'm gonna do it all legal, with a pen and not a gun. Now get off my land."

One bullet went over Fox Running's head. Way high. He knew he should leave, but he had to reply to the taunts.

"You seek to bury The People. You do not see that the wind is sweeping this valley free of people like you, who live only to destroy. If you kill all The People, the rocks will come alive and fight you. And if you smash all the rocks, the Star Warriors in the sky will fight you. And there will be a place in this valley where no one will hunt and shoot a Cheyenne for being a Cheyenne. And if it comes while the sun bleaches your bones as they witness it, I shall be glad."

"Not afraid of your heathen spirits, Injun," Sanders replied.

Fox Running snapped off two shots toward a group of men who were still out of range but moving in to close off any escape. He turned Coyote Horse around to run away. This time.

August 15, 1883, Lame Deer, Montana
John Dooley walked when he was troubled. Not far. Not fast. The leg wound from the war took care of that. He was certain Sanders was sending them into a trap with the information he'd provided. It would take no

effort at all for Sanders to tell the men living on Wolf Mountain that Fox Running was coming, or to ensure his own men were there waiting.

"He could post twenty men there and kill all of us," he had told his Cheyenne friend. "Just because he claimed they were soldiers or former soldiers doesn't mean you can believe him. You took a foolhardy risk confronting him, and all you did was let Sanders know he should be on his guard. Think, lad. This Montana Territory keeps trying to get itself admitted as a state. Sanders wants to be important. He doesn't want any blood on his wee white hands. If he sends you into the gun sights of some army renegades, there may not be anyone who can say what he's been doing. He's using you to do some dirty work of his own, you can be sure. Let it alone, lad. Let it alone."

Dooley knew there was more to the death of Amos Greene than anyone would admit to him but grudgingly agreed to mouth the lie the family and Fox Running would tell the army. His larger concern was to stop Fox Running before the younger man ended up dead.

Fox Running was impatient. They had argued until Dooley left the cabin, which Dooley had cleaned the best he could, Fox

Running being a stranger to cleanliness except for his pistols.

Walking a beat in Boston was simple. Watch the bad ones and protect the good ones. Here in Montana, everything was confusion. Except Mairead, who spent more and more time during the day at the cabin, for her own safety. If any good had come from this, it was that in the final days before the school opened, he could say he was doing his job by being there to protect her as he helped finish the schoolroom. In fact, he should be there now. Her advice had been good. He walked faster.

Katherine McGillicuddy put the stack of papers in order as she prepared to read through them once again. John Dooley was a dutiful correspondent who made up in polite phrases for what he left out in information. Annie Campbell, whose sketch of Little Wolf at the soldier's funeral was among the most moving images she had ever drawn, had written a longer, informal, fast-paced letter that explained the vast amount of trouble actually taking place all around Fox Running.

Katherine could see a plan developing to throttle what seemed to be the *de facto* creation of a reservation. Fox Running was fighting back — perhaps too hard from the tone of concern registered by Dooley, but perhaps with that instinct that comes from knowing there is only one choice, as Annie's letter implied.

It would be a good time for her to remind those in the War Department who knew her that if they wanted the contributions to keep coming that helped underwrite the costs of Fort Keogh, they should not abandon the course Captain Evans had set of being fair and impartial. Yes, she would send those letters. And she would continue to keep that wild young man and his friend Dooley in her prayers.

"Hello, Farleigh."

Victor Farleigh was staying at the boardinghouse run by Elinor Planksworth, one of the earliest settlers in Lame Deer. Now in her seventies, she took in guests to help pay her costs for food and the upkeep of the house she shared with Jack, her husband of forty-seven years.

"Mrs. Planksworth," Fox Running added, nodding politely.

She knew him as the Indian who had some manners, but she still wasn't sure about living so close to them. She tried a neutral smile.

"Does this man owe you money?" Fox Running inquired.

"Oh no," she said. "They all pay in advance. A week at a time."

"Well then, you will be the one who gains, because there are five days left in this week, and Mr. Farleigh is leaving." Fox Running paused. "Now."

Farleigh scowled. "You can't —"

Fox Running's right hand shot out to grab Farleigh by the coat. "We shall continue this outside so as not to damage the furniture," he said. He thrust Farleigh half out the door that he had not shut behind him on his way in. "You have a choice, Farleigh. Leave or die," he said as they reached the street. "I do not know how Bigelow found you, nor do I care. The army does not care about your tale. I have told them everything."

"I want fifty dollars."

"If you came on the train to Sickles, I shall buy your ticket. If you came on a horse, get it."

Farleigh itched to reach for the gun in the black leather holster at his right hip. "I'll leave," he said, raising his hands. "Bigelow was hiring, and when I heard what you did to him, I thought he might give me a little extra if I told him what I had on you. Just looking out for myself. Nothing personal."

"Let me walk you to the stable," Fox Running said. When they got there, he admonished Farleigh to leave and never return, then started back along the road. *I am getting old,* he thought as he walked, counting. At eight, he turned.

Farleigh was reaching for his gun. His face registered panic as Fox Running's eyes met his. He fumbled for the pistol. Fox Running waited. Farleigh lifted the weapon from its holster and raised it. Even at a distance of thirty feet, Fox Running could see the gun shaking.

"Shall I come closer?" he called. "Will that help?"

He moved toward Farleigh, anger making him stride faster. Twenty feet. Fifteen. He stopped. The gun was shaking worse.

"Put that away. Leave," Fox Running commanded. This time, he turned away and did not look back.

August 19, 1883, Lame Deer, Montana
Fox Running had been seven. The drought that had dried up almost every water hole, spring, and small creek had ended in a deluge. The People — who had taken these events as a sign that they had drifted from the spirits and must draw closer to them — had gathered to give thanks that the spirits

understood they were sorry for their sins. On that day, the usual thumping rhythms of the dance drum yielded pride of place to some Cheyenne women, including Fox Running's mother, who played the flute. The music soared like an injured bird returning to the wild and danced like young raccoons in spring. He had never heard the song again, but it never left his head.

On this day, he was humming it as Dooley eyed him suspiciously.

Fox Running was reading the latest issue of the *Western Territories News,* which regularly chronicled the exploits of the Cheyenne Kid, a distorted, slanted telling of the adventures Fox Running either did have or would have had if he were an evil, twisted, death-dealing gunfighter as proclaimed by the paper. Usually, the paper was balled up page by page and thrown in the fire amid a deluge of Cheyenne and Lakota words whose meaning Dooley never inquired about.

This day was different. Although Fox Running had been in a good mood since his run-in with Farleigh, one he did not share with Dooley lest he have to spill a tale he thought Dooley did not know about, this level of happiness was well out of character.

Dooley could not keep still.

"And why, lad, are you singing and chipper while reading that garbage? We buried the good captain just days ago. What can be so lovely that you think you're a bird flying?" Dooley said.

Their luck had been running sour. The army had ruled that Evans's killer mistook him for Dooley and that, therefore, his death was an accident. Dooley and Fox Running assumed that any investigation was ruled out because of where it might lead. The army had also pulled back its men from Lame Deer to the friendlier confines of Fort Keogh on the excuse that it was safer.

Dooley had hoped the lull in activity would be a good time to get his friend to understand he needed to be more careful. They'd exchanged more than a few heated words on the subject.

But today, Fox Running held up the paper as though their luck was changing. "Because, Mr. Dooley, they have made a mistake. At last, they have made a mistake!"

August 21, 1883, Miles City, Montana
The Grand Hotel in Miles City might not have been described that way by its guests. As the nearest hotel to Fort Keogh, it was in constant demand by the many civilian visitors not important enough to be offered

accommodations at the fort. There was thus little motivation for new paint, wallpaper, mattresses, or other improvements.

However, with two stories and twelve rooms, it was one of the fast-growing community's larger attractions and played host to many whose names in the guest book were known far and wide. For the past two weeks, the hotel had been the home of famous writer Carson McAllister of the *Western Territories News.* He had let slip to the staff that when his current schedule of articles was complete, he would begin a lecture tour in Cheyenne before moving to St. Louis and then the East. The lectures would focus on his hardships and efforts to tell the story of the deadly Cheyenne Kid, whose latest exploits included ambushing a dozen men who rode for a local rancher.

McAllister was tapping the pointed, upturned end of his waxed mustache as he contemplated the foolscap paper before him. This account would follow the Kid's recent effort to murder the rancher by riding into his ranch yard while an accomplice fired from behind, a clear violation of the rules of proper killing. In it, the Cheyenne Kid would be chased by a posse. Readers always liked posses. It was standard stuff, but he had stopped while waiting for his meal to arrive. He would be done today, and another chapter of his return to his rightful prominence would be completed.

A knock at the door announced the arrival of his dinner. Due to his fame, he no longer ate in the dining room. He had also paid the staff to ensure those coming up to his room were properly screened. The woman with the pipe who said she loved him and wanted him to be her husband in a cabin had scared him with her intensity.

"Come in. Set it there," he said, pointing. No reply. The staff could be so stupid! He turned around, and his eyes widened. An Indian? Who in their right mind would send an Indian with his dinner? Did they never read what he wrote?

"Take that away and send the manager," he commanded. "You may leave."

"I do not think so," the Indian said, setting down the tray. He was young and wiry, and as he shucked off the coat he had been wearing that was clearly too big for him, McAllister could see two guns. His eyes immediately went to the Indian's face. It bore many marks, as though someone had fired a shotgun into it, but there was also a telltale scar that sliced from his forehead between his eyes. This was Fox Running, the young man McAllister had transformed into the

Cheyenne Kid, whom he had last seen on the Great Sioux Reservation multiple humiliations ago.

"What do you want?" His bluster covered his fear.

"I would like to kill you," Fox Running replied calmly, moving to a chair to sit. "Perhaps I will show you my fast draw and put a bullet dead center in your forehead, which I understand I do very well, and very often. I do wish I was wittier, though. I like the ones who kill six people and make jokes."

"All I do is write," he said. "I entertain people."

"Do you remember last year at Pine Ridge when you wanted them to take me? When they thought you were writing the truth? I was shot then. Do you know what being shot feels like, Carson? Would you like to learn how little it is like a 'stinging burn' leaving a 'fiery red trail' that does nothing to impede one's ability to shoot people?"

He blanched. "No. I mean, I'm sorry."

"Carson, I know you have been receiving information about me. You could not have written your last story without hearing from someone who was either involved in the shooting or who heard about it from the very few people who knew of it. That's how

I knew you had to be close by. Miles City is the largest community here, and the only one with a decent hotel for a man of your reputation, so I knew where I could find you."

"What do you want?"

"Carson, you know me. You know I have a short temper. I have decided I no longer want to read about the Cheyenne Kid."

"But —"

"If I ever do, after the story you are going to write, nothing will stop me from finding you and killing you, regardless of where you seek to take your miserable drunken hide. I do not care who you write for or where you write, or what name you might use. I will find you. Us Injun trackers, you know, Carson. We always find our prey. Do you understand, Carson?"

Fox Running had risen and now loomed over the sitting writer, who nodded.

"I need to hear you say it, Carson."

"No. Yes. I mean, yes. The Cheyenne Kid series is through."

"I am so glad we have an understanding, Carson. I know you have a deadline to meet. I have a new series of three articles for you. These will allow you to file for this week and the next two, and then vanish."

He reached inside his shirt, pulled out a

sheaf of papers, and handed them over. Captain Evans had been writing about the group of soldiers who were working to push out the Cheyenne. He must have known after his trip to Miles City, just before his murder, that he had gone too far to remain unpunished. Fox Running had taken the few words he could make out from the blood-covered piece of paper they had pulled from under Evans's body and added what he could surmise. He had also gone through what he could find of Evans's mail and orders sent down to him while he was at Lame Deer. He wished now that he'd treated Evans less like a soldier and more like a friend, but he would do what he could to make sure that Evans had not died for nothing.

When McAllister finished reading the papers, he was white as a ghost. "I . . . I can't write this."

"Why not, Carson? Is it even close to the lies you tell about me?"

"No. No. I know it is true. It's all true. It must be. I have heard this over and over . . . all this, and more. I was told some of them considered Evans a renegade. But they will kill me."

"Or I will kill you now," said Fox Running, slowly pulling his revolver from its holster. "Any last words, Carson?"

"No, no. No!" McAllister sputtered. "Don't shoot me. I will have it sent. Just as you wrote it."

"Many people get lost in San Francisco, I hear," Fox Running said. "A new name, perhaps a face without a mustache, and there will be a place for you. You have money. If you leave soon, you will have your health. If you leave very soon. The moment those are filed. Are we agreed?"

"Yes!"

"Now read this again, Carson, and tell me what I have left out, especially names. And when you are through, you will tell me who has been giving you information for your most recent articles. This is very important to me, Carson. You see, I could have these next articles telegraphed to the East in your name, the way you have been doing while you are here, and no one would know the difference."

"You are threatening me."

"Yes, Carson. I am. I am glad you know that. I hope that will help you make the right decision."

McAllister wanted a drink. He wanted to run. He wanted to find any place in the hotel room to get away from the relentless glare of Fox Running's eyes.

He lowered his gaze and scanned what would be his final pieces until he became someone else in San Francisco or some other place. And then he talked.

August 23, 1883, Miles City, Montana
As revelations about a secret society within the army occupied readers of the *Western Territories News,* Fox Running and Dooley divided forces. Fox Running returned to Miles City after conferring with Dooley, waiting for someone connected to the army ring to come looking for McAllister.

Dooley remained in Lame Deer, where he continued to deal with disputes referred by the army, under the temporary command of Lieutenant Eric Moore, who had not yet visited Lame Deer. Moore had sent word that seemed to imply he would prefer not to work with the agency and said any further investigation of the deaths of Rawlins and Greene should wait until the army made some decisions.

Dooley was uneasy. Fox Running knew Dooley was reluctant to leave Mairead, and that there were other pressures on him that he hadn't shared. Dooley had spoken to Fox Running often of trying to talk through his differences with Sanders and the others who opposed a reservation instead of settling everything with a gun. Fox Running guessed it was Mairead's voice speaking, trying to be sure Dooley did not end up a victim. Other thoughts he kept to himself, for now. He would wait until the time was right.

Three days after the first piece exposed the secret society, Fox Running — who continued to occupy the hotel room McAllister had rented for another two weeks — heard footsteps moving as stealthily down the hall as three to four booted white men could manage. He was glad McAllister had packed a valise and left. Fox Running hoped he would never see the reporter again.

If the hotel had decent walls, perhaps the approaching men's whispers would not have been audible. Then again, cavalry soldiers were noted for one thing — a charge.

They did not let him down. They came storming through the door, which popped back and then sagged on its hinges as it slammed into the wall, sending pieces of wood flying amid a cloud of plaster dust.

Fox Running had set up the desk, which was to the right of the door as they entered, to look as though someone had just left it. He'd theatrically left one shoe under the bed, which might be effective if whoever came for McAllister knew the manner of man they were hunting.

However, they did not come to talk; they came to kill, with guns drawn.

"Surrender!" one man called out as he and the rest clustered between the desk and the bed.

"Drop the guns," said Fox Running, with the over-enunciation he knew was often needed to get a message into minds that were not prone to listening.

It was a wasted effort. The first shot came as he was speaking, the second boomed right after it.

Fox Running had set up a small barricade of a nightstand and a washstand and dove to his left behind it as two bullets flew over his head and slammed through the thin wall. He fired back blindly twice, lifting his head to sight the next shot as three more bullets plowed into the wood of the washstand and a fourth splintered the nightstand in his face. The noise was deafening in the confines of the room, and powder from the guns in the small space obscured vision.

Fox Running fired until his first revolver was empty, then dropped it to draw the second. More bullets chewed into his barricade as he rolled away from it and, prone on the floor, fired all six bullets at the remaining three men.

One man was left standing. He had used

all his bullets. Fox Running wanted him alive. He pulled a knife from his belt and moved toward his target. The man swung his revolver at Fox Running's head. Fox Running ducked and slashed at him across the middle. The man yelped in pain.

"Drop the gun," Fox Running hissed. "Drop it."

The man threw the gun at him, then reached for Fox Running's knife. Fox Running dodged the gun but could not get his knife hand loose from the man's grip, even when he pulled at the man's arms. He let his legs go out from under him, and they both fell to the floor. Fox Running head butted the man in the face. Again. The assailant's grip relaxed slightly. Fox Running drove his knee into the man's stomach, pulled his knife arm free, and rolled away.

"I don't want . . . to kill you," Fox Running gasped. "Give up."

The man had spotted one of his companions' guns on the floor and was moving, crab-like, towards it on hands and knees. He reached the weapon and turned, then slumped back with a gurgle as the knife hit his chest. A line of blood, followed by a stream, came from his mouth as he fell back with his hand frozen on the trigger.

Fox Running pounded the floor. He'd

wanted someone to use to learn more about whoever was threatening Cheyenne farmers, not just more dead bodies. He knew he had little choice, but as he looked at the all-but-destroyed room, he knew that these men — all of whom looked as though they had ridden the Plains as soldiers for years — were only sent to do a chore.

He got up to leave before what passed for the law in Miles City was called. First, he reloaded both his guns. Then he skimmed through every dead man's pockets. He left enough money to cover coffins for them. He found a crude map of Miles City and a map of what had to be their cabin in Lame Deer. And a note that read, in part, *S says he will be there.* Sanders? His shoulders sagged. If so, it would only mean that someone who openly hated the Cheyenne was linked with the soldiers. Nothing more.

Boots! He moved to the window. It would be a dangerous leap from the second floor. Better face up to it. He could try to talk his way out first.

"What are you doing . . ." The man filling the doorway was not the law. The former soldiers must have had someone watching.

"Arms up," said Fox Running. The man complied. "We need to talk. Your friends are past talking. Look for yourself if you do not believe me. But first, lower your gun to the floor."

The man began to lower his arms. Fox Running knew what was going to happen. "Do not! Do not!"

But the man did not listen. He clawed for his gun. Fox Running drew his own and shot. At a range of four feet, he could hardly miss. The man spun as the bullet entered his leg. Even as he hit the floor, he drew his revolver and sent a wild bullet into the ceiling. Fox Running's second shot ended it.

This one's inside coat pocket was stuffed with papers, but Fox Running knew this was not the time to read them. If the law in Miles City was not already on its way, it would be soon. It was time to leave.

Chapter Fifteen

August 24, 1883, Lame Deer, Montana
"So ye learned nothing?" Dooley was cross. He tried to explain to Fox Running that the existence of a network of former soldiers who were threatening Cheyenne farmers was not a surprise, and with Evans dead, the army was no longer interested in learning that men who fought Indians in uniform continued to do so after they left the cavalry.

The only thing that had saved Fox Running from going to jail for the gunplay in Miles City was how careful he had been in getting in and out of the hotel unseen. With no witnesses and no survivors, there was no one to tell the tale. Dooley tried to convince his friend he had pushed the matter as far as it could go, and to let the issue rest.

"I think it might be over, lad. The way the army sees it, Evans strayed too far onto the side of the Cheyenne. There is talk his murder might have been something with a woman, and not with anything else. They're closing ranks, laddie. Canna ye see that? It might be time to just protect what we have."

"Is this Mairead talking?" Fox Running said coldly.

Dooley knew nothing ignited Fox Running's rage as much as anyone trying to push him around, but he kept going just the same. This wasn't the Indian School, it was life — and it could be death. "Lad, the fight over who controls this valley is bigger than you and bigger than me. It runs all the way to Washington. The best we can do is do what Miss McGillicuddy wanted, and try to keep these small things from getting out of hand while we live to see tomorrow. Think for a minute. We have had killings that could have set the whole shootin' match of Cheyenne and settlers at each other's throats, and we found a way to keep that from happening. When we started, we would have said that was a big accomplishment!"

"There is too much hate."

"Maybe the Cheyenne who used to kill whites and the whites who used to kill Indians are not living in perfect peace and harmony, lad, but who is? If you get too close to the fire, you will get burned. Leave it for Two Moon to fret about. I do not want you hurt, lad. This is more than anyone can control."

Fox Running understood there was some wisdom in what Dooley said. In an odd, ugly way, the past weeks of the summer had brought some Indian and white settlers together as they realized they were all being threatened, while not allowing anything to divide them more than their competing dreams already did. The railroad would never want the Indians to be given land; the small traders and merchants who dealt with Indians as customers would favor a reservation. The Cheyenne themselves were at odds over the size and location, with some wanting the land by the river and others the land by Rosebud Creek where Little Wolf had settled.

"I suppose you are right, Mr. Dooley. I need to visit Cut Sky. She returned to her father after I tried to confront Sanders. There are things we need to speak about. I shall be back in two days. No longer."

Dooley nodded. "Lad, show some sense and look at making a life here with the lass. You have prime land where you can build a house. It takes time. You cannot hope to fight them all forever. You can do nothing for anyone when you are dead."

■ ■ ■ ■

August 25, 1883, Tongue River Breaks

Cut Sky shook her head at Fox Running as they sat at the edge of a cave overlooking a creek that curved in a series of S-shapes down one of the tree-covered hills in the Tongue River Breaks.

"You are an odd Cheyenne, Fox Running," she teased. "You spend every minute of your life helping the Cheyenne have land, a reservation, a place where they can never be pushed off to someplace else. You have almost killed yourself for this over and over, and I know I can speak until owls fly in daylight and I will never stop you. But you never join your people. You have never been to any Cheyenne gathering. You did not go to the Sun Dance or any other dance. You shun the harvest festival. You never speak in council; you hardly speak to anyone among the Cheyenne except Rides a Crow. Should I be jealous of her?"

He shrugged. He was too tired for a clever answer.

"When I was in Boston, I was a Cheyenne. I was never more of a Cheyenne than when they tried to beat and shame it out of me. But the truth, Cut Sky, is that I was only living among the Cheyenne for a small part of my life. Since the year before the Custer fight, for these past eight years, I have lived away from the Cheyenne more than I have lived with them. Some Cheyenne words, I have forgotten, and I use Lakota words instead. My time in the world of the white man changed me. I hated my school, but I learned from it. I fit at the edges of the Cheyenne, the Lakota and the white world, but in the middle of none of them. It is like the sheepdog seeking to be one with the sheep. The dog's job is not to be a sheep but protect them. I have come to believe the spirits made me not to be in the middle of The People, but to protect them."

He took her hand. "I have spent all these years fighting," he said. "Fighting soldiers. Fighting someone. Mr. Dooley fears I fight because I love fighting. He may be right. But I know, Cut Sky, that men who want to destroy the Cheyenne are there, as though a thousand warriors were gathering behind high hills while we are unaware. I know that in these weeks before the winter closes in, something will happen that can destroy any hopes of the government creating a reservation. I know they dare not wait until the spring. They choose a new Great White Father next year, and this changes all the things they do in their government. And yet I might as well shoot at the sky because, other than Sanders, who sneered at me when I confronted him and sent us to chase others, I do not know who is the unseen enemy gathering, even though I know he is close."

"What have you asked of my father?"

"Your father? I am planning to ask for you, Cut Sky!"

She dismissed that comment with a wave of her hand. "Yes, yes, yes. As soon as you can pay my bride price, and I am sure you have not even started that conversation!"

"I..."

"Do not," she warned. "Do not explain to me how running here and there is more important than I am."

She laughed as he looked truly tongue tied and lost and took pride in having defeated him in a contest of words.

"What I meant was whether you asked him to help you put together the pieces you have. The Bandit King knows much."

During their meal, Blue Feather told Fox Running that Golden Turtle and the widow of Amos Greene had formed some kind of partnership to work their lands jointly, with everyone sharing in the profits. The creation of a Cheyenne-white partnership was the talk of the valley, he said. It had put to rest rumors that Greene was killed by an Indian. The army had explained that the same group of men who killed Rawlins killed Greene. Fox Running recalled the difficult time he had persuading Dooley to simply let it drop, because his friend suspected there was something below the surface, but in the wake of Evans's murder, there were other priorities.

"Yet you are not surprised," Blue Feather said as he studied Fox Running. "What do you know of this?"

Cut Sky knew Fox Running had been part of whatever took place involving Golden Turtle that led to the army no longer investigating his neighbor's death. She could see Fox Running did not wish to either lie or explain.

"Is it true my bride price is ten thousand cows and a horse?" she asked her father with exaggerated innocence. She roared with laughter as Blue Feather reacted, coughing and spitting out his stew.

"It is customary to discuss the bride price without the bride present," he replied, clutching at the shreds of his dignity, when he could speak again.

"Well, this oaf," she gestured at Fox Running, "is slow to talk. Shall we start talking now, so that I am not old and hunched before you do?"

"I gather from this you plan to marry my daughter?" Blue Feather asked, enjoying the sight of Fox Running taken aback.

"I do have money," Fox Running replied. He pulled a small cloth purse from the pocket of his coat. "I am not at all sure what she is worth . . ."

"The way that is said, I do not like," Cut Sky interjected.

". . . but this may be a start."

Blue Feather looked at the coins, at first casually and then with interest.

"Eyes grow old," he said. "Daughter, put more wood on the fire, and then look at these." He dropped five coins into her left hand.

She examined them closely, on each side.

"They are very unusual," she said. "They are all identical. They all have a scratch on them across the man's face."

"And what kind of coin is this?" he asked. "A daughter of mine should know!"

She shrugged. "I have never seen one like this. It is copper, not silver, but it is big."

"It is an English penny," he said. "An old one. A very old one. For ten years, my daughter, I have traded goods for goods, and sometimes for coins, and I have seen these perhaps once before. Now to find five, and all with the same mark upon them, is more than a coincidence. Where did these come from?"

"Are they of great value?" asked Fox Running.

"No," said Blue Feather. "Perhaps they would buy things in England, but out here they are not common and not worth very much."

"The coins came from the men I shot in Miles City," he said. "Each had one coin on him."

"Then you have found something of interest," said Blue Feather. He looked at his daughter a moment as the fire flared and illuminated her face. He touched her hair tenderly. "Perhaps even more important than the bride price of my daughter."

Cut Sky smiled at Blue Feather. She had lost her blood family but found a better one. She had been blessed. Was she so foolish she might throw all that away?

"I have known men before who belong to groups that wish to keep their purpose and membership secret, to have objects on them that identify them," Blue Feather said. "The men in the group you are seeking use these coins to identify themselves."

"How is that important?" asked Fox Running.

"If there are enough men that they do not all know each other, it means you are fighting a large group of people, and that new people may be coming to join them."

"What should I do?"

"For now, nothing. Cut Sky, bring Owl Face to me." She left. "Owl Face has a gift. He can draw well and draw what others tell him. The railroad comes through Sickles. Men come. Men go. He can watch to see who comes and goes. He can see who is new in the town these past weeks. He can learn all you might need to know about who your enemy is. Then you can see what they look like, and perhaps know who it is you are fighting, so you can end this and then get to important matters."

Fox Running's face reflected his confusion.

Blue Feather laughed. "Discussing Cut Sky's bride price, of course!"

"Roads divide," Blue Feather mumbled.

"What are you talking about, Father?"

Fox Running had returned to Lame Deer. His visit had troubled Blue Feather, who saw that when those who opposed the reservation and those who wanted it collided, straddling both sides in some middle ground would be all but impossible.

"He would give up everything for this dream of the Cheyenne having a reservation here in this valley," he said. "Does that dream burn hot within you as well?"

"Not as with him, but in a different way. There must be a place, Father, where being an Indian does not mean being kicked aside, where being Cheyenne or Lakota does not mean you can be killed without anyone caring. I see the way all these white men support one another against us. There must be a place where we can support one another against them. Perhaps that sounds" — she waved her hands — "silly and simple, but if all these hateful men fear this, Father, then I must be for it."

"I am not a warrior, Cut Sky, nor have I been one for many years. The path I have followed twists from light to dark. I have survived; I have tried to help you survive as well. Survival, Child, is a business that is not sung about at the circle, or celebrated in the stories. It is ugly; it is dirty. It is like peeling the innards of the buffalo; yet without survival, there is nothing."

"Father, what is wrong?"

"I have long told you when you stammered to tell me something you had done wrong that it was better to get it out, and I find myself disobeying my own advice! The men who have been riding and killing, the men who now fight Fox Running, are men to whom I have sold guns and ammunition."

"Father!"

"I have sold many guns to many men, Child. Some good; many bad. I have told myself that those who seek guns will find them. It is even true. Yet now I find myself in a position where the guns I sold could be turned upon one I love."

He touched her hair.

"But I am also in a place where I may be able to help Fox Running, because I can contact those he fights and arrange a meeting where he could take them by surprise. Yet, if I do this, it may be the end of my time, for those with whom I have dealt are vicious and powerful. Even from the glimmers of what I can learn, I know the ones he fights here are part of something bigger. And yet, for all that, I am a man standing on a hill as the wind blows, knowing that what is to come will tear up much of what has been and yet feeling in the wind something true, strong, and good and urging it to blow stronger and harder and longer until everything it touches is scoured clean."

Cut Sky embraced Blue Feather.

"Father, I know you have done what was necessary for me. I would be lying if I told you I did not like being the daughter of the Bandit King, and that I do not know how you earned your name! I do not care if you sold guns to them; the evil caused is theirs, by what they have done. So, Father, shall we scheme together?"

Howard Porter was a man beset. He had not responded to the past two telegrams from Boston demanding answers about his report. It had been going so well for his first few days, but it had tailed off. His ability to write what his employer wanted was fading in an inverse relationship to his own understanding of the issues and people.

Many Cheyenne chafed at the restrictions this new life placed upon them, particularly young men who wanted to make names for themselves as their fathers had done. As a man who had dealt more than once with gangs of young thugs in Boston, he knew the impulse to do violence was not confined to Indians in their teens!

Then there was that young Indian who worked in the general store. Harry Miller had made some reference to there being a problem that resulted in him taking on the boy. The first time Porter asked the boy to find something, he had almost acted afraid. The old man running the store had a white boy there for a while, but he was clearly lazy and not willing to work. The Indian boy had become helpful and polite and was learning to talk better English. Perhaps people who were shooting at each other up until a few years ago and were now neighbors just needed more time than anyone wanted to give them.

He also was coming to believe that much of the unrest was stirred by outsiders who wanted to provoke violence. It would not take much. Only one spark. Then the army would have no choice, and all the small steps in the world would not matter. Guns would do all the talking.

August 30, 1883, Lame Deer, Montana
Mairead Cullihan was pleased. John had proposed, and she had accepted. It had taken longer than she expected, but everything was under control. She had agreed that, unless there was some terrible weather, the next time the traveling minister arrived — which should be November — they would be married and then go back East for a few months.

She was writing that, and other important

news, in a letter to be delivered to her friends, so they could know when all the preparations would need to be completed. As she waited with John in the cabin, she thought life was moving along just perfectly.

Fox Running, as usual, was off somewhere again — as he had been for days on end. He could rarely stay still. She had come to realize he was very different from most of the Cheyenne. He had lived among the Cheyenne, Lakota, and whites so much that he didn't quite fit with any of them, although he seemed to believe strongly in Cheyenne spirits. She had met Cut Sky, who for all she could see was almost never more than a few feet away from a rifle. Civilized? Hardly! Still, John liked them, and they were very loyal to him. As they should be! They could all be dead by now. Only she knew how much they really owed him and, of course, her.

Dooley was pacing. Mairead's smiles from time to time were welcome, but he wanted to get this over with. The lad adjusted poorly to changes, and the news of the marriage might disturb him. Fox Running had sent word when he arrived in Lame Deer that he needed to stop at the army camp and would be coming to the cabin once that errand was over.

The latch lifted, and the door swung slowly open.

"Lad?"

Fox Running stood there with his hand on the gun worn at his right hip. He stepped into the doorway, but no further. "How long, Mr. Dooley? How long?"

"Lad, I . . ."

"Empty your pockets, Mr. Dooley. Let me see the coin you carry to identify yourself to your compatriots. Or should I call you Sean?"

There was not a sound in the cabin as Dooley, face ashen, looked at Fox Running.

"I do not know what this is . . ." Mairead began as she started to rise.

"Shut your mouth and sit down, Woman," Fox Running snarled. "I know you are a part of it. More than a small part." He looked back at Dooley. "Your pockets, Mr. Dooley?"

Dooley complied, and in moments a large copper coin with a scratch across the face of the man on it was lying on the table.

"When did ye know?" Dooley had gone red in the face.

"These past weeks, your voice changed from seeking justice, to seeking something that would not endanger anyone, to implying that the men who oppose the Cheyenne have a point. It was slow, but as I heard it, I realized your words were being shaped by someone else — someone who has her own agenda, or should I say the agenda of the people who sent her here to spy for them?"

He looked at Mairead. "You tell a wonderful lie, but Annie Campbell, the writer, was at Fort Keogh the other week when I was in Miles City. You said she was your friend. She never heard of you. I know that white people lie all the time, so I did not think much of this, but she was curious and asked about you of people she knew in Boston. Meanwhile, Blue Feather had one of his men draw the people who were coming and going from Sickles, people who seemed suspicious. Owl Face noted that the red hair was unlike anything he had ever seen."

He walked over to the table Dooley had built to replace the one ruined when Evans was killed. He slapped down a sketch that was clearly a drawing of Mairead.

"She met with this man." He set down another drawing. They bore a strong resemblance.

Dooley was looking at Mairead as if hoping for help. She raised her chin and defiantly stared at Fox Running. "I am organizing a school. I meet with many people."

"But this man is in charge of the men who

live on Wolf Mountain and have been intimidating the Cheyenne. Your brother, I assume?"

She did not answer.

Dooley said, "Lad, this is all wrong. I need to tell you something . . ."

"Miss Campbell found out quite a bit," Fox Running continued. "Remind me never to get on her bad side. It seems that a certain Michael McGillicuddy, Miss McGillicuddy's uncle, has funded the Loyal Legion of Faithful Pioneers, which on the surface supports the army by sending soldiers socks and such. Michael McGillicuddy has spoken often in Boston about the need to exterminate Indians. One of Miss Campbell's friends found a clipping in which a Thomas Cullihan spoke about the need to first eliminate the Cheyenne before they could get a reservation, and then later to break up the Lakota reservation entirely. He said it could be done by men with determination to honor the memory of George Armstrong Custer. He said only more money was needed to complete what was already begun." He tapped the second of Owl Face's sketches, next to Mairead's on the table. "Thomas Cullihan is one of the men who comes and goes from Sickles."

Fox Running glared at Dooley.

"Why, Mr. Dooley? Why did you listen to her? How could you close your eyes to all around you and do this to me?"

Dooley shook his head. "Lad, ye dinna see. The army men, like so many of ye who want the world in your pocket tomorrow, are fighting over the land. They were going to kill ye, lad, if ye did not slow down. I spoke for ye, but then ye did that deed with the newspaper man and exposed them. There is no need for a reservation, just reason, if ye'd all just let it happen over time. In twenty years, there would be no fight over it. It would come natural. If the Northern Cheyenne stopped demanding, these men would stop pushing back."

Fox Running touched a loop of leather around his right wrist.

"Do you know where this came from? Do you?!" Dooley shook his head. "This spring, after Morning Shadow and the Lakota rejected me, I went for a time to Hat Creek, where The People were slaughtered in the January after they escaped from Indian Territory. I went to the ditch where men and women and children died because they were Cheyenne who would not live under someone's thumb. There was a tiny moccasin and around it was this piece of leather. I have worn this since that day to remind myself,

Mr. Dooley, that listening to fine talk and soft words is to forget that those who speak those words slaughtered men, women, and children who wanted to live free as Cheyenne."

"That was in the past," Dooley said.

"It is never in the past," Fox Running replied. "To you, it is history, like your Rising of '98 is to me. I was there, Mr. Dooley. I talked to those people; I saw them. I will not allow it to ever happen again."

"Lad, ye do not see clearly because you are a zealot. If we can cool the fires here, lad, there can be peace."

"And was getting rid of me how you would cool those fires?"

"Lad, I —"

"Do I need to show you Owl Face's sketch of Sean O'Farrell?" Fox Running said, recalling the name sung in the opening line of "The Rising of the Moon." "Do I need to tell you that the men I killed in Miles City met with him while I was there; that they came not for a drunken writer, but for me? I have killed men for less, Mr. Dooley."

"Lad, ye do not understand. No one was supposed to be hurt. Mairead promised me her brother would not harm ye. They were sent to tell ye that ye are facing odds you cannot beat. To pound sense into your thick skull! Ye started it and killed them! There needs to be order here, and not chaos! It was a noble gesture to turn the Cheyenne loose in the valley without a stick of a plan, but it was too late. There are other men already here. There must be another place where this would work better."

"And if this can be shown to fail . . ."

"It *has* failed, lad. Have we had fifty complaints in the months we've been here? They are rising, not falling. The army is unsure they want to work with us, which means that whatever you've done may all be wasted. Grand dreams do not always come true. Give up all this reservation talk, stop trying to fight men who can out-gun you fifty to one, go off with that girl and live your life. They will kill you, lad. You want too much of fighting! Think of what the army is doing. Has anyone asked in days about the Rawlins man or Amos Greene? If tackling the men who are killers — or who they think are killers — is too big a job for the army, how can you even think of fighting? Use your head! How did life end for that man Crazy Horse you glorify? He was nothing but a killer, lad, who killed people until he died that way!"

"Did Crazy Horse raid Boston and seek to kill children in their homes?" Fox Running retorted.

"Look at what happened to Evans when he was caught between, lad!"

Mairead broke in. "John has been protecting you, you ungrateful savage! He has tried to avoid anyone getting hurt, and there are those who have made life hard for him, but he never complained, because he spoke for you. Yes, I have intervened, because John is a good man, and he deserves to be happy. As John said, look at what happened to Captain Evans! That will happen to anyone who gets in the way!"

"Do you mean the man you helped kill?" said Fox Running, ice creeping into his tone. "Ruffled Badger told me a white handkerchief was tied to the window that afternoon. He said he had seen it before, now and then when the captain was there, but only when John was not present."

"You have no proof of anything!"

"That is not a denial. I leave it for Mr. Dooley to decide if you are safe and trustworthy," said Fox Running. "You are right that I have no proof. If I did, I would kill you."

Dooley glared. "Lad, watch the things ye say. I am to marry the lady."

Fox Running looked at him. "Mr. Dooley, I owe you a great deal. I know you honestly believe that what you are doing is for the best, and I am in the wrong, but I believe it is time we part ways. I do not trust *her*. I will follow the road I take; you will follow yours. I hope the spirits hold you closely, for even in this hour you are my friend, even though while you are under her spell, I cannot have you watching my back."

He glared at Mairead. "Tell your brother and all those who come for me that I will come for them, and that even if I have no one else, I will have the spirits that led three hundred Northern Cheyenne through thousands of soldiers, and I will not be defeated. If they kill me, Mr. Dooley, I will die knowing that for once in my life I fought for something more than myself."

For a moment, as he looked at the heartbroken face of John Dooley, Fox Running recalled songs in Boston, meals in Lame Deer, and trust that time and years had made valuable. All gone. He stepped back and slammed the door behind him.

The storm that had been building over the Tongue River Valley finally broke. Coyote Horse shied at the lightning. Fox Running did not. Even as the winds snapped tree branches and limbs, the slump-shouldered rider guided Coyote Horse through the downpour and across the rivulets that turned into creeks for a few hours. During the last storm, he and John Dooley had listened to rain hitting the cabin's roof, sheepishly grinned when the thunder and lightning grew close, and ridden it out. Another flash. Somewhere, a tree fell. Fox Running rode on, for this was now a world without dry places.

Mairead Cullihan assured John Dooley that Fox Running would soon regret his outburst and apologize and talked about wedding plans. She reminded him there was a chaplain at Fort Keogh.

There had been some difficult moments between them. Mairead admitted she had only met Annie Campbell Collins in passing at an event, but said she had dropped the name in hopes of being more easily accepted. She stressed that the kind of peace they wanted for the valley was exactly what her brother wanted as well and reminded Dooley of the risks he took to meet with her brother and his supporters.

"It is never easy being a peacemaker," she told him. "That is why I admire you so much."

Dooley stared into the fire as rain pounded on the cabin, turning Lame Deer into a quagmire. He was recalling the basement that held the detention rooms at the Indian School of Boston, a young and angry Cheyenne who took the worst beatings they could give and never gave an inch, and the way the two of them would sing Irish rebel songs together. That was the past. He looked down at the head of the woman nestled in his arm as they sat by the fire on the bench he had made for them and thought about the future.

August 31, 1883, Sickles, Montana
Sam Rickett had asked every day. Except for the day there was a hand-written note about the army man, every day he had the same answer. Until this one. The telegram had four numbers on it. That meant six of the ten people on his list would be spared. The other four would die. Now he could do the job he was paid for and leave this place behind. About time.

August 31, 1883, Lame Deer, Montana
Howard Porter noticed the horse outside his boardinghouse. It was the most beautiful horse he had ever seen. The glossy black mare eyed him casually after he descended. He had the oddest feeling the horse was waiting for him. His experiences with horses

had been uniformly negative, but he approached this one without fear.

"Isn't she beautiful?" It was the little girl, Spotted Dawn, who was more full of happiness than any ten children Porter had ever known in Boston. She sliced her hair to ribbons when trimming it, but she was so full of life that on her it looked good. She had refused to let Porter mope on the bad days and came by to cheer him up. She had insisted he take a meal with her family. The food was better than his landlady served. "She is a spirit horse, I can tell!"

Porter smiled indulgently. There were spirit animals everywhere, the Cheyenne said, whatever that meant. Living so close to nature, he supposed it made sense they had myths about the animals that were such a part of their lives. Harmless superstition. Spirit horses, they said, roamed the land and helped preserve the Northern Cheyenne. Well, this horse was certainly far above any other he had seen, so why not let her think it was something special?

"She wants us to ride her!" the little girl said.

Porter panicked. He had fallen off most horses he ever rode, and those were tame, saddled animals. This horse had no saddle. He would fall off and die!

The horse's eye turned upon him, as if reacting to his fears and assuring him there would be no tricks.

Spotted Dawn was already on the mare's back, even though she was far smaller than the horse. She reached down her hand. "Please, Busy Writer," she said. "She wants us to ride with her! Please? Don't let me ride her alone!"

Porter closed his eyes. Opened them. This was not a dream.

"Perhaps," he said, as a flurry of happily unfocused instructions about mounting descended upon him. He looked up and down the street to see if anyone would be watching him make a fool of himself. One deep swallow, and he tried the first leap of his life since he was a boy.

August 31, 1883, along Rosebud Creek
In her dream, the man entered Rides a Crow's lodge without ceremony. Once, he had been the Sweet Medicine Chief of the Northern Cheyenne and helped lead The People from Indian Territory to the Tongue River Valley. Now, Little Wolf lived in self-imposed exile, his punishment for having shot a fellow Cheyenne to death.

"Would it be good for The People if I were dead?" he asked in the dream.

"No," she replied instantly. "We may not be able to follow you any longer, but we love you."

"If a man killed me, would it be good or bad?"

"A white man?"

"Yes."

"The People would not tolerate this, Little Wolf," she said. "They would fight to the death to avenge you."

"Many would die."

"To kill those responsible, yes."

"I go to the Rosebud every morning at dawn. I pray there. I think of the road to the Milky Way there. I ask the spirits a question. I wonder what answer the spirits might send, and if it is not the one I have expected, I will let the spirits decide."

The dream faded, and she was awake, with the child staring. Rides a Crow wondered if she had spoken aloud while asleep or whether at some level Wrapped in a Blanket shared in her visions.

"Put sticks on the fire, little one," Rides a Crow told her. "The spirits and I must talk long this night, for dawn comes soon."

Howard Porter was certain that, despite cheating death in his successful attempt to mount the horse, he would fall off and die somewhere along the path to wherever they were going. But as the horse walked gently, he learned how to sway with the animal as it moved through Lame Deer. Cheyenne men, women, and children waved. They smiled and called greetings.

"They know this is a special horse, and if we are on it, we must be special!" Spotted Dawn chirped, telling Porter that some of the Cheyenne phrases were blessings on them both.

Porter realized neither of them was actually guiding the horse. He had thought the girl held the reins, but there were none to hold. He thought about jumping off, but feared that would mean a broken leg or a busted skull, so great was the height of the mare's back. Spotted Dawn's chatter had faded as they approached a place with a low stone wall around it. He recognized it. This was where they had buried Evans, and the entire Cheyenne community had turned out for the funeral of an army officer.

There was a wooden cross for Evans, and also a stone. At one time, when he first came to Lame Deer, Porter had wondered if the Indians used the stone for human sacrifice.

"It is there so everyone will understand," said Spotted Dawn, as if reading his mind.

"This is where Dull Knife is buried."

Dull Knife! The man responsible for depredations all the way across Kansas; the chief who helped fight Custer; the man who was assumed to be dead and returned to life after the escape from Fort Robinson; the man who told his people to be good farmers when they finally returned home.

"The spirit horse wanted you to see this," the girl said, hopping down from the horse to sit on the wall, dangling her bare feet. "Mama has told me why Dull Knife is a hero. Should I tell you? I think the spirit horse wants you to know, and that is why she brought us here."

"Yes," said Porter, following suit and sitting on the wall. "I think I would like to hear it. I think I need to hear it."

Chapter Sixteen

September 5, 1883, Lame Deer, Montana
The fine day was lost on John Dooley as he walked Mairead to his cabin after her school lessons were over. Last week's storm had been followed by days when the air was thick and heavy, but another storm the night before had swept all that away. Now the air was clear and the trees greener.

She only kept the children a few hours, understanding that boys and girls did not take lightly to being indoors until the weather was too unpleasant to do anything else. Then she would walk home with him and make dinner before he walked her back to the school building as dusk was falling.

It was a pleasant routine, but this day his mind drifted to Fox Running, as it had often in the past few days. The Cheyenne had spent so much of his life fighting everything that stood in his way, he had never learned there were some battles he could not fight.

Dooley had hoped he could somehow bridge the divide between what the young man wanted and what was realistic, but either he had failed, or it was a chasm too wide and deep to be spanned. Each day brought him a different conclusion. He had no idea where Fox Running was. He had asked Spotted Dawn to let him know if the lad was seen, but the little girl and her friends had not laid eyes on him in the week since he left. The girl was full of the marvel of the spirit horse, and the funny man it came for, but nothing else.

Now, however, she was running towards them. She must have seen Fox Running! Dooley felt conflicting emotions. He missed the younger man, for they had been friends, but he did not want another argument. He waited to hear the news, then realized the girl was focused on Mairead.

"Mary Ed! Mary Ed!"

Displeasure passed swiftly across Mairead's face before it was replaced with a smile.

Spotted Dawn reached them. "I forgot! I forgot! Walking Wolf brought me a message for you from your friend!" she chattered, handing Mairead a folded piece of paper.

Mairead's brow furrowed as she scanned what Dooley could see were several lines scrawled in pencil. "What is it?" he asked her.

"Thank you for delivering this," Mairead told Spotted Dawn, with a slight edge in her voice. "Remember we said in private? That means when we are alone. Now go to your lodge and do your chores."

The small girl's ever-present smile faded.

"On wi' ye now, Grasshopper," Dooley said, squatting down to be face to face with the girl and showing her a smile he did not feel. "When the chores end, dinner begins!"

"Thank you, Big Bear," she said, hugging him, and then darted off.

They walked on in silence. The activities of Tom Cullihan were a subject they avoided. Dooley had tried to reach out to the men working with her brother in hopes of finding a way to reach a peaceful solution, and at Mairead's urging, but with Fox Running now gone, he had no interest in the ongoing battle over the future of the Cheyenne and their quest for a reservation. That was a fight for others, not him. He disliked the former soldiers and vowed he would tolerate them if he must, but never join them. The lad had not understood he would never betray their friendship. Dooley was determined he was going to find happiness, and if others wanted to throw away their lives in hate, they could do so!

As they reached the cabin, he held the door open. Mairead entered, unpinning her hat and tossing it on the table before taking the pins out of her hair and letting it fall loose to her shoulders, just the way John liked it.

"That paper seemed to upset you. From the wee girl. Was the note bad news?" he asked as he went to build up the fire.

"It was nothing that should upset us, John. We have so little time alone."

Dooley busied himself with the fire. There was tension in Mairead's tone. Tension only meant one thing. "From your brother it was?"

"Well, if you must know. When Fox Running left here after saying those horrible things, I warned Tom he might be coming after them."

"But I thought we agreed . . ."

"I sent the note before we talked, my dear," she said, smiling. "He is my brother, after all."

Dooley felt uneasy. Although he could understand the bonds of family, her claim was not quite how he recalled the conversation. "What happened, Mairead?"

"Nothing to distress yourself over. No, nothing ever happens to that Indian!"

She shook her hair again after her outburst and smiled at Dooley. "Would you like pie tonight, John? The apples that grow here are not New England apples, but they will have to do, I fear! We should bring some decent apples back here after our honeymoon."

Dooley felt a hole growing inside. He could sense when a lie was in the air — and not the harmless ones a woman tells a man. This was something darker. He asked again.

"Apparently, he went to see that wild woman, Cut Sky."

"And?" Something was wrong. Fox Running sought out Cut Sky the way lightning sought out dead trees, to ignite a fire. That alone would not generate a note that had so obviously upset Mairead.

"And what? Your friend is still among the living." Her voice hardened. "Which is more than I can say for those he killed escaping from Tom and his men. They wounded him, at least. Tom was sure of it."

"He's hurt?"

"Tom is fine."

"I mean the lad."

"You mean an Indian brave who would kill me if I was not under your protection. You will protect me, won't you? Oh dearest, do you know how much even the mention of his name scares me?"

Her voice quivered. He thought he saw wetness in her eyes. Dooley wanted to be done with all of it — all the hatred, all the violence.

"Ahh, lass," he said in resignation at the mess life had become. He took a step towards her. She poked the tiny piece of white paper sticking out of the left sleeve of her dress further under the cuff before lifting her head with a smile for him.

A wall of suspicion hit Dooley in the face.

"Can I see yon note?" he said. "If another man is sending you sweet things, I want to be sure I tell the man he is poaching."

She stepped back.

"John. Really. Don't be silly. It was from Tom. Silly men playing silly games. Let them all go fight each other. We have better things to do with our lives."

Her eyes weighed the impact of her words. She risked a step closer. Another.

Dooley's right hand shot out to grip her left wrist. With his free hand, he pried loose the note. He read it out loud. " 'You were right. He came to see her. Your ambush almost worked. I think I hit him. He killed Kelly and Farley, wounded Crothers. Get more information out of that Irishman. We need to finish this.' "

Silence followed. For just a moment, Dooley hoped a rational explanation might be forthcoming. Then he realized he was only fooling himself.

"Ye set men to kill him." Along with dismay, Dooley's voice held a trace of wonder. "Ye told me they never wanted him dead."

"After the horrible things he said, how can you even think of letting him live? You know as well as I that one day he will be there at the doorway with those two guns of his in his hands. They are all unable to control themselves! Some of them try, but they are still savages, John. I know at that school you pitied him, and you tried to do right for him out here, but he'll always be just another brave on the warpath, no matter what."

She paused, as if trying to find the right words to placate Dooley. "In some ways, John, it's a mercy to kill him. He's a wild animal who has become a danger to himself and everyone around him. Now, will you get the flour for me? It's on the top shelf."

"Ye lied to me. Ye used me," Dooley said. The voice in his head that sounded much like Fox Running, and that had never stilled since their fight, was growing louder now. "Ye're with them and not with me. He was right. I was a fool! Ye fooled me!"

"You're talking out of your head. You don't know what you're saying. I know this has been hard on you, because you tried to be his friend, but soon everything will be settled. You know how I feel about you, John." She touched his cheek.

He stepped back. "I want you to write to your brother. Or we'll go see him. I won't have Fox Running killed. I can't allow that. Reservations and politics and that nonsense is one thing. My friend is another. It's early enough we can ride to Sickles tonight."

"John, I don't think you understand. There are so many people involved, and this is so much bigger than you know. Even if I wanted to, I couldn't change it. Gears have already begun turning that cannot be stopped. An inspector is here now. He'll send a report to Washington that the Cheyenne are violent and up in arms, which they will be when Fox Running and those chiefs of theirs get what they have coming. Then there will be peace."

She moved toward the table where she'd left her purse. "Don't waste your time on him. The Indians have to die to make way for civilization. Some of them also deserve it. Fox Running is one of them. Tom's uncle hired someone to make sure of that, along with the other ringleaders who are in the way. Tom has a list. It's out of anyone's hands now and is nothing that should trouble us."

"No, Mairead, no. Fox Running trusted me. I'm going to warn him, wherever he is! I will deal with you later." He started toward the door.

"No, you will not." It was not the words that stopped him but the click of the hammer on the small revolver in her hand. She was pointing it steadily at him.

Dooley had been reaching for the door latch. He froze as he slowly came to grips with the extent to which he had been betrayed.

"Mairead, whatever your brother is making you do, turn away from it. More bloodshed, more death, 'tis all he wants. The dead won't bring the peace our children need."

"Spare me," she snarled, sweeping the pie dish off the table with her left hand while the gun remained steady in her right. Dooley watched the shards fly, then turned back to see a face he knew and loved lose its warmth and change into a snake-eyed visage he had never seen before.

"John, you are a sad and simple soul. Let me open your eyes before you meet with a tragic accident. My 'brother' is not my brother. Tom is my husband. He and I share a common purpose — that the Cheyenne who have slaughtered whites for so many years get what they deserve, and that this valley is not handed to them on a silver platter. When we came out from Boston, we knew all about your little agency with your Indian friend, and we knew just what could drive you two apart! Once this new inspector's report is submitted — and there is no chance of a reservation for those Indians, and your little agency is no more — I can stop pretending to be some simpering, silly woman who actually likes this flea-infested, dust-ravaged hole and go back East to live like a civilized person. Once we collect what we will be paid, that is. In another world you might have been a sweet, dull man to marry, but I do not want sweet and dull in my life, especially the dull part."

Dooley stood frozen, unbelieving. "You never . . ."

"You are so lonely, it was simple to let you see what you wanted to see. I am sorry you put that Indian ahead of me. It was inevitable some accident would forestall our marriage, but I had hoped someone else would do the work. Men are unreliable. You were too good for your own survival, John. These people look up to you. I am sorry."

"Ye will not succeed."

"Goodbye, John."

Dooley reached for the fireplace poker as the first of three shots rang out.

September 6, 1883, along Rosebud Creek
Sam Rickett lugged the heavy Sharps rifle with him. It would kill at ten times the distance, but it was his job to be sure. Rosebud Creek was swollen from the recent rains as it raced along in muddy swirls over downed tree limbs. It was no secret to him that the man he was killing was both famous and infamous, but it meant nothing. It was a job.

Little Wolf rose before dawn, as always, with the feeling of caked visions on his brain — the feeling that often came when he was leading The People home. The visions, the dream life, the connection to the spirit world — he had walked away from them when he did what was right, yet still they came unbidden. He wondered more than once if the dust of the Spirit Walker had rubbed off on him.

He slogged through the muddy track. The early September heat would dry it within a day, but the hot days were nearing the end. In a few weeks, the moon would begin to turn the waters cold, and then hard, and then The People would endure winter. They would have their own corn to eat this year. It was not buffalo meat, but The People were alive because of it.

The creek rushed like a wild young man, overflowing the place he usually sat. He found another. The log was damp, but what were wet britches in a life like his? He looked to the east, where the sun would soon rise in the parti-colored sky. He closed his eyes. He began to pray.

Sam Rickett watched Little Wolf. He knew the man's story, envied his harmony in disgrace. At least he'd die happy. Rickett put the rifle to his shoulder and sighted on Little Wolf's head through the scope. Nope. Branch in the way. He needed to move. The flood had changed everything just a little, and he wanted this to be one clean, perfect shot. He had planned it out, which target in which order. The man he never expected to see on the list would come next. Then Two Moon. Then the one he had been watching the closest, and fearing the most.

At last. A clean line of sight. He raised the rifle again. Perfect. He loaded the weapon. It was a one-shot model, but one shot was all a man needed with a bullet that size. Now he was ready.

As he sighted the gun, he realized he was not alone. He had not heard footsteps. Little

Wolf was still sitting with his eyes closed. Rickett turned to see who had approached.

The wolf looking back had the most intelligent eyes of any animal Rickett had ever seen, as though it knew what he was doing.

"Git, critter," he said.

The wolf stayed. For a moment, Rickett thought about throwing something at the animal to get it to move. Its stare was unnerving. He took a quick step toward it, as if in threat. Instead of backing up, the wolf moved closer. It was staring up at Rickett with the most malevolent glare the gunfighter had ever seen.

Rickett had a rifle that could kill at more than half a mile. He had a Colt at his hip. He knew both were useless against a creature on the verge of springing for his throat. The man who had faced down more than thirty men knew fear.

Then his mind began responding to his emotions. He was letting the Cheyenne talk of spirits get to him. This wolf was an animal. Nothing more. One swift kick, and it would turn tail and run.

Then it growled — a long, slow, deadly sound. It knew what he was thinking. It was warning him.

Rickett was paid to kill, not die. Part of his mind told him the wolf was protecting the former Cheyenne leader, while another part said the animal was defending territory, nothing more. They did that. Just because it had never shown up before didn't mean anything.

Rickett looked across the muddy creek. Little Wolf still sat in prayer.

The wolf's muscles were tensed to spring. Death glared up at him.

Rickett told himself he needed to be practical; that he was not afraid; that backing away from the edge was the right decision for a man in the business of death.

"I'll be back," he told the Indian and the wolf. "I'll be back."

Rickett slung the Sharps over his right shoulder. The animal backed away. Rickett thought of using the Colt to kill it, but the gunfire would alert Little Wolf and probably others. He knew the Indian lived apart from the rest.

Dawn would come again tomorrow. No one came or went. Little Wolf would be there.

As the sun crested the hills to the east, Rickett walked into the brush. He needed to get to Lame Deer quickly. His second target's routine was predictable. He took one look back, in case. The wolf was still there. Watching. Waiting. Rickett moved into the deeper brush to get his horse and ride.

Long after he had gone, Little Wolf opened his eyes. Across the fast-flowing creek he saw the wolf looking back. He recalled the spirit wolf of the journey, the things that were said. This animal could be one and the same. He felt joy for a reason he did not understand.

"Greetings, old spirit friend," Little Wolf called. "May the spirits bless you."

The wolf barked a greeting back, melted into the bushes and trees, and vanished from sight.

Sam Rickett stalked through the lodges and rude buildings of Lame Deer. The big Irishman never broke his routine. Every morning he walked to the school, and every afternoon he walked the teacher to his home. However, the school was not in session. The teary-eyed little Cheyenne girl insisted she did not know where the teacher had gone.

He reached the cabin. He had always believed it was bad luck to go back to the scene of a shooting. He couldn't help but look at the window. No signal this time, but he didn't expect one. His Colt in his right hand, he lifted the latch with the other and shoved the door open.

The cabin was empty. There was blood — a lot of it, too fresh to have been from that army officer they wanted dead. Someone else had died here. He wondered if someone had done his job for him. He moved on, shutting the door behind him. He was feeling the edge of frustration. The day was not going as planned. When plans fell apart, luck walked in, and he did not want anyone on his list to be lucky this day.

Two Moon always had a crowd around his lodge. This day was no different. Rickett had known from the start this would be the biggest risk, because Two Moon's emergence from his lodge varied widely day to day. Between the crowds, nearby lodges, and the open space where the lodges were packed, he did not have the option of finding a safe, distant place and then picking off the man when he emerged.

Instead, he told one of the women he assumed were wives that he was from the East to see the chief. Once he entered the lodge, he would have his opportunity. None of the men around the lodge ever had guns, so in the confusion that would follow, anyone trying to stop him would be easy to kill.

He waited. And waited. Indians had no proper sense of time, he knew. He was getting itchy. He still had work to do.

Finally, he was called and strode into the lodge, ducking his head. As his eyes adjusted to the dimness, he saw that next to the plainly dressed chief opposite him was the same wolf he had seen by Little Wolf's praying spot. The simple plan he had worked out in his head died. This was not a wolf marking territory. This was another warning. This was whatever ungodly spirits protected these Indians telling him that they would take his life before he would touch their leaders. Rickett had learned from the wild Comanches much about Indian religion. Their spirits came to Earth with a vengeance when they did so. This was not killing cowboys and drunks, or even men for pay. This was a fight he would lose, and one where he would feel teeth tearing at his skin and his soul. No money on Earth was worth this.

The wolf rose. Its lips quivered, showing its teeth. Rickett mumbled something about what a great Injun the chief was and backed out. He looked over his shoulder as he left. The wolf was not following him. Rickett got the message: he could live, or he could try to kill men who were protected by something beyond anything he knew.

One more name. He would give that one

a try, but if that didn't work out — and he wasn't entirely sure it would, because he had to find the man all over again — a sensible man would leave this place and go back to Texas, or find a spot in New Mexico or Colorado where no one knew him. And the people who hired him could go to the devil, which was where he was heading if he did not get away from the Tongue River Valley.

September 6, 1883, Sickles, Montana
The main street in Sickles was barely two hundred yards long. Fox Running waited on the wooden duckboards that lined the entrance to the general store. He could not explain how he knew the time for his moment to face death had come, but he knew. Coyote Horse knew, too. The horse had nuzzled him a few times as they waited. He did not bother stabling the animal. He might need him. Or not.

The man riding lazily in the saddle into Sickles checked his mount's stride briefly when he saw the Indian. At least this made it easy, but it made him wonder who was pursuing whom. Rickett saw Fox Running pet the horse that was loosely tied to the rail and run his hand down its mane before looking steadily at him. He dismounted and led his animal next to the roan. The Indian was short and not much to look at in a batch of cast-off rags. He could shoot, though. Rickett had seen it.

Fox Running recalled seeing the man dozens of times. "Thank you for putting your horse near mine. This way, the animals will be safe," he said.

Rickett did not reply. He was not used to conversation with men before he killed them.

"What is your name, friend?" Fox Running asked.

"Why?" replied Rickett.

"For your grave."

"Sam Rickett."

"Texas," replied Fox Running. He knew more than that. Rickett had killed more than thirty men in Texas alone. The newspapers had made him famous, even more famous than the Cheyenne Kid, as the deadliest gun for hire in Texas. He had never been wounded, let alone defeated. A lick of unease coursed through Fox Running that needed to be stifled. "You were famous there. You should have stayed. Then you would not die here in Montana."

"Big talk."

"Let us get this over with," Fox Running said, as though the gunfight was an item on a list of things to accomplish. "I have much to do. Do you prefer one side or the other? I only ask that we stay away from the horses. This is not their fight."

Rickett had fought men who were drunk, who were angry, who were determined and deadly. He had never fought anyone this nonchalant before, as though stepping out to kill or be killed was just another day's work. He wondered if the spirits he had faced in Lame Deer would protect this Cheyenne, too. Then he dismissed the fear as the product of too little sleep and bad food. He pointed to his right, toward the hotel.

"I do not wish to kill you," said the Indian. "I do not know you. I do not hate you. You may still leave."

"Just business," replied Rickett. "Got hired to do a job. Planning on keeping my word." The gray-tipped mustache twitched in what might have been the beginning of a smile. "Happy to oblige if you don't want to kill anybody."

One side of Fox Running's mouth jerked in reaction to the gunman's words. He turned his back on Rickett and walked slowly to the left as Rickett found a place he liked to the right.

As the low-key drama was building, the

people of Sickles found windows and doorways. A crowd gathered by the Copper Penny saloon, well down the street out of range.

Rickett's long-barreled .44 had a longer range and better accuracy than the guns most cowboys carried. A man needed an advantage to stay alive. The Indian would be expecting to fire away at fifteen or twenty feet. Rickett would get in the first shot well before that.

Except the little Cheyenne wasn't waiting. He'd started moving almost as soon as Rickett found a spot the gunfighter liked. Give that man credit for nerve. Shame the men Rickett respected the most were some of the ones he had put in the ground — the ones who stood tall and were men to the end. He reminded himself: *kill him first, then tell yourself he was brave.*

Fox Running walked slowly. One of Cullihan's men had managed to hit his right foot in the ambush. Fox Running ignored the pain, as the limp became part of the rhythm of his approach. Like drums sounding for war, there was a pulse that built within as his eyes focused on the man who wanted to kill him. His hand would do what it knew how to do, as if a separate being. He did not understand what flowed through him;

he accepted it and used it. Once, some time back, he had dived into a deep lake in Wyoming. The way he had heard sounds while he was under the water reminded him of moments like this. Everything was distant. Muted. Unimportant.

The spirits had brought him here. He had come to believe they would lead him to do what was best for The People. Poor John Dooley could never understand. *No. Not now. Focus.* He had never before faced a man he knew was faster and deadlier with a gun. *Cut Sky . . . No. Not now.*

Ice coated Rickett's nerves. He'd been thrown off balance by that wolf, but this was his world. He owned any street he walked. Maybe two more steps.

Fox Running felt the flow of energy within him. Yes! There was always a way. The air felt sharp and clear as he breathed it in. His hands felt light. His eyes keen. Just a few more steps.

Rickett reached down. The barrel of the .44 was clearing the holster. The flash of sunlight by his eyes jarred him. The gun wavered as he ducked. The knife sailed wide well over his head as he leveled his gun at the Cheyenne, hearing the Indian's gun explode seconds after he pulled the trigger.

The spectators at the Copper Penny

almost needed to cover their ears as the two men traded shots. They saw Fox Running bent over but still firing. Rickett was weaving in place until one final shot hit him. He staggered and fell.

The dust of the street had a dark line on it as Fox Running moved, limping from a bullet that had hit his right ankle. Blood flowed from his left arm, struck twice and now dangling as though useless. One shot had nipped his left side. He was certain a bullet had nicked his neck. Another would have shot off his hat, had he been wearing one.

Rickett had four bullets in him — one that had skimmed his left thigh, one in his stomach, one that had nicked his right calf, and the final one that had plowed into his chest.

Fox Running staggered to where Rickett lay. Dead. He limped past the Texas killer's body. Past. He tried to bend but fell to his knees as he picked up the knife he had thrown. Gasping for breath, he looked back down the street, where the crowd still waited.

"Coyote Horse," he whispered. "I need you."

The crowd had started moving closer to Rickett when the Indian's horse bucked by the post where it had been tied. When the reins were free, it walked to where the Cheyenne gunman knelt bleeding, droplets leaking from his left hand to the dirt. Some of the witnesses insisted the horse knelt for the rider to mount; others claimed that was a tall tale. But all said that, once he was on the horse's back, he sat tall, blood matted but proud, as the animal clip-clopped down the street until horse and rider were lost to view.

September 7, 1883, along Rosebud Creek
Howard Porter had tried to brush some of the dirt off his suit. He had three times tried to gather the nerve, and this was his fourth.

"Please do not go away again," sang the voice of Rides a Crow as she came walking down the path to stand before him with a welcoming smile on her face. "It has been forever since I bit off the head of a man. Him, perhaps, not so long," she added, gesturing at the wolf that dozed in the morning sun.

Porter was uncertain how to reply. No words seemed right.

"There is much you wish to understand. I hope I may teach you," she said. "I am very happy you have come. I wanted to speak with you, but it had to be you who wanted to hear what I have to say."

Porter found himself returning her smile. What had seemed a silly conversation a few moments ago now made perfect sense. He did want to learn. He needed to understand.

September 7, 1883, Tongue River Breaks
"Fool!"

Cut Sky was scolding as she worked. "The bullet went through your arm. It almost hit the bones. I do not think it broke them, but it should have."

Fox Running had come to the same conclusion as he pitched in the saddle on the ride to Blue Feather's camp. He had been wounded before but never with this level of pain. He could not tell how damaged the arm was because it hurt so much.

The wound in his side was minor. An inch or two the wrong way and he would have been dead, a word Cut Sky seemed inordinately fond of using as she scolded him. "And look at this!" She pulled at his hair. He yelped. "It is the hair by my neck, Cut Sky. My head will not turn that far."

"Something cut a lot of this, you fool warrior! He shot you in your hair! Do you realize how close you came to being killed?"

"Very close," replied Fox Running. "Are you going to bandage my hair?"

He was sitting on a log as she tended him. She angrily squatted down at his eye level.

"Do you not care that you almost died? You could have bled to death. You will not walk right for days! Is creating this reservation more important than your life?"

"I do not wish to die, Cut Sky, but I will not run from it if it is required."

Blue Feather appeared. Cut Sky looked up at him. "Father! Will you talk sense to this . . . this . . ."

"I believe talking sense to either of you is much like telling the wind to blow backwards," Blue Feather observed.

"What have you learned?" Fox Running asked anxiously.

Blue Feather reported that Owl Face had ridden in from Sickles just moments ago. Rickett had been staying in Sickles for weeks and would ride out for hours. He kept to himself, and no one really knew what he did, but no one cared much, either. Most of the townsfolk believed he was scouting for the army, or the railroad. When they went through the few things in his saddlebags, they found drawings of several people in and around Sickles — including Captain Evans, Two Moon, Little Wolf, Fox Running, Rides a Crow, and Golden Turtle. Each sketch was given a number, but not named. Rickett had saved a message dated from a few days before Evans was killed that simply had his number on it.

"A few days ago, he got another telegram with four numbers on it," Blue Feather explained. "Three of them belonged to you, Two Moon, and Little Wolf. There was one more. Your friend John Dooley."

"Mr. Dooley? But he was working with them!"

"Perhaps not as much as you thought," Blue Feather said. "I have sent to Lame Deer to learn more. If this man killed Two Moon . . ."

"He did not," replied Fox Running.

"How do you know?"

"Coyote Horse is a spirit horse. The spirit horses and spirit wolf were anxious today, but if the chief was dead, they would be distraught."

"You ride a spirit horse?" Blue Feather asked.

"He was a gift from Rides a Crow," Fox Running explained. "I am not sure if she wanted me to better connect to the spirits or to have them keep an eye on me."

"Well, someone should!" Cut Sky interrupted. "Enough talk. Enough war. Enough guns. You are going to eat stew, and then you are going to rest. Father, you will not put new ideas of foolishness in his head, because if you get him shot after eating my stew and it all drains out onto the ground, I shall be very angry!"

September 24, 1883, Tongue River Breaks
Fox Running took a deep breath and swallowed his nerves. He would rather face Rickett again than do what came next. His left arm was still weak, but it was usable if he could endure the pain.

"Cut Sky." She was laboring over the process of making a buckskin shirt for him for the winter and had banished him from her father's lodge so she might work uninterrupted.

"Out!" she said. "Or do you want to freeze?"

"We need to talk."

She knew the tone. He had been idle for almost a week. She had expected he would want to go search for Dooley, who, along with his woman, was missing. No one had seen them in days, even before Rickett tried to kill Little Wolf and Two Moon.

"Two Moon asked the army to search for your friend," she said. "What can you do that they cannot?"

There was silence. Then he said, "I am not going to look for Mr. Dooley. I am going to finish what these men who left the army started." She drew breath to argue. He held up his left hand, a pained look on his face. "We cannot wait. They know everything they planned has failed. We know where they are. We need to find them before they scatter. I have a plan."

"Is this as good as your plan that led to Bigelow getting killed, or that almost got you killed when you went to scare Sanders and failed? Or the one that almost got you killed facing that gunman?"

"One teacher at the Indian school used to tell a joke that in some famous man's plays, the entire plot was that everyone died. This is a better plan, and perhaps at some school one day, someone will learn about it. Wait until you hear it."

CHAPTER SEVENTEEN

September 25, 1883, Tongue River Breaks, Montana

Blue Feather recalled what it had felt like to be a warrior. Exciting. Fearful. It was so different a life that he wondered at times if he had actually lived it. He had ridden a horse rarely since his accident. He had grown heavy, and mounting with a leg that refused to work was humbling except when it was totally humiliating.

He was not sure how this venture would end. He could fire a gun. There was nothing wrong with his hands and eyes. But he had not fired from the back of a horse in so long, he would be unable to hit anything he aimed at. If this plan of Fox Running's went the least bit awry, he would be one of those who would never see another day.

He had thought of how to draw these men into an ambush. He knew them; he could fool them. Then Fox Running blasted those illusions to shreds, refusing to allow Cut Sky's father to risk his life. Blue Feather had allowed this, and for all that he reproached himself as a coward, he also knew the younger man was right when he said the risks of failure outweighed the odds of success.

He had, however, conspired with his daughter and the man she appeared to be willing to risk her life with as they planned how to carry out what had to be the most foolish escapade he had ever known. Fox Running, who he was certain had sustained more injuries than the young man claimed, had infused Blue Feather's men with the spirit to risk themselves. Even men who were usually immune to fancy words were ready to fight. Owl Face had not believed, when first told, that Fox Running was even alive, let alone planning something that Owl Face ended up volunteering for, even at his age.

Did they really have a choice? Perhaps they could live in the shadows where black and white overlapped into gray and eke out a living in the years to come, but whether they were full-blood Northern Cheyenne or mongrels who were part this and part that and all of nothing, they all knew that if the Northern Cheyenne could cling to their toehold in the Tongue River Valley, there might be hope yet that life could be good. It would never be what it was when the Plains were free of railroads and wires, but to live openly in dignity was a call too loud for anyone to ignore. As long as men who would and could kill at any time were free to do so, no one was safe.

And so he planned and plotted, hiding his fears from Cut Sky, so she would not tell him he should leave this foolish scheme to younger men. Oh, it was nice at times to have men call him the Bandit King as though he could make goods appear from thin air, and he ate better than most while he traded in this and that. But, as Fox Running had spent more and more time with his daughter, Blue Feather had come to realize that he longed for just a taste of that fire that seemed to consume them both.

The spirits had granted him many good things in a life that could have ended years ago. He asked them to grant him the courage to at least act on the outside as though he were all his daughter would want, even if on the inside there was a man wondering why he was risking his life for the same kind of idealistic notion for which he had mocked so many for so long.

■ ■ ■ ■

September 27, 1883, Wolf Mountain, Montana

Cut Sky was ready. Her left hand rested in Fox Running's good one as they looked at the cabin nestled amid the slopes. Fox Running was wishing for one cannon that could wipe out all its occupants and end any risk to Cut Sky.

"This dream. The People. The price is high," she said.

"Nothing good comes cheaply," came his rote reply. His eyes were focused on the landscape, measuring distances to know how fine he could cut what was to come and survive it.

They were quiet as they looked down at the small ranch where, by the count of Blue Feather's scouts, at least twenty men were living. Fox Running did not ask how Blue Feather knew this, or so much about them that he could outline a plan to trap them. The Bandit King's secrets and whatever as-yet-undiscovered sins his past — and present — might contain were not Fox Running's to probe.

He felt worn and tired. His left arm was almost useless when it came to shooting a gun, and he could not walk very far. The dark circles beneath his eyes were prominent again. He felt so weary he wanted it to end but knew he had to share with Cut Sky and all of Blue Feather's men a determination and energy that, on this day, he did not have.

"Believe, Cut Sky. Believe." He let go of her hand. "And shoot straight."

She watched him slowly ride up to the cabin. She was unsure about his first request, but she could guarantee the second.

"Hello, the house!"

Fox Running knew he was within rifle range but trusted that curiosity and overconfidence would stay the shot that could kill him. The smile on his face was not from mirth; it bloomed unbidden when he risked everything, as though doing that was the greatest joy he could have.

The door to the house opened. Fox Running could see men at the glass-less windows.

"My name is Fox Running," he called out. "I hear you have business with me."

"Names are cheap," the man in the doorway called out. "Come closer so we can see it's you!"

"Why do you not all come out of your hiding place?" Fox Running called back. "Are all of you afraid of one Cheyenne? Do you think I can do to you what my people did to Custer? Or are all white soldiers really cowards?"

He continued inventing whatever insults came to mind to inflame them. The man in the doorway moved out a few steps. Other men crowded behind him.

Finally, the man in the doorway interrupted him. "Heard enough."

"I have much more to say, Thomas!"

"How do you know my name?"

"You know mine. It is only fair I know yours. Your so-called sister told me." Fox Running paused for effect. "Before I scalped your wife."

The final word had barely come out of his mouth when the guns opened from the window. Coyote Horse needed no urging. The animal had already danced away, moving back far enough to make the range difficult for all but the best shots.

"Coyote Horse, when the spirit horses gather, this will be a tale to tell."

In his mind, he was sure he heard Cut Sky screaming above the gunfire as he charged the cabin, firing a Winchester in what he was certain were wild shots as he galloped towards it and then away. He looked behind him to see men streaming out of the house and toward the corral where their horses were kept. He reined in Coyote Horse, awkwardly reloaded the rifle, and sent a few more shots their way. Then, as the riders headed toward him, he rode into the woods and along the trail. They could not find the trap without a guide, after all.

As Coyote Horse cut sharply to the right, Fox Running heard the first volley. The shots nipped leaves over his head. Blue Feather's men were better at stealing than shooting, but from the cover of the woods, they were firing on targets that were not firing back — the men chasing Fox Running into the trap he had prepared for them.

Then he heard more guns. Too many! Something was wrong. Coyote Horse dodged and picked his way through the trees; low hanging branches left their marks on Fox Running's face.

As he rode unseen in the thick woods, he saw what had happened. Cullihan's men had formed into two groups. Blue Feather's men attacked the first group and closed in to finish them off. Their lack of patience was their undoing as the second group attacked. Fox Running still had some shells in the rifle, so he opened up from the heavy timber on Cullihan's men. Luck was with him. He hit one.

The man he took to be Cullihan saw him and pointed. Fox Running turned Coyote Horse away. They would follow him and leave Blue Feather's men for later.

One tree shivered as bullets struck it. He galloped out of the woods. The change from the shade of the trees to the bright sunlight of the clearing disoriented him at first. There was a rocky outcrop to the left, uphill across a rock-strewn field. He made for it, dismounted, and swatted Coyote Horse, telling the animal to run for its life.

He limped up the rocky hill. A volley behind him made him cry out as Coyote Horse stumbled. Then the animal righted itself and was gone out of range.

Cullihan's men were yelling as they dismounted to chase Fox Running up the slope. Cut Sky materialized from the trees, one rifle in her hands, another at her feet. She sent two shots at the men, making them take cover as she picked up the second rifle and ran to join Fox Running.

He rose from his hiding place.

"No!" Cut Sky pointed behind him.

Three men on horseback had ridden through the trees to the top of the slope. They started down, picking their way through the rocks as they closed in from above while a handful of other men closed in from below.

"Uphill or downhill?" he asked her.

"Downhill." She pointed at the larger group as she traded the 1860 Henry rifle she had carried for the Sharps rifle she had dropped. Owl Face had stolen it from the things Rickett left behind. She dug a bullet from the bag slung at her waist, locked the bullet in place with the bolt, took quick aim, and fired.

The boom of the gun deafened them both, and the recoil jarred Cut Sky. One of the men advancing up the hill pitched backwards. The others paused again to take cover.

Fox Running stood back to back with Cut Sky behind the rocks. One rifle bullet whined above his head, fired by a man coming down from the top of the hill. It was a long range to be accurate with a pistol, but Fox Running had been firing guns since he was a child. He aimed low and pulled the trigger. The bullet sparked against the rocks at the feet of the center rider's horse. It shied, hitting the animal next to it, which reared. The next round of shots from the men went wide.

Cut Sky fired twice more with the Sharps rifle. Still the men came.

"Take the riders!" Fox Running called.

They changed positions.

The men coming down could not move faster for fear of their horses losing their footing. Cut Sky killed one and narrowly missed a second. The two remaining riders dismounted, moving closer now as they used rocks for cover.

"They are coming!" she called.

"Take my other pistol!"

The men advancing up the hill took advantage of the lull in firing to charge Fox Running and Cut Sky's position. Their shots while running went wide. Fox Running had time to aim and used it. Soon only two men were coming from below. Cut Sky fired the pistol every time anything moved. At least one more man went down.

Their pistols clicked on empty barrels. Cut Sky dove for the Henry, which still had shells. Fox Running drew his knife and tried to charge the two men who were covering the final few open feet, but his right leg buckled when a bullet sprayed rocks at his injured ankle.

A rifle blast in his ear singed his temple. He turned to see a man advancing on Cut Sky. The knife flew. The blade sunk deep into the advancing man's right thigh. His pistol tumbled down next to him.

Cut Sky had launched herself at one attacker. Fox Running reached for the gun that had fallen near him. A bullet struck his right hand. The world turned white with pain. Something stung his shoulder. His left hand clawed a man's blood-slick leg, pain radiating through his arm as he tried to pull the man down. He could hear screaming and wondered whose voice it was.

His wounded right hand touched metal. His fingers were swollen and clumsy, but he turned with the pistol in his unsteady grip and pointed it at a man standing over Cut Sky as her knife flashed in the sunlight. He pulled the trigger. Once. Twice. Even with a bad hand it was hard to miss at that range. The man went down.

Fox Running scrambled on all fours next to Cut Sky. Blood dripped from her mouth, and more blood was smeared all over her face. She held her side as she tried to rise.

Fox Running tried to stand over her, then knelt as he braced for a final charge, gun raised as blood from a cut over his eye obscured his vision. He tried to blink away the blood to see who was charging them. He did not know if there were even any bullets left. At least they would die together.

Cut Sky could barely see from the blood in her eyes. Fox Running was next to her. She turned to fire her rifle at a sound behind her. Then the cursing white man was upon her. The muzzle flash of Fox Running's pistol flared brightly before everything went dark.

Fox Running clicked on emptiness. He threw the gun at an approaching figure he could barely see, then clawed at the rock formation with bloody fingers, desperate for something to throw. Hands reached around him in a bear grip. He tried to resist, but he had no strength left.

"Stop ye!" the voice screamed in his ear as he ineffectually brought his useless right foot down on the boot of the man who held him. Distant gunfire erupted.

"Did I not tell ye this foolishness would be the death of ye?" John Dooley said as he spun Fox Running around, causing the Cheyenne to stumble and fall. "Foxy, it's me, John Dooley! Stop ye!"

Fox Running's wavering vision focused on the friend he had lost as Dooley's fretful face looked down on him. He must be dead. His spirit must be leaving now. He could feel a smile from somewhere rising to greet Dooley's spirit. At least they could be friends again in the world to come.

"I told you . . . Cheyenne . . . outstubborn the Irish," Fox Running slurred. He saw Cut Sky's bloody face and inert form. "I am sorry, Cut Sky," he whispered. "I loved you. I shall hold you . . . Seana."

He reached out to touch her and collapsed over her body.

September 29, 1883, Tongue River Breaks
Water. He was swimming. He had not done that since he was a boy. Perhaps when he surfaced, his mother would be alive. He had never said goodbye. And his sister. There she was!

"He wakes."

The blurred face in his vision was not his mother or sister. It was a white man. Did the Cheyenne let whites in Seana? The land of the dead should be a place of peace, not war.

A hand smoothed back his hair. A big, rough hand. It touched the leather around his right wrist. "Aye." Then the presence was gone.

"Who is there?"

A gust of wind had moved the entrance flap of the lodge.

"Who is it?" He flailed for a gun, or tried to, but his arm would not move.

Voices came to him from outside the lodge. "He does not die easily."

The voice was familiar. Was it a ghost? Did

death send haunting visions? Had they all died?

" 'Tis but stubbornness," another voice said. "When you shoot a Cheyenne in the head, it only makes him angry."

That voice he knew also. "Mr. Dooley?" he croaked, repeating his friend's name over and over, louder and louder until the lodge flap moved.

"So formal we are, lad," Dooley said as he entered the lodge where Fox Running had flirted with death but rejoined the living. "What is it we will have to endure before you call me John?"

"Am I alive?"

"Not ready for the dancin', but yes."

"Cut Sky?"

"She is well, lad. She was shot a bit in this fool's escapade of yours, but she pulled through and is going to be fine. She's sleeping."

"See her? Have to."

"When it is light, lad. Let her rest. 'Tis the middle of the night, and with you wobbly as a foal you'd fall in the fire and there would go my dinner, or breakfast, or whatever it is they are cooking."

Fox Running was quiet.

"Still with me, lad? What do you remember?"

Fox Running listed the fragments he could recall. Dooley nodded along.

"Blue Feather's men knocked most of them down, but there were more than thirty in the whole kit and caboodle, lad. Me and the army had gotten there in the morning, but we were a mile and more away, where there's another ranch that has been used by some manner of thieves. Someone must have got word to that man who knows the turn of every leaf, because Blue Feather, shot in one hand and galloping for all he was worth, even lame like he is, found us about the same time that fool horse of yours did. Then we heard the guns, but it was mostly over. There was a group still looking to either run away or fight, but they decided to run when the army showed up. They didn't get far. There will be none telling the tale."

After this somber recitation, Dooley's face split with a grin. "Did I tell you about the surprise? Their own man who had come out to write some report about how terrible the Cheyenne were ended up turning against them. They kidnapped him to get him to finish it, and he was the only one left in the house after all Cullihan's men rode off. He was very talkative. Little bald man. You mentioned him a long time ago. He has decided not to go back East and face that miserable fellow who is your friend Miss McGillicuddy's uncle. He is staying to teach school. Apparently little Grasshopper is already the teacher's pet."

There was one thing Fox Running still had to know. "Why are you here, Mr. Dooley? I thought . . . we argued . . ."

"Lad, a pretty face can make a man a fool. The man we thought was her brother was her husband." Fox Running chose not to let Dooley know he had already worked that out. "When I learned they were still trying to kill you, and that she had lied to me and used me, well, there was a permanent parting of the ways."

Fox Running frowned, unsure what Dooley meant. The Irishman explained. "She tried to kill me, lad, and I returned the favor. Not meaning to kill a woman, but she had a gun, and there was not much for it. I took her body to Fort Keogh, because she had connections, and it needed to be reported proper, and the lieutenant came down with some friends. Want to hear a man rave? Ask the lieutenant about army politics. It all came right in the end, although he seems a little less willing than the captain to be fooled. We came to Wolf Mountain after because we knew ye could not leave it alone, and ye would be starting the entertainment without us."

"Sorry for . . ."

"Lad, you told me once you had done stupid and foolish things, and your spirits or the grace of God or whatever one wishes to call it saved you from your mistakes. Even are we now, and we will not speak of it again."

Fox Running held his damaged left arm and bandaged right hand out to Dooley. They wobbled with the effort it took to hold them up. Dooley took them, then released them.

Fox Running managed a smile. "I will fight for the Cheyenne until the breath has left my body, John Dooley, but I will be your friend for an hour longer."

Dooley wiped away a tear.

"Good Irish ways ye're learnin'. And I, lad. And I."

October 1, 1883, Boston, Massachusetts
Katherine McGillicuddy strode through the clerks at her uncle's office, swatting aside any arms that reached to stop her with a lead-centered walking stick that she often carried in public. When she encountered a locked door that separated her from his inner sanctum, she smashed the frosted glass

with the stick, sending pieces flying and the few clerks that dared approach her behind their desks for cover.

"What is this outrage?" Michael McGillicuddy demanded, his balding head and red angry face turned toward her.

"I will not desist," she said. "I know what you have done. God who judges all of us knows what you have done. You tried to kill the Northern Cheyenne by using those stupid former soldiers as your weapons, but they will not be killed, because God and right and I are all on their side, you foul, evil man! I shall meet with President Arthur if need be to get him to approve a reservation in the Tongue River Valley. I have just come from creating a trust fund so that when I am dead, Uncle Michael, everything I have will help those people you want to wipe from the face of the Earth. You can kill me now, and you will lose, Uncle! You are never going to win, never!"

A clerk, bolder than the rest, loomed up behind her.

"Move or I will turn your head into jelly," she said without turning around, brandishing the stick.

Her uncle attempted a sneer. "You are upset, Niece. Have a glass of sherry and lie on the couch until your fit passes. Women are, after all, unsuited to the work of a man."

"That is true," she said. "A man would come to kill you. One may yet. After all, do not forget that Fox Running knows Boston and would no doubt be pleased to come calling on the man who hates his people so much you want them all dead!"

Smash! The stick pulverized a large shard of glass that had survived the initial onslaught. "If you want war, Uncle, you have one, and no matter how much you think your connections and your bribes will help you, I know who history will regard as nothing more than a force of evil who killed a great people for selfish gain!" She threw a newspaper cutting on his desk — an article that reported the deaths of several former army officers killed in a shootout aimed at starting an Indian war. "I'm sure you've read this already. It is not the only such story. Annie Campbell Collins has published others in various magazines, telling how the Northern Cheyenne are trying to work with their neighbors, and how their white neighbors want peace, but a few renegade army officers only wanted war — wanted it so badly they hired the murder of one of their own. Perhaps you recall the name — Captain Evans."

Silence reigned for a few seconds. She

turned and stalked from the room, leaving her uncle behind with his bellows of rage.

October 10, 1883, Tongue River Breaks
The first frost was not far off as Cut Sky sat with Fox Running by the pool where they often went to be alone. Both could finally walk unaided, but neither had touched a gun in days. Fox Running's right hand had suffered many small bones broken by the bullet that wounded him, although his left arm was now usable, despite the pain. John Dooley had gone back to Lame Deer, where he promised to give away the cabin he had built, vowing that, when the spring came, he would build two new ones on the land Fox Running had purchased — one for himself and one for any couple that might need it in the event they could stop shooting things long enough to be decently married according to the customs of one people or the other.

Blue Feather's stature had risen. That the Bandit King of the Cheyenne could defeat Custer's men made him a legend. He had feared at first his white customers and partners might keep their distance, but they still came to him — for the stories, if not for whatever business might need transacting in the shadows of the Tongue River Breaks.

The time since the fight at Wolf Mountain had been eventful. Faced with outrage that its soldiers were fighting private wars, the War Department, which only learned about the incident second hand through a steady stream of telegrams from readers of Katherine McGillicuddy's publications, weeded out those still serving whose membership in a secret group might compromise their ability to follow army policy. Officers were instructed to ban former soldiers from their forts if those soldiers fomented violence against the Indians. The army would keep the peace, or so the men were now told. No one actually believed the group's claws were drawn, but at least it would not be officially supported.

Nor was there any official record of anything that took place on Wolf Mountain. Dooley had urged the army to let the wind of rumor carry the tale. After Dooley used his full power of persuasion to share with Moore his concern that any time outsiders knew anything about the complexities of the Tongue River Valley it made matters worse, Moore agreed. The less a soldier was caught up in politics, the better. When Colonel Shepard in Denver asked about tales of a fight, after the Eastern papers published accounts unfavorable to the army, Moore said a group of bandits and thieves with some past connections to the army had fallen out with other outlaws, which he decided was as close to the truth as anyone outside the valley needed to know. The army waited for the publicity to subside. Those who had been putting money into the secret group pondered a different course of action. The Cheyenne endured.

Sanders had gone back to his fine home in Cheyenne, Wyoming, for the winter, having failed in his efforts to control the valley. Small ranchers who had stood with him in the summer when it seemed the Cheyenne were killing whites had changed their tunes now that they saw he was close to those who wanted to keep the blood flowing in the Tongue River region. Every rancher might want more land, but they all wanted peace more than anything else.

Epilogue

October 25, 1883, Tongue River Valley, Montana

Fox Running could feel the pulse of the spirits throbbing, demanding, commanding. He was weak. From time to time, he suffered blurry vision caused by the rock chips that hit his eyes during the shootout. His body creaked as it worked, as though he were an elder. He had not tried to hold a gun. Even the thought hurt.

Then he recalled Crazy Horse telling him victory only came when one's enemy was truly routed, not just wounded. A warrior did not wait. A warrior acted. Pain was the price a warrior paid to be a warrior. As long as Sanders thought he had won, and was safe to try again, the summer's work was not finished.

"There is something I must do," Fox Running said to Cut Sky after a day of intense talking to himself. What he was thinking might not even be possible, but it had to be attempted. "I have thought of this as I lay healing. The snows will fall soon, and no one can travel, but this cannot wait until the spring. I will not do it without your blessing."

He omitted that he also needed her in case his body was not up to what his spirit demanded.

"You are learning," she said. "You learn slowly, but you are learning."

He told her.

She grinned at the wickedness and daring of it. "Only if I come with you."

October 30, 1883, Cheyenne, Wyoming
The engraved plaque on the iron fence read *Box S,* but there was little of a cattle ranch in the mansion that sat along Millionaire's Row in the boom town of Cheyenne. As long as beef was king, those who profited from it lived like royalty. Better.

The house proclaimed that Ronald Sanders was rich and powerful. Still, after he came back from a summer in Montana, the servants noticed some changes. The boss might swagger as much as ever, but the large, fine house with two floors of polished wood and gleaming brass fixtures now had men with guns guarding it all day, and a man walking the manicured grounds at night. Strangers entering had to state their business at the outer gate instead of being welcomed at the door and told to "get down and come in."

As the days of early fall grew into the season of longer nights, Sanders also had a man in the house with a gun. Just in case. In case of what, he never said, but in the kitchen where the staff gathered to talk quietly, there were stories told of wild Cheyenne Indians who might one day show up on the doorstep. The cowboys who came and went with Sanders had spread word that Sam Rickett, the fastest gun in Texas, had been killed up in the Tongue River Valley in a gunfight that must have involved Injun trickery. No mortal man could get the drop on Sam Rickett.

On this night, Sanders, now used to the security he had fashioned for himself, had stayed up late looking at his business accounts and ledgers. He admitted to some concern that if a dip in prices ever came along, the empire he was building would collapse in a hurry. Some men were already setting money aside for the day that would happen, but Sanders was a survivor. He poured himself another generous helping of the Mexican wine that was brought in for him and walked up the curving staircase to his vast second-floor bedroom, where he had ordered the maids to always have candles and oil lamps lit once the sun went down.

The room was dark. One of the maids would have to be beaten or fired, he told himself, if only to remind them he was the boss. He knew there was talk about the changes since his return from Montana. He didn't want his employees to think he was getting soft. He lit one of the oil lamps on the dresser.

The first thing he saw was that one of his favorite hats was missing from its place on the hat rack. Big and wide brimmed, to him it conveyed authority. He had not worn it often, mostly when fine ladies came to dinner. He wondered which servant had been dared into pulling a stunt like this.

A maid had left something on the bed. A piece of paper, folded. It had not been there an hour or two ago when he went outside to smoke a cigar in the walled-in garden. As he picked it up, something fell and rolled onto the floor.

He held the note close to the lamp. It read, *We will see you again. Another night.* It was signed, *Fox Running and Cut Sky.* Next to the names was a small drawing of a running fox and a much larger one of a dark cloud with a thunderbolt through it.

Sanders looked around the room. Someone's idea of a joke? He would fire them all!

He looked closer. Some things on the bed had fallen from the paper. Four teeth. Painted black. And, on the floor, just at the edge of the pool of light from the lamp, lay a bullet for a .45.

In his secure house, Ronald Sanders felt fear and wondered for just a moment whether the spirits the Cheyenne talked about were real.

November 9, 1883, Tongue River Breaks
A cold wind blew outside the cave where Fox Running lived. He and Cut Sky had been back for a few days, having made the trip just in time before bitter winds set in. Dooley had been horrified at the idea of two people who still could barely move attempting the stunt they had in mind but ended up conspiring with them so they could take trains instead of riding from Sickles to Cheyenne. Fox Running was not sure how this happened, until Dooley mentioned with an impish grin that Katherine McGillicuddy had an interest in a railroad. The rest, Dooley said, was nothing more than Miss McGillicuddy forcing other

people to do her bidding, something she did well and enjoyed.

"I believe when she demanded special trains, lad, every railroad in America lined up and snapped to!" he said, once Dooley could assure himself and Katherine that no further violence was planned as part of the trip.

Dooley had been glad to have a purpose, for time lay heavy on his hands as he thought of how badly he had been fooled. How easy it was for one woman to manipulate him.

While they were gone, word had filtered through Paul Collins, Annie's husband and the army's official liaison to Two Moon, that opposition to a reservation for the Cheyenne was fading, and that he expected the Great White Father would act before he left office at the end of the next year.

Blue Feather had laughed when presented with the wide-brimmed hat. "It is a bride price like no other," Cut Sky chimed in.

Blue Feather's condition for his daughter's wedding had been that Fox Running live through the winter with them in their camp, so that he and Cut Sky could have time when they were not at war with the world to see if they actually liked each other, a condition Fox Running gladly accepted.

"More stew, more work," Cut Sky had carped at the time.

Now she stood at the entrance to the small cave, watching the dark-gray clouds move in from the north. Around her left wrist she wore a leather bracelet made for her by Rides a Crow and given to her upon their return. "The spirits shall walk with you both," Rides a Crow had said. "When the world of men makes you forget the spirits are with you, this is to remind you that, but for them, your road would already have ended."

She touched the leather and looked Fox Running in the eye. "We could have killed him," she said.

He shook his head. "It would have been murder. It would not have been justice. It would be a good thing if he were to die, but I fear another would just take his place. And, with my hand the way it is, I do not think I could risk a gunfight. Perhaps in time, but not now."

"Will he be back?"

"Him or one like him. But he will never be the same, because like most men who prey on those who are weaker, he is a coward inside. It is not finished, Cut Sky." Fox Running gazed out as the snow began to fall in a curtain that in time would bury the schemes of men until spring. "No matter what we have done, it is not over. They will come again."

The sound of a Henry rifle being cocked filled the cave.

Fox Running looked at Cut Sky's blazing eyes as she spoke.

"Let them come. I am ready."

HISTORICAL NOTE

In 1882, General Nelson Miles urged the Northern Cheyenne to begin settling the Tongue River Valley. Prior to that, the survivors of the 1877 exile to Indian Territory in the south and the 1878–1879 Northern Cheyenne Exodus back to Montana had lived around Fort Keogh, at the north end of the valley. Conflicts emerged between Indians and white settlers, many resulting in violence and some in death. It was not until November 1884, when President Chester A. Arthur was all but out of office, that an executive order was signed creating the Northern Cheyenne Reservation. Even that did not bring peace, because the reservation area included land occupied by white settlers. It was not until 1892 and dozens of conflicts later that new reservation boundaries were proposed that would expand the Northern Cheyenne Reservation, ensure that the pattern of Cheyenne and non-

Native American ownership would end, and give the Northern Cheyenne full control of the land. Bureaucracy being what it was — and is — action to implement the recommendations did not come until 1900, when President William McKinley signed the order to create an expanded, homogenous Northern Cheyenne Reservation.

ABOUT THE AUTHOR

Rusty Davis is a freelance writer whose first five novels, *Wyoming Showdown, Black Wind Pass, Rakeheart, Spirit Walker,* and *Cheyenne Gun,* were published by Five Star. From the West he saw on TV and in the movies as a child to the rugged hills and endless vistas of the Laramie and Bighorn Mountains he saw as an adult, the stories of the men and women who fought nature when not battling each other have always captivated him. After a long trail of understanding that began with Custer's defeat was illuminated by the many writers who saved the sagas of the Cheyenne and Lakota from obscurity, and was made real by firsthand experience with Native Americans, Rusty wanted to write stories that offered a different perspective on the experiences of the Northern Cheyenne and other Nations.

Rusty is currently writing the next chapters in the series of books chronicling the adventures of Fox Running, his friend John Dooley, and the blazing-spirited Cut Sky as they try to bring justice to the Tongue River Valley in a time of sorrow and strife. Rusty can be reached by emailing him at rustywork777@gmail.com.

The employees of Thorndike Press hope you have enjoyed this Large Print book. All our Thorndike, Wheeler, and Kennebec Large Print titles are designed for easy reading, and all our books are made to last. Other Thorndike Press Large Print books are available at your library, through selected bookstores, or directly from us.

For information about titles, please call:
 (800) 223-1244

or visit our website at:
 gale.com/thorndike

To share your comments, please write:
 Publisher
 Thorndike Press
 10 Water St., Suite 310
 Waterville, ME 04901